HARLAN COBEN

TELL
NO ONE

WHEELER
PUBLISHING, INC.
ROCKLAND, MA

★ AN AMERICAN COMPANY ★

Published in Large Print by arrangement with Delacorte Press, an imprint
of The Bantam Dell Publishing Group, a division of Random House, Inc.,
in the United States and Canada.

Wheeler Large Print Book Series.

Set in 16 pt Plantin.

Library of Congress Cataloging-in-Publication Data

Coben, Harlan, 1962-
  Tell no one / Harlan Coben.
     p. (large print) cm.(Wheeler large print book series)
  ISBN 1-58724-063-7 (hardcover)
  1. Physicians—Fiction. 2. Large type books. I. Title. II. Series

[PS355.O225 T45   2001b]
813′.54—dc21

                                                     2001026349
                                                          CIP

Small said, "But what about when we are dead and gone, will you love me then, does love go on?"

Large held Small snug as they looked out at the night, at the moon in the dark and the stars shining bright. "Small, look at the stars, how they shine and glow, some of the stars died a long time ago. Still they shine in the evening skies, for you see, Small, love like starlight never dies...."
—Debi Gliori
No Matter What
(Bloomsbury Publishing)

ACKNOWLEDGMENTS

Right then. Before we start, I'd like to introduce the band:

- editor extraordinaire Beth de Guzman, as well as Susan Corcoran, Sharon Lulek, Nita Taublib, Irwyn Applebaum, and the rest of the prime-time players at Bantam Dell

- Lisa Erbach Vance and Aaron Priest, my agents

- Anne Armstrong-Coben, M.D., Gene Riehl, Jeffrey Bedford, Gwendolen Gross, Jon Wood, Linda Fairstein, Maggie Griffin, and Nils Lofgren for their insight and encouragement

- and Joel Gotler, who pushed and prodded and inspired

There should have been a dark whisper in the wind. Or maybe a deep chill in the bone. Something. An ethereal song only Elizabeth or I could hear. A tightness in the air. Some textbook premonition. There are misfortunes we almost expect in life— what happened to my parents, for example— and then there are other dark moments, moments of sudden violence, that alter everything. There was my life before the tragedy. There is my life now. The two have painfully little in common.

Elizabeth was quiet for our anniversary drive, but that was hardly unusual. Even as a young girl, she'd possessed this unpredictable melancholy streak. She'd go quiet and drift into either deep contemplation or a deep funk, I never knew which. Part of the mystery, I guess, but for the first time, I could feel the chasm between us. Our relationship had survived so much. I wondered if it could survive the truth. Or for that matter, the unspoken lies.

The car's air-conditioning whirred at the blue

MAX setting. The day was hot and sticky. Classically August. We crossed the Delaware Water Gap at the Milford Bridge and were welcomed to Pennsylvania by a friendly toll collector. Ten miles later, I spotted the stone sign that read LAKE CHARMAINE—PRIVATE. I turned onto the dirt road.

The tires bore down, kicking up dust like an Arabian stampede. Elizabeth flipped off the car stereo. Out of the corner of my eye, I could tell that she was studying my profile. I wondered what she saw, and my heart started fluttering. Two deer nibbled on some leaves on our right. They stopped, looked at us, saw we meant no harm, went back to nibbling. I kept driving and then the lake rose before us. The sun was now in its death throes, bruising the sky a coiling purple and orange. The tops of the trees seemed to be on fire.

"I can't believe we still do this," I said.

"You're the one who started it."

"Yeah, when I was twelve years old."

Elizabeth let the smile through. She didn't smile often, but when she did, *pow*, right to my heart.

"It's romantic," she insisted.

"It's goofy."

"I love romance."

"You love goofy."

"You get laid whenever we do this."

"Call me Mr. Romance," I said.

She laughed and took my hand. "Come on, Mr. Romance, it's getting dark."

Lake Charmaine. My grandfather had come up with that name, which pissed off my grandmother to no end. She wanted it named for her. Her name was Bertha. Lake Bertha. Grandpa wouldn't hear it. Two points for Grandpa.

Some fifty-odd years ago, Lake Charmaine had been the sight of a rich-kids summer camp. The owner had gone belly-up and Grandpa bought the entire lake and surrounding acreage on the cheap. He'd fixed up the camp director's house and tore down most of the lakefront buildings. But farther in the woods, where no one went anymore, he left the kids' bunks alone to rot. My sister, Linda, and I used to explore them, sifting through their ruins for old treasures, playing hide-and-seek, daring ourselves to seek the Boogeyman we were sure watched and waited. Elizabeth rarely joined us. She liked to know where everything was. Hiding scared her.

When we stepped out of the car, I heard the ghosts. Lots of them here, too many, swirling and battling for my attention. My father's won out. The lake was hold-your-breath still, but I swore I could still hear Dad's howl of delight as he cannonballed off the dock, his knees pressed tightly against his chest, his smile just south of sane, the upcoming splash a virtual tidal wave in the eyes of his only son. Dad liked to land near my sunbathing mother's raft. She'd scold him, but she couldn't hide the laugh.

I blinked and the images were gone. But I remembered how the laugh and the howl and the splash would ripple and echo in the stillness of our lake, and I wondered if ripples and echoes like those ever fully die away, if somewhere in the woods my father's joyful yelps still bounced quietly off the trees. Silly thought, but there you go.

Memories, you see, hurt. The good ones most of all.

"You okay, Beck?" Elizabeth asked me.

I turned to her. "I'm going to get laid, right?"

"Perv."

She started walking up the path, her head high, her back straight. I watched her for a second, remembering the first time I'd seen that walk. I was seven years old, taking my bike—the one with the banana seat and Batman decal—for a plunge down Goodhart Road. Goodhart Road was steep and windy, the perfect thoroughfare for the discriminating Stingray driver. I rode downhill with no hands, feeling pretty much as cool and hip as a seven-year-old possibly could. The wind whipped back my hair and made my eyes water. I spotted the moving van in front of the Ruskins' old house, turned and—first pow—there she was, my Elizabeth, walking with that titanium spine, so poised, even then, even as a seven-year-old girl with Mary Janes and a friendship bracelet and too many freckles.

We met two weeks later in Miss Sobel's second-grade class, and from that moment on—please don't gag when I say this—we were soul mates. Adults found our relationship both cute and unhealthy—our inseparable tomboy-kickball friendship morphing into puppy love and adolescent preoccupation and hormonal high school dating. Everyone kept waiting for us to outgrow each other. Even us. We were both bright kids, especially Elizabeth, top students, rational even in the face of irrational love. We understood the odds.

But here we were, twenty-five-year-olds, married seven months now, back at the spot when at the age of twelve we'd shared our first real kiss.

Nauseating, I know.

We pushed past branches and through humidity thick enough to bind. The gummy smell of pine clawed the air. We trudged through high grass. Mosquitoes and the like buzzed upward in our wake. Trees cast long shadows that you could interpret any way you wanted, like trying to figure out what a cloud looked like or one of Rorschach's inkblots.

We ducked off the path and fought our way through thicker brush. Elizabeth led the way. I followed two paces back, an almost symbolic gesture when I think about it now. I always believed that nothing could drive us apart—certainly our history had proven that, hadn't it?—but now more than ever I could feel the guilt pushing her away.

My guilt.

Up ahead, Elizabeth made a right at the big semi-phallic rock and there, on the right, was

5

our tree. Our initials were, yup, carved into the bark:

E.P.

+

D.B.

And yes, a heart surrounded it. Under the heart were twelve lines, one marking each anniversary of that first kiss. I was about to make a wisecrack about how nauseating we were, but when I saw Elizabeth's face, the freckles now either gone or darkened, the tilt of the chin, the long, graceful neck, the steady green eyes, the dark hair braided like thick rope down her back, I stopped. I almost told her right then and there, but something pulled me back.

"I love you," I said.

"You're already getting laid."

"Oh."

"I love you too."

"Okay, okay," I said, feigning being put out, "you'll get laid too."

She smiled, but I thought I saw hesitancy in it. I took her in my arms. When she was twelve and we finally worked up the courage to make out, she'd smelled wonderfully of clean hair and strawberry Pixie Stix. I'd been overwhelmed by the newness of it, of course, the excitement, the exploration. Today she smelled of lilacs and cinnamon. The kiss moved like a warm light from the center of my heart. When our tongues met, I still felt a jolt. Elizabeth pulled away, breathless.

"Do you want to do the honors?" she asked.

She handed me the knife, and I carved the

thirteenth line in the tree. Thirteen. In hindsight, maybe there had been a premonition.

It was dark when we got back to the lake. The pale moon broke through the black, a solo beacon. There were no sounds tonight, not even crickets. Elizabeth and I quickly stripped down. I looked at her in the moonlight and felt something catch in my throat. She dove in first, barely making a ripple. I clumsily followed. The lake was surprisingly warm. Elizabeth swam with clean, even strokes, slicing through the water as though it were making a path for her. I splashed after her. Our sounds skittered across the lake's surface like skipping stones. She turned into my arms. Her skin was warm and wet. I loved her skin. We held each other close. She pressed her breasts against my chest. I could feel her heart and I could hear her breathing. Life sounds. We kissed. My hand wandered down the delicious curve of her back.

When we finished—when everything felt so right again—I grabbed a raft and collapsed onto it. I panted, my legs splayed, my feet dangling in the water.

Elizabeth frowned. "What, you going to fall asleep now?"

"Snore."

"Such a man."

I put my hands behind my head and lay back. A cloud passed in front of the moon, turning the blue night into something pallid and gray. The air was still. I could hear Elizabeth getting out of the water and stepping onto the dock. My eyes tried to adjust. I could barely make out her naked silhouette. She was, quite simply, breathtaking. I watched her bend at the waist and wring the water out of her hair. Then she arched her spine and threw her head back.

My raft drifted farther away from shore. I tried to sift through what had happened to me, but even I didn't understand it all. The raft kept moving. I started losing sight of Elizabeth. As she faded into the dark, I made a decision: I would tell her. I would tell her everything.

I nodded to myself and closed my eyes. There was a lightness in my chest now. I listened to the water gently lap against my raft.

Then I heard a car door open.

I sat up.

"Elizabeth?"

Pure silence, except for my own breathing.

I looked for her silhouette again. It was hard to make out, but for a moment I saw it. Or I thought I saw it. I'm not sure anymore or even if it matters. Either way, Elizabeth was standing perfectly still, and maybe she was facing me.

I might have blinked—I'm really not sure about that either—and when I looked again, Elizabeth was gone.

My heart slammed into my throat. "Elizabeth!"

No answer.

The panic rose. I fell off the raft and started

swimming toward the dock. But my strokes were loud, maddeningly loud, in my ears. I couldn't hear what, if anything, was happening. I stopped.

"Elizabeth!"

For a long while there was no sound. The cloud still blocked the moon. Maybe she had gone inside the cabin. Maybe she'd gotten something out of the car. I opened my mouth to call her name again.

That was when I heard her scream.

I lowered my head and swam, swam hard, my arms pumping, my legs kicking wildly. But I was still far from the dock. I tried to look as I swam, but it was too dark now, the moon offering just faint shafts of light, illuminating nothing.

I heard a scraping noise, like something being dragged.

Up ahead, I could see the dock. Twenty feet, no more. I swam harder. My lungs burned. I swallowed some water, my arms stretching forward, my hand fumbling blindly in the dark. Then I found it. The ladder. I grabbed hold, hoisted myself up, climbed out of the water. The dock was wet from Elizabeth. I looked toward the cabin. Too dark. I saw nothing.

"Elizabeth!"

Something like a baseball bat hit me square in the solar plexus. My eyes bulged. I folded at the waist, suffocating from within. No air. Another blow. This time it landed on the top of my skull. I heard a crack in my head, and it felt as though someone had hammered a nail through my temple. My legs buckled and I dropped to my knees. Totally disoriented now, I put my hands against the sides of my head and tried to cover up. The next blow—the final blow—hit me square in the face.

I toppled backward, back into the lake. My eyes closed. I heard Elizabeth scream again—she screamed my name this time—but the sound, all sound, gurgled away as I sank under the water.

1

Eight Years Later

Another girl was about to break my heart.

She had brown eyes and kinky hair and a toothy smile. She also had braces and was fourteen years old and—

"Are you pregnant?" I asked.

"Yeah, Dr. Beck."

I managed not to close my eyes. This was not the first time I'd seen a pregnant teen. Not even the first time today. I've been a pediatrician at this Washington Heights clinic since I finished my residency at nearby Columbia-Presbyterian Medical Center five years ago. We serve a Medicaid (read: poor) population with general family health care, including obstetrics, internal medicine, and, of course, pediatrics. Many people believe this makes me a bleeding-heart do-gooder. It doesn't. I like

11

being a pediatrician. I don't particularly like doing it out in the suburbs with soccer moms and manicured dads and, well, people like me.

"What do you plan on doing?" I asked.

"Me and Terrell. We're real happy, Dr. Beck."

"How old is Terrell?"

"Sixteen."

She looked up at me, happy and smiling. Again I managed not to close my eyes.

The thing that always surprises me—always—is that most of these pregnancies are not accidental. These babies want to have babies. No one gets that. They talk about birth control and abstinence and that's all fine and good, but the truth is, their cool friends are having babies and their friends are getting all kinds of attention and so, hey, Terrell, why not us?

"He loves me," this fourteen-year-old told me.

"Have you told your mother?"

"Not yet." She squirmed and looked almost all her fourteen years. "I was hoping you could tell her with me."

I nodded. "Sure."

I've learned not to judge. I listen. I empathize. When I was a resident, I would lecture. I would look down from on high and bestow upon patients the knowledge of how self-destructive their behavior was. But on a cold Manhattan afternoon, a weary seventeen-year-old girl who was having her third kid with a third father looked me straight in the eye and spoke an indisputable truth: "You don't know my life."

It shut me up. So I listen now. I stopped playing Benevolent White Man and became a better doctor. I will give this fourteen-year-old and her baby the absolute best care possible. I won't tell her that Terrell will never stay, that she's just cut her future off at the pass, that if she is like most of the patients here, she'll be in a similar state with at least two more men before she turns twenty.

Think about it too much and you'll go nuts.

We spoke for a while—or, at least, she spoke and I listened. The examining room, which doubled as my office, was about the size of a prison cell (not that I know this from first-hand experience) and painted an institutional green, like the color of a bathroom in an elementary school. An eye chart, the one where you point in the directions the Es are facing, hung on the back of the door. Faded Disney decals spotted one wall while another was covered with a giant food pyramid poster. My fourteen-year-old patient sat on an examining table with a roll of sanitary paper we pulled down fresh for each kid. For some reason, the way the paper rolled out reminded me of wrapping a sandwich at the Carnegie Deli.

The radiator heat was beyond stifling, but you needed that in a place where kids were frequently getting undressed. I wore my customary pediatrician garb: blue jeans, Chuck Taylor Cons, a button-down oxford, and a bright Save the Children tie that screamed 1994.

I didn't wear the white coat. I think it scares the kids.

My fourteen-year-old—yes, I couldn't get past her age—was a really good kid. Funny thing is, they all are. I referred her to an obstetrician I liked. Then I spoke to her mother. Nothing new or surprising. As I said, I do this almost every day. We hugged when she left. Over her shoulder, her mother and I exchanged a glance. Approximately twenty-five moms take their children to see me each day; at the end of the week, I can count on one hand how many are married.

Like I said, I don't judge. But I do observe.

After they left, I started jotting notes in the girl's chart. I flipped back a few pages. I'd been following her since I was a resident. That meant she started with me when she was eight years old. I looked at her growth chart. I remembered her as an eight-year-old, and then I thought about what she'd just looked like. She hadn't changed much. I finally closed my eyes and rubbed them.

Homer Simpson interrupted me by shouting, "The mail! The mail is here! Oooo!"

I opened my eyes and turned toward the monitor. This was Homer Simpson as in the TV show *The Simpsons*. Someone had replaced the computer's droning "You've got mail" with this Homer audio wave. I liked it. I liked it a lot.

I was about to check my email when the intercom's squawking stopped my hand. Wanda, a receptionist, said, "You're, uh, hmm, you're, uh...Shauna is on the phone."

14

I understood the confusion. I thanked her and hit the blinking button. "Hello, sweetums."

"Never mind," she said. "I'm here."

Shauna hung up her cellular. I stood and walked down the corridor as Shauna made her entrance from the street. Shauna stalks into a room as though it offends her. She was a plus-size model, one of the few known by one name. Shauna. Like Cher or Fabio. She stood six one and weighed one hundred ninety pounds. She was, as you might expect, a head-turner, and all heads in the waiting room obliged.

Shauna did not bother stopping at Reception and Reception knew better than to try to stop her. She pulled open the door and greeted me with the words "Lunch. Now."

"I told you. I'm going to be busy."

"Put on a coat," she said. "It's cold out."

"Look, I'm fine. The anniversary isn't until tomorrow anyway."

"You're buying."

I hesitated and she knew she had me.

"Come on, Beck, it'll be fun. Like in college. Remember how we used to go out and scope hot babes together?"

"I never scoped hot babes."

"Oh, right, that was me. Go get your coat."

On the way back to my office, one of the mothers gave me a big smile and pulled me aside. "She's even more beautiful in person," she whispered.

"Eh," I said.

"Are you and she..." The mother made a together motion with her hands.

"No, she's already involved with someone," I said.

"Really? Who?"

"My sister."

We ate at a crummy Chinese restaurant with a Chinese waiter who spoke only Spanish. Shauna, dressed impeccably in a blue suit with a neckline that plunged like Black Monday, frowned. "Moo shu pork in a tortilla shell?"

"Be adventurous," I said.

We met our first day of college. Someone in the registrar's office had screwed up and thought her name was Shaun, and we thus ended up roommates. We were all set to report the mistake when we started chatting. She bought me a beer. I started to like her. A few hours later, we decided to give it a go because our real roommates might be assholes.

I went to Amherst College, an exclusive small-Ivy institution in western Massachusetts, and if there is a preppier place on the planet, I don't know it. Elizabeth, our high school valedictorian, chose Yale. We could have gone to the same college, but we discussed it and decided that this would be yet another excellent test for our relationship. Again, we were doing the mature thing. The result? We missed each other like mad. The separation deepened our commitment and gave our love a new distance-makes-the-heart-grow-fonder dimension.

Nauseating, I know.

Between bites, Shauna asked, "Can you baby-sit Mark tonight?"

Mark was my five-year-old nephew. Sometime during our senior year, Shauna started dating my older sister, Linda. They had a commitment ceremony seven years ago. Mark was the by-product of, well, their love, with a little help from artificial insemination. Linda carried him to term and Shauna adopted him. Being somewhat old-fashioned, they wanted their son to have a male role model in his life. Enter me.

Next to what I see at work, we're talking *Ozzie and Harriet*.

"No prob," I said. "I want to see the new Disney film anyway."

"The new Disney chick is a babe and a half," Shauna said. "Their hottest since Pocahontas."

"Good to know," I said. "So where are you and Linda going?"

"Beats the hell out of me. Now that lesbians are chic, our social calendar is ridiculous. I almost long for the days when we hid in closets."

I ordered a beer. Probably shouldn't have, but one wouldn't hurt.

Shauna ordered one too. "So you broke up with what's-her-name," she said.

"Brandy."

"Right. Nice name, by the way. She have a sister named Whiskey?"

"We only went out twice."

"Good. She was a skinny witch. Besides, I got someone perfect for you."

"No, thanks," I said.

"She's got a killer bod."

"Don't set me up, Shauna. Please."

"Why not?"

"Remember the last time you set me up?"

"With Cassandra."

"Right."

"So what was wrong with her?"

"For one thing, she was a lesbian."

"Christ, Beck, you're such a bigot."

Her cell phone rang. She leaned back and answered it, but her eyes never left my face. She barked something and flipped the mouthpiece up. "I have to go," she said.

I signaled for the check.

"You're coming over tomorrow night," she pronounced.

I feigned a gasp. "The lesbians have no plans?"

"I don't. Your sister does. She's going stag to the big Brandon Scope formal."

"You're not going with her?"

"Nah."

"Why not?"

"We don't want to leave Mark without us two nights in a row. Linda has to go. She's running the trust now. Me, I'm taking the night off. So come over tomorrow night, okay? I'll order in, we'll watch videos with Mark."

Tomorrow was the anniversary. Had Elizabeth lived, we'd be scratching our twenty-first line in that tree. Strange as this might sound, tomorrow would not be a particularly hard day for me. For anniversaries or holidays or Elizabeth's birthday, I get so geared up that I usually handle them with no problems. It's the "regular" days that are hard. When I flip with the remote and stumble across a classic episode of *The Mary Tyler Moore Show* or *Cheers*. When I walk through a bookstore and see a new title by Alice Hoffman or Anne Tyler. When I listen to the O'Jays or the Four Tops or Nina Simone. Regular stuff.

"I told Elizabeth's mother I'd stop by," I said.

"Ah, Beck..." She was about to argue but caught herself. "How about after?"

"Sure," I said.

Shauna grabbed my arm. "You're disappearing again, Beck."

I didn't reply.

"I love you, you know. I mean, if you had any sort of sexual appeal whatsoever, I probably would have gone for you instead of your sister."

"I'm flattered," I said. "Really."

"Don't shut me out. If you shut me out, you shut everyone out. Talk to me, okay?"

"Okay," I said. But I can't.

I almost erased the email.

I get so much junk email, spam, bulk emails, you know the drill, I've become quite handy

19

with the delete button. I read the sender's address first. If it's someone I know or from the hospital, fine. If not, I enthusiastically click the delete button.

I sat at my desk and checked the afternoon schedule. Chock-full, which was no surprise. I spun around in my chair and readied my delete finger. One email only. The one that made Homer shriek before. I did the quick scan, and my eyes got snagged on the first two letters of the subject.

What the—?

The way the window screen was formatted, all I could see were those two letters and the sender's email address. The address was unfamiliar to me. A bunch of numbers @comparama.com.

I narrowed my eyes and hit the right scroll button. The subject appeared a character at a time. With each click, my pulse raced a bit more. My breathing grew funny. I kept my finger on the scroll button and waited.

When I was done, when all the letters showed themselves, I read the subject again and when I did, I felt a deep, hard thud in my heart.

"Dr. Beck?"

My mouth wouldn't work.

"Dr. Beck?"

"Give me a minute, Wanda."

She hesitated. I could still hear her on the intercom. Then I heard it click off.

I kept staring at the screen:

To: dbeckmd@nyhosp.com
From: 13943928@comparama.com

Subject: E.P.+ D.B ///////////////////

Twenty-one lines. I've counted four times already.

It was a cruel, sick joke. I knew that. My hands tightened into fists. I wondered what chicken-shitted son of a bitch had sent it. It was easy to be anonymous in emails—the best refuge of the techno-coward. But the thing was, very few people knew about the tree or our anniversary. The media never learned about it. Shauna knew, of course. And Linda. Elizabeth might have told her parents or uncle. But outside of that...

So who sent it?

I wanted to read the message, of course, but something held me back. The truth is, I think about Elizabeth more than I let on—I don't think I'm fooling anyone there—but I never talk about her or what happened. People think I'm being macho or brave, that I'm trying to spare my friends or shunning people's pity or some such nonsense. That's not it. Talking about Elizabeth hurts. A lot. It brings back her last scream. It brings back all the unanswered questions. It brings back the might-have-beens (few things, I assure you, will devastate like the might-have-beens). It brings back the guilt, the feelings, no matter how irrational, that a stronger man—a better man—might have saved her.

They say it takes a long time to comprehend a tragedy. You're numb. You can't adequately accept the grim reality. Again, that's not true. Not for me anyway. I understood the full implications the moment they found Elizabeth's body. I understood that I would never see her again, that I would never hold her again, that we would never have children or grow old together. I understood that this was final, that there was no reprieve, that nothing could be bartered or negotiated.

I started crying immediately. Sobbing uncontrollably. I sobbed like that for almost a week without letup. I sobbed through the funeral. I let no one touch me, not even Shauna or Linda. I slept alone in our bed, burying my head in Elizabeth's pillow, trying to smell her. I went through her closets and pressed her clothes against my face. None of this was comforting. It was weird and it hurt. But it was her smell, a part of her, and I did it anyway.

Well-meaning friends—often the worst kind—handed me the usual clichés, and so I feel in a pretty good position to warn you: Just offer your deepest condolences. Don't tell me I'm young. Don't tell me it'll get better. Don't tell me she's in a better place. Don't tell me it's part of some divine plan. Don't tell me that I was lucky to have known such a love. Every one of those platitudes pissed me off.

They made me—and this is going to sound uncharitable—stare at the idiot and wonder why he or she still breathed while my Elizabeth rotted.

I kept hearing that "better to have loved and lost" bullshit. Another falsehood. Trust me, it is not better. Don't show me paradise and then burn it down. That was part of it. The selfish part. What got to me more—what really hurt—was that Elizabeth was denied so much. I can't tell you how many times I see or do something and I think of how much Elizabeth would have loved it and the pang hits me anew.

People wonder if I have any regrets. The answer is, only one. I regret that there were moments I wasted doing something other than making Elizabeth happy.

"Dr. Beck?"

"One more second," I said.

I put my hand on the mouse and moved the cursor over the Read icon. I clicked it and the message came up:

To: dbeckmd@nyhosp.com
From: 13943928@comparama.com
Subject: E.P.+ D.B ///////////////////

Message: Click on this hyperlink, kiss time, anniversary.

A lead block formed in my chest.
Kiss time?

It was a joke, had to be. I am not big on cryptic. I'm also not big on waiting.

I grabbed the mouse again and moved the arrow over the hyperlink. I clicked and heard the primordial modem screech the mating call of machinery. We have an old system at the clinic. It took a while for the Web browser to appear. I waited, thinking *Kiss time, how do they know about kiss time?*

The browser came up. It read error.

I frowned. Who the hell sent this? I tried it a second time, and again the error message came up. It was a broken link.

Who the hell knew about kiss time?

I have never told anyone. Elizabeth and I didn't much discuss it, probably because it was no big deal. We were corny to the point of Pollyanna, so stuff like this we just kept to ourselves. It was embarrassing really, but when we kissed that first time twenty-one years ago, I noted the time. Just for fun. I pulled back and looked at my Casio watch and said, "Six-fifteen."

And Elizabeth said, *"Kiss time."*

I looked at the message yet again. I started getting pissed now. This was way beyond funny. It's one thing to send a cruel email, but...

Kiss time.

Well, kiss time was 6:15 P.M. tomorrow. I didn't have much choice. I'd have to wait until then.

So be it.

I saved the email onto a diskette just in case. I pulled down the print options and hit

Print All. I don't know much about computers, but I know that you could sometimes trace the origin of a message from all that gobbledygook at the bottom. I heard the printer purr. I took another look at the subject. I counted the lines again. Still twenty-one.

I thought about that tree and that first kiss, and there in my tight, stifling office I started to smell the strawberry Pixie Stix.

2

At home, I found another shock from the past.

I live across the George Washington Bridge from Manhattan—in the typical American-dream suburb of Green River, New Jersey, a township with, despite the moniker, no river and shrinking amounts of green. Home is Grandpa's house. I moved in with him and a revolving door of foreign nurses when Nana died three years ago.

Grandpa has Alzheimer's. His mind is a bit like an old black-and-white TV with damaged rabbit-ear antennas. He goes in and out and some days are better than others and you have to hold the antennas a certain way and not move at all, and even then the picture does the intermittent vertical spin. At least,

25

that was how it used to be. But lately—to keep within this metaphor—the TV barely flickers on.

I never really liked my grandfather. He was a domineering man, the kind of old-fashioned, lift-by-the-bootstraps type whose affection was meted out in direct proportion to your success. He was a gruff man of tough love and old-world machismo. A grandson who was both sensitive and unathletic, even with good grades, was easily dismissed.

The reason I agreed to move in with him was that I knew if I didn't, my sister would have taken him in. Linda was like that. When we sang at Brooklake summer camp that "He has the whole world in His hands," she took the meaning a little too much to heart. She would have felt obligated. But Linda had a son and a life partner and responsibilities. I did not. So I made a preemptive strike by moving in. I liked living here well enough, I guess. It was quiet.

Chloe, my dog, ran up to me, wagging her tail. I scratched her behind the floppy ears. She took it in for a moment or two and then started eyeing the leash.

"Give me a minute," I told her.

Chloe doesn't like this phrase. She gave me a look—no easy feat when your hair totally covers your eyes. Chloe is a bearded collie, a breed that appears far more like a sheepdog than any sort of collie I've ever seen. Elizabeth and I had bought Chloe right after we got married. Elizabeth had loved dogs. I hadn't. I do now.

Chloe leaned up against the front door. She looked at the door, then at me, then back at the door again. Hint, hint.

Grandpa was slumped in front of a TV game show. He didn't turn toward me, but then again, he didn't seem to be looking at the picture either. His face was stuck in what had become a steady, pallid death-freeze. The only time I saw the death-freeze melt was when he was having his diaper changed. When that happened, Grandpa's lips thinned and his face went slack. His eyes watered and sometimes a tear escaped. I think he is at his most lucid at the exact moment he craves senility.

God has some sense of humor.

The nurse had left the message on the kitchen table: CALL SHERIFF LOWELL.

There was a phone number scribbled under it.

My head began to pound. Since the attack, I suffer migraines. The blows cracked my skull. I was hospitalized for five days, though one specialist, a classmate of mine at medical school, thinks the migraines are psychological rather than physiological in origin. Maybe he's right. Either way, both the pain and guilt remain. I should have ducked. I should have seen the blows coming. I shouldn't have fallen into the water. And finally, I somehow summoned up the strength to save myself—shouldn't I have been able to do the same to save Elizabeth?

Futile, I know.

I read the message again. Chloe started

whining. I put up one finger. She stopped whining but started doing her glance-at-me-and-the-door again.

I hadn't heard from Sheriff Lowell in eight years, but I still remembered him looming over my hospital bed, his face etched with doubt and cynicism.

What could he want after all this time?

I picked up the phone and dialed. A voice answered on the first ring.

"Dr. Beck, thank you for calling me back."

I am not a big fan of caller ID—too Big Brother for my tastes. I cleared my throat and skipped the pleasantries. "What can I do for you, Sheriff?"

"I'm in the area," he said. "I'd very much like to stop by and see you, if that's okay."

"Is this a social call?" I asked.

"No, not really."

He waited for me to say something. I didn't.

"Would now be convenient?" Lowell asked.

"You mind telling me what it's about?"

"I'd rather wait until—"

"And I'd rather you didn't."

I could feel my grip on the receiver tighten.

"Okay, Dr. Beck, I understand." He cleared his throat in a way that indicated he was trying to buy some time. "Maybe you saw on the news that two bodies were found in Riley County."

I hadn't. "What about them?"

"They were found near your property."

"It's not my property. It's my grand-father's."

"But you're his legal custodian, right?"

"No," I said. "My sister is."

"Perhaps you could call her then. I'd like to speak with her too."

"The bodies were *not* found on Lake Charmaine, right?"

"That's correct. We found them on the western neighboring lot. County property actually."

"Then what do you want from us?"

There was a pause. "Look, I'll be there in an hour. Please see if you can get Linda to come by, will you?"

He hung up.

The eight years had not been kind to Sheriff Lowell, but then again, he hadn't been Mel Gibson to begin with. He was a mangy mutt of a man with features so extra-long hangdog that he made Nixon look as though he'd gotten a nip and tuck. The end of his nose was bulbous to the nth degree. He kept taking out a much-used hanky, carefully unfolding it, rubbing his nose, carefully refolding it, jamming it deep into his back pocket.

Linda had arrived. She leaned forward on the couch, ready to shield me. This was how she often sat. She was one of those people who gave you their full, undivided attention. She fixed you with those big brown eyes and you could look nowhere else. I'm definitely biased, but Linda is the best person I know. Corny, yes, but the fact that she exists gives me hope for this world. The fact that she loves me gives me whatever else I have left.

We sat in my grandparents' formal living room, which I usually do my utmost to avoid. The room was stale, creepy, and still had that old-people's-sofa smell. I found it hard to breathe. Sheriff Lowell took his time getting situated. He gave his nose a few more swipes, took out a pocket pad, licked his finger, found his page. He offered us his friendliest smile and started.

"Do you mind telling me when you were last at the lake?"

"I was there last month," Linda said.

But his eyes were on me. "And you, Dr. Beck?"

"Eight years ago."

He nodded as though he'd expected that response. "As I explained on the phone, we found two bodies near Lake Charmaine."

"Have you identified them yet?" Linda asked.

"No."

"Isn't that odd?"

Lowell thought about that one while leaning forward to pull out the hanky again. "We know that they're both male, both full-grown, both white. We're now searching through missing persons to see what we can come up with. The bodies are rather old."

"How old?" I asked.

Sheriff Lowell again found my eyes. "Hard to say. Forensics is still running tests, but we figure they've been dead at least five years.

They were buried pretty good too. We'd have never found them except there was a landslide from that record rainfall, and a bear came up with an arm."

My sister and I looked at each other.

"Excuse me?" Linda said.

Sheriff Lowell nodded. "A hunter shot a bear and found a bone next to the body. It'd been in the bear's mouth. Turned out to be a human arm. We traced it back. Took some time, I can tell you. We're still excavating the area."

"You think there may be more bodies?"

"Can't say for sure."

I sat back. Linda stayed focused. "So are you here to get our permission to dig on Lake Charmaine property?"

"In part."

We waited for him to say more. He cleared his throat and looked at me again. "Dr. Beck, you're blood type B positive, isn't that right?"

I opened my mouth, but Linda put a protective hand on my knee. "What does that have to do with anything?" she asked.

"We found other things," he said. "At the grave site."

"What other things?"

"I'm sorry. That's confidential."

"Then get the hell out," I said.

Lowell did not seem particularly surprised by my outburst. "I'm just trying to conduct—"

"I said, get out."

Sheriff Lowell didn't move. "I know that your wife's murderer has already been brought to justice," he said. "And I know it must hurt like hell to bring this all up again."

"Don't patronize me," I said.

"That's not my intent."

"Eight years ago you thought I killed her."

"That's not true. You were her husband. In such cases, the odds of a family member's involvement—"

"Maybe if you didn't waste time with that crap, you would have found her before—" I jerked back, feeling myself choking up. I turned away. Damn. Damn him. Linda reached for me, but I moved away.

"My job was to explore every possibility," he droned on. "We had the federal authorities helping us. Even your father-in-law and his brother were kept informed of all developments. We did everything we could."

I couldn't bear to hear another word. "What the hell do you want here, Lowell?"

He rose and hoisted his pants onto his gut. I think he wanted the height advantage. To intimidate or something. "A blood sample," he said. "From you."

"Why?"

"When your wife was abducted, you were assaulted."

"So?"

"You were hit with a blunt instrument."

"You know all this."

"Yes," Lowell said. He gave his nose another wipe, tucked the hanky away, and started pacing. "When we found the bodies, we also found a baseball bat."

The pain in my head started throbbing again. "A bat?"

Lowell nodded. "Buried in the ground with the bodies. There was a wooden bat."

Linda said, "I don't understand. What does this have to do with my brother?"

"We found dried blood on it. We've typed it as B positive." He tilted his head toward me. "Your blood type, Dr. Beck."

We went over it again. The tree-carving anniversary, the swim in the lake, the sound of the car door, my pitifully frantic swim to shore.

"You remember falling back in the lake?" Lowell asked me.

"Yes."

"And you heard your wife scream?"

"Yes."

"And then you passed out? In the water?"

I nodded.

"How deep would you say the water was? Where you fell in, I mean?"

"Didn't you check this eight years ago?" I asked.

"Bear with me, Dr. Beck."

"I don't know. Deep."

"Over-your-head deep?"

"Yes."

"Right, okay. Then what do you remember?"

"The hospital," I said.

"Nothing between the time you hit the water and the time you woke up at the hospital?"

33

"That's right."

"You don't remember getting out of the water? You don't remember making your way to the cabin or calling for an ambulance? You did all that, you know. We found you on the floor of the cabin. The phone was still off the hook."

"I know, but I don't remember."

Linda spoke up. "Do you think these two men are more victims of"—she hesitated—"KillRoy?"

She said it in a hush. KillRoy. Just uttering his name chilled the room.

Lowell coughed into his fist. "We're not sure, ma'am. KillRoy's only known victims are women. He never hid a body before—at least, none that we know about. And the two men's skin had rotted so we can't tell if they'd been branded."

Branded. I felt my head spin. I closed my eyes and tried not to hear any more.

3

I rushed to my office early the next morning, arriving two hours before my first scheduled patient. I flipped on the computer, found the strange email, clicked the hyperlink. Again it came up an error. No surprise really. I stared at the message, reading it over and over as though I might find a deeper meaning. I didn't.

Last night, I gave blood. The DNA test would take weeks, but Sheriff Lowell thought they might be able to get a preliminary match earlier. I pushed him for more information, but he remained tight-lipped. He was keeping something from us. What, I had no idea.

As I sat in the examining room and waited for my first patient, I replayed Lowell's visit. I thought about the two bodies. I thought about the bloody wooden bat. And I let myself think about the branding.

Elizabeth's body was found off Route 80 five days after the abduction. The coroner estimated that she'd been dead for two days. That meant she spent three days alive with Elroy Kellerton, aka KillRoy. Three days. Alone with a monster. Three sunrises and sunsets, scared and in the dark and in immense agony. I try very hard not to think about it. There are some places the mind should not go; it gets steered there anyway.

KillRoy was caught three weeks later. He confessed to killing fourteen women on a spree that began with a coed in Ann Arbor and ended with a prostitute in the Bronx. All fourteen women were found dumped on the side of the road like so much refuse. All had also been branded with the letter K. Branded in the same way as cattle. In other words, Elroy Kellerton took a metal poker, stuck it in a blazing fire, put a protective mitt on his hand, waited until the poker turned molten red with heat, and then he seared my Elizabeth's beautiful skin with a sizzling hiss.

My mind took one of those wrong turns, and images started flooding in. I squeezed my eyes shut and wished them away. It didn't work. He was still alive, by the way. KillRoy, I mean. Our appeals process gives this monster the chance to breathe, to read, to talk, to be interviewed on CNN, to get visits from do-gooders, to smile. Meanwhile his victims rot. Like I said, God has some sense of humor.

I splashed cold water on my face and checked the mirror. I looked like hell. Patients started filing in at nine o'clock. I was distracted, of course. I kept one eye on the wall clock, waiting for "kiss time"—6:15 P.M. The clock's hands trudged forward as though bathed in thick syrup.

I immersed myself in patient care. I'd always had that ability. As a kid, I could study for hours. As a doctor, I can disappear into my work. I did that after Elizabeth died. Some people point out that I hide in my work, that I choose to work instead of live. To that cliché I respond with a simple "What's your point?"

At noon, I downed a ham sandwich and Diet Coke and then I saw more patients. One eight-year-old boy had visited a chiropractor for "spinal alignment" eighty times in the past year. He had no back pain. It was a con job perpetrated by several area chiropractors. They offer the parents a free TV or VCR if they bring their kids in. Then they bill

Medicaid for the visit. Medicaid is a wonderful, necessary thing, but it gets abused like a Don King undercard. I once had a sixteen-year-old boy rushed to the hospital in an ambulance—for routine sunburn. Why an ambulance instead of a taxi or subway? His mother explained that she'd have to pay for those herself or wait for the government to reimburse. Medicaid pays for the ambulance right away.

At five o'clock, I said good-bye to my last patient. The support staff headed out at five-thirty. I waited until the office was empty before I sat and faced the computer. In the background I could hear the clinic's phones ringing. A machine picks them up after five-thirty and gives the caller several options, but for some reason, the machine doesn't pick up until the tenth ring. The sound was somewhat maddening.

I got online, found the email, and clicked on the hyperlink yet again. Still a no-go. I thought about this strange email and those dead bodies. There had to be a connection. My mind kept going back to that seemingly simple fact. I started sorting through the possibilities.

Possibility one: These two men were the work of KillRoy. True, his other victims were women and easily found, but did that rule out his killing others?

Possibility two: KillRoy had persuaded these men to help him abduct Elizabeth. That might explain a lot. The wooden bat, for one thing, if the blood on it was indeed mine. It also put to rest my one big question mark

37

about the whole abduction. In theory, KillRoy, like all serial killers, worked alone. How, I'd always wondered, had he been able to drag Elizabeth to the car and at the same time lie in wait for me to get out of the water? Before her body surfaced, the authorities had assumed there had been more than one abductor. But once her corpse was found branded with the K, that hypothesis was finessed. KillRoy could have done it, it was theorized, if he'd cuffed or somehow subdued Elizabeth and then gone after me. It wasn't a perfect fit, but if you pushed hard enough, the piece went in.

Now we had another explanation. He had accomplices. And he killed them.

Possibility three was the simplest: The blood on the bat was not mine. B positive is not common, but it's not that rare either. In all likelihood, these bodies had nothing to do with Elizabeth's death.

I couldn't make myself buy it.

I checked the computer's clock. It was hooked into some satellite that gave the exact time.

6:04.42 P.M.

Ten minutes and eighteen seconds to go.

To go to what?

The phones kept ringing. I tuned them out and drummed my fingers. Under ten minutes now. Okay, if there was going to be a change in the hyperlink, it would have probably happened by now. I put my hand on the mouse and took a deep breath.

My beeper went off.

38

I wasn't on call tonight. That meant it was either a mistake—something made far too often by the clinic night operators—or a personal call. It beeped again. Double beep. That meant an emergency. I looked at the display.

It was a call from Sheriff Lowell. It was marked Urgent.

Eight minutes.

I thought about it but not for very long. Anything was better than stewing with my own thoughts. I decided to call him back.

Lowell again knew who it was before he picked up. "Sorry to bother you, Doc." Doc, he called me now. As though we were chums. "But I just have a quick question."

I put my hand back on the mouse, moved the cursor over the hyperlink, and clicked. The Web browser stirred to life.

"I'm listening," I said.

The Web browser was taking longer this time. No error message appeared.

"Does the name Sarah Goodhart mean anything to you?"

I almost dropped the phone.

"Doc?"

I pulled the receiver away and looked at it as though it had just materialized in my hand. I gathered myself together a piece at a time. When I trusted my voice, I put the phone back to my ear. "Why do you ask?"

Something started coming up on the computer screen. I squinted. One of those sky cams. Or street cam, I guess you'd call this one.

They had them all over the Web now. I sometimes used the traffic ones, especially to check
out the morning delay on the Washington
Bridge.

"It's a long story," Lowell said.

I needed to buy time. "Then I'll call you
back."

I hung up. Sarah Goodhart. The name
meant something to me. It meant a lot.

What the hell was going on here?

The browser stopped loading. On the monitor, I saw a street scene in black and white.
The rest of the page was blank. No banners
or titles. I knew you could set it up so that you
grabbed only a certain feed. That was what we
had here.

I checked the computer clock.

6:12.18 P.M.

The camera was pointing down at a fairly
busy street corner, from maybe fifteen feet off
the ground. I didn't know what corner it was
or what city I was looking at. It was definitely a major city, though. Pedestrians flowed
mostly from right to left, heads down, shoulders slumped, briefcases in hand, downtrodden at the end of a workday, probably
heading for a train or bus. On the far right, I
could see the curb. The foot traffic came in
waves, probably coordinated with the changing
of a traffic light.

I frowned. Why had someone sent me this
feed?

The clock read 6:14.21 P.M. Less than a
minute to go.

40

I kept my eyes glued to the screen and waited for the countdown as though it were New Year's Eve. My pulse started speeding up. Ten, nine, eight...

Another tidal wave of humanity passed from right to left. I took my eyes off the clock. Four, three, two. I held my breath and waited. When I glanced at the clock again, it read:

6:15.02 P.M.

Nothing had happened—but then again, what had I expected?

The human tidal wave ebbed and once again, for a second or two, there was nobody in the picture. I settled back, sucking in air. A joke, I figured. A weird joke, sure. Sick even. But nonetheless—

And that was when someone stepped out from directly under the camera. It was as though the person had been hiding there the whole time.

I leaned forward.

It was a woman. That much I could see even though her back was to me. Short hair, but definitely a woman. From my angle, I hadn't been able to make out any faces so far. This was no different. Not at first.

The woman stopped. I stared at the top of her head, almost willing her to look up. She took another step. She was in the middle of the screen now. Someone else walked by. The woman stayed still. Then she turned around and slowly lifted her chin until she looked straight up into the camera.

My heart stopped.

I stuck a fist in my mouth and smothered a scream. I couldn't breathe. I couldn't think. Tears filled my eyes and started spilling down my cheeks. I didn't wipe them away.

I stared at her. She stared at me.

Another mass of pedestrians crossed the screen. Some of them bumped into her, but the woman didn't move. Her gaze stayed locked on the camera. She lifted her hand as though reaching toward me. My head spun. It was as though whatever tethered me to reality had been severed.

I was left floating helplessly.

She kept her hand raised. Slowly I managed to lift my hand. My fingers brushed the warm screen, trying to meet her halfway. More tears came. I gently caressed the woman's face and felt my heart crumble and soar all at once.

"Elizabeth," I whispered.

She stayed there for another second or two. Then she said something into the camera. I couldn't hear her, but I could read her lips.

"I'm sorry," my dead wife mouthed.

And then she walked away.

4

Vic Letty looked both ways before he limped inside the strip mall's Mail Boxes Etc. His gaze slid across the room. Nobody was watching. Perfect. Vic couldn't help but smile. His scam was foolproof. There was no way to trace it back to him, and now it was going to make him big-time rich.

The key, Vic realized, was preparation. That was what separated the good from the great. The greats covered their tracks. The greats prepared for every eventuality.

The first thing Vic did was get a fake ID from that loser cousin of his, Tony. Then, using the fake ID, Vic rented a mailbox under the pseudonym UYS Enterprises. See the brilliance? Use a fake ID *and* a pseudonym. So even if someone bribed the bozo behind the desk, even if someone could find out who rented the UYS Enterprises box, all you'd come up with was the name Roscoe Taylor, the one on Vic's fake ID.

No way to trace it back to Vic himself.

From across the room, Vic tried to see in the little window for Box 417. Hard to make out much, but there was something there for sure. Beautiful. Vic accepted only cash or money orders. No checks, of course. Nothing that could be traced back to him. And whenever he picked up the money, he wore a disguise.

Like right now. He had on a baseball cap and a fake mustache. He also pretended to have a limp. He read somewhere that people notice limps, so if a witness was asked to identify the guy using Box 417, what would the witness say? Simple. The man had a mustache and a limp. And if you bribed the dumb-ass clerk, you'd conclude some guy named Roscoe Taylor had a mustache and a limp.

And the real Vic Letty had neither.

But Vic took other precautions too. He never opened the box when other people were around. Never. If someone else was getting his mail or in the general vicinity, he'd act as though he was opening another box or pretend he was filling out a mailing form, something like that. When the coast was clear—and only when the coast was clear—would Vic go over to Box 417.

Vic knew that you could never, ever be too careful.

Even when it came to getting here, Vic took precautions. He'd parked his work truck—Vic handled repairs and installations for CableEye, the East Coast's biggest cable TV operator—four blocks away. He'd ducked through two alleys on his way here. He wore a black windbreaker over his uniform coverall so no one would be able to see the "Vic" sewn over the shirt's right pocket.

He thought now about the huge payday that was probably in Box 417, not ten feet from where he now stood. His fingers felt antsy. He checked the room again.

44

There were two women opening their boxes. One turned and smiled absently at him. Vic moved toward the boxes on the other side of the room and grabbed his key chain—he had one of those key chains that jangled off his belt—and pretended to be sorting through them. He kept his face down and away from them.

More caution.

Two minutes later, the two women had their mail and were gone. Vic was alone. He quickly crossed the room and opened his box.

Oh wow.

One package addressed to UYS Enterprises. Wrapped in brown. No return address. And thick enough to hold some serious green.

Vic smiled and wondered: Is that what fifty grand looks like?

He reached out with trembling hands and picked up the package. It felt comfortably heavy in his hand. Vic's heart started jack-hammering. Oh, sweet Jesus. He'd been running this scam for four months now. He'd been casting that net and landing some pretty decent fish. But oh lordy, now he'd landed a friggin' whale!

Checking his surroundings again, Vic stuffed the package into the pocket of his windbreaker and hurried outside. He took a different route back to his work truck and started for the plant. His fingers found the package and stroked it. Fifty grand. Fifty thousand dollars. The number totally blew his mind.

By the time Vic drove to the CableEye plant, night had fallen. He parked the truck in the back and walked across the footbridge to his own car, a rusted-out 1991 Honda Civic. He frowned at the car and thought, Not much longer.

The employee lot was quiet. The darkness started weighing against him. He could hear his footsteps, the weary slap of work boots against tar. The cold sliced through his windbreaker. Fifty grand. He had fifty grand in his pocket.

Vic hunched his shoulders and hurried his step.

The truth was, Vic was scared this time. The scam would have to stop. It was a good scam, no doubt about it. A great one even. But he was taking on some big boys now. He had questioned the intelligence of such a move, weighed the pros and cons, and decided that the great ones—the ones who really change their lives—go for it.

And Vic wanted to be a great one.

The scam was simple, which was what made it so extraordinary. Every house that had cable had a switch box on the telephone line. When you ordered some sort of premium channel like HBO or Showtime, your friendly neighborhood cable man came out and flicked a few switches. That switch box holds your cable life. And what holds your cable life holds all about the real you.

Cable companies and hotels with in-room movies always point out that your bill will not list the names of the movies you watch. That might be true, but that doesn't mean they don't know. Try fighting a charge sometime. They'll tell you titles until you're blue in the face.

What Vic had learned right away—and not to get too technical here—was that your cable choices worked by codes, relaying your order information via the cable switch box to the computers at the cable company's main station. Vic would climb the telephone poles, open the boxes, and read off the numbers. When he went back to the office, he'd plug in the codes and learn all.

He'd learn, for example, that at six P.M. on February 2, you and your family rented *The Lion King* on pay-per-view. Or for a much more telling example, that at ten-thirty P.M. on February 7, you ordered a double bill of *The Hunt for Miss October* and *On Golden Blonde* via Sizzle TV.

See the scam?

At first Vic would hit random houses. He'd write a letter to the male owner of the residence. The letter would be short and chilling. It would list what porno movies had been watched, at what time, on what day. It would make it clear that copies of this information would be disseminated to every member of the man's family, his neighbors, his employer. Then Vic would ask for $500 to keep his mouth shut. Not much money maybe, but Vic thought it was the perfect amount—high enough to give Vic some serious green yet low enough so that most marks wouldn't balk at the price.

Still—and this surprised Vic at first—only about ten percent responded. Vic wasn't sure why. Maybe watching porno films wasn't the stigma it used to be. Maybe the guy's wife already knew about it. Hell, maybe the guy's wife watched them with him. But the real problem was Vic's scam was too scattershot.

He had to be more focused. He had to cherry-pick his marks.

That was when he came up with the idea of concentrating on people in certain professions, ones who would have a lot to lose if the information came out. Again the cable computers had all the info he needed. He started hitting up schoolteachers. Day care workers. Gynecologists. Anyone who worked in jobs that would be sensitive to a scandal like this. Teachers panicked the most, but they had the least money. He also made his letters more specific. He would mention the wife by name. He would mention the employer by name. With teachers, he'd promise to flood the Board of Education and the parents of his students with "proof of perversion," a phrase Vic came up with on his own. With doctors, he'd threaten to send his "proof" to the specific licensing board, along with the local papers, neighbors, and patients.

Money started coming in faster.

To date, Vic's scams had netted him close to forty thousand dollars. And now he had landed his biggest fish yet—such a big fish that at first Vic had considered dropping the matter altogether. But he couldn't. He couldn't just walk away from the juiciest score of his life.

Yes, he'd hit someone in the spotlight. A big, big big-time spotlight. Randall Scope. Young, handsome, rich, hottie wife, 2.4 kids, political aspirations, the heir apparent to the Scope fortune. And Scope hadn't ordered just one movie. Or even two.

During a one-month stint, Randall Scope had ordered twenty-three pornographic films.

Ee-yow.

Vic had spent two nights drafting his demands, but in the end he stuck with the basics: short, chilling, and very specific. He asked Scope for fifty grand. He asked that it be in his box by today. And unless Vic was mistaken, that fifty grand was burning a hole in his windbreaker pocket.

Vic wanted to look. He wanted to look right now. But Vic was nothing if not disciplined. He'd wait until he got home. He'd lock his door and sit on the floor and slit open the package and let the green pour out.

Serious big-time.

Vic parked his car on the street and headed up the driveway. The sight of his living quarters—an apartment over a crappy garage—depressed him. But he wouldn't be there much longer. Take the fifty grand, add the almost forty grand he had hidden in the apartment, plus the ten grand in savings...

The realization made him pause. One hundred thousand dollars. He had one hundred grand in cash. Hot damn.

He'd leave right away. Take this money and head out to Arizona. He had a friend out there, Sammy Viola. He and Sammy were going to start their own business, maybe open a restaurant or nightclub. Vic was tired of New Jersey.

It was time to move on. Start fresh.

Vic headed up the stairs toward his apartment. For the record, Vic had never carried out his threats. He never sent out any letters to anyone. If a mark didn't pay, that was the end of it. Harming them after the fact wouldn't do any good. Vic was a scam artist. He got by on his brains. He used threats, sure, but he'd never carry through with them. It would only make someone mad, and hell, it would probably expose him too.

He'd never really hurt anyone. What would be the point?

He reached the landing and stopped in front of his door. Pitch dark now. The damn lightbulb by his door was out again. He sighed and heaved up his big key chain. He squinted in the dark, trying to find the right key. He did it mostly through feel. He fumbled against the knob until the key found the lock. He pushed open the door and stepped inside and something felt wrong.

Something crinkled under his feet.

Vic frowned. Plastic, he thought to himself. He was stepping on plastic. As though a painter had laid it down to protect the floor or something. He flicked on the light switch, and that was when he saw the man with the gun.

"Hi, Vic."

Vic gasped and took a step back. The man in front of him looked to be in his forties. He was big and fat with a belly that battled against the buttons of his dress shirt and, in at least one place, won. His tie was loosened and he had the worst comb-over imaginable—eight braided strands pulled ear to ear and greased against the dome. The man's features were soft, his chin sinking into folds of flab. He had his feet up on the trunk Vic used as a coffee table. Replace the gun with a TV remote and the man would be a weary dad just home from work.

The other man, the one who blocked the door, was the polar opposite of the big guy—in his twenties, Asian, squat, granite-muscular and cube-shaped with bleached-blond hair, a nose ring or two, and a yellow Walkman in his ears. The only place you might think to see the two of them together would be on a subway, the big man frowning behind his carefully folded newspaper, the Asian kid eyeing you as his head lightly bounced to the too-loud music on his headset.

Vic tried to think. Find out what they want. Reason with them. You're a scam artist, he reminded himself. You're smart. You'll find a way out of this. Vic straightened himself up.

"What do you want?" Vic asked.

The big man with the comb-over pulled the trigger.

Vic heard a pop and then his right knee exploded. His eyes went wide. He screamed and crumbled to the ground, holding his knee. Blood poured between his fingers.

"It's a twenty-two," the big man said, motioning toward the gun. "A small-caliber weapon. What I like about it, as you'll see, is that I can shoot you a lot and not kill you."

With his feet still up, the big man fired again. This time, Vic's shoulder took the hit. Vic could actually feel the bone shatter. His arm flopped away like a barn door with a busted hinge. Vic fell flat on his back and started breathing too fast. A terrible cocktail of fear and pain engulfed him. His eyes stayed wide and unblinking, and through the haze, he realized something.

The plastic on the ground.

He was lying on it. More than that, he was bleeding on it. That was what it was there for. The men had put it down for easy cleanup.

"Do you want to start telling me what I want to hear," the big man said, "or should I shoot again?"

Vic started talking. He told them everything. He told them where the rest of the money was. He told them where the evidence was. The big man asked him if he had any accomplices. He said no. The big man shot Vic's other knee. He asked him again if he had accomplices. Vic still said no. The big man shot him in the right ankle.

An hour later, Vic begged the big man to shoot him in the head.

Two hours after that, the big man obliged.

5

I stared unblinking at the computer screen.

I couldn't move. My senses were past overload. Every part of me was numb.

It couldn't be. I knew that. Elizabeth hadn't fallen off a yacht and assumed drowned, her body never found. She hadn't been burned beyond recognition or any of that. Her corpse had been found in a ditch off Route 80. Battered, perhaps, but she had been positively IDed.

Not by you...

Maybe not, but by two close family members: her father and her uncle. In fact, Hoyt Parker, my father-in-law, was the one who told me that Elizabeth was dead. He came to my hospital room with his brother Ken not long after I regained consciousness. Hoyt and Ken were large and grizzled and stone-faced, one a New York City cop, the other a federal agent, both war veterans with beefy flesh and large, undefined muscles. They took off their hats and tried to tell me with the semidistant empathy of professionals, but I didn't buy it and they weren't selling too hard.

So what had I just seen?

On the monitor, flows of pedestrians still spurted by. I stared some more, willing her to come back. No dice. Where was this anyway?

A bustling city, that was all I could tell. It could be New York for all I knew.

So look for clues, idiot.

I tried to concentrate. Clothes. Okay, let's check out the clothes. Most people were wearing coats or jackets. Conclusion: We were probably somewhere up north or, at least, someplace not particularly warm today. Great. I could rule out Miami.

What else? I stared at the people. The hairstyles? That wouldn't help. I could see the corner of a brick building. I looked for identifiable characteristics, something to separate the building from the norm. Nothing. I searched the screen for something, anything, out of the ordinary.

Shopping bags.

A few people were carrying shopping bags. I tried to read them, but everyone was moving too fast. I willed them to slow down. They didn't. I kept looking, keeping my gaze at knee level. The camera angle wasn't helping here. I put my face so close to the screen, I could feel the heat.

Capital R.

That was the first letter on one bag. The rest was too squiggly to make out. It looked written in some fancy script. Okay, what else? What other clues could I—?

The camera feed went white.

Damn. I hit the reload button. The error screen returned. I went back to the original email and clicked the hyperlink. Another error.

My feed was gone.

I looked at the blank screen, and the truth struck me anew: I'd just seen Elizabeth.

I could try to rationalize it away. But this wasn't a dream. I'd had dreams where Elizabeth was alive. Too many of them. In most, I'd just accept her return from the grave, too thankful to question or doubt. I remember one dream in particular where we were together— I don't remember what we were doing or even where we were—and right then, in mid-laugh, I realized with breath-crushing certainty that I was dreaming, that very soon I'd wake up alone. I remember the dream— me reaching out at that moment and grabbing hold of her, pulling her in close, trying desperately to drag Elizabeth back with me.

I knew dreams. What I had seen on the computer wasn't one.

It wasn't a ghost either. Not that I believe in them, but when in doubt, you might as well keep an open mind. But ghosts don't age. The Elizabeth on the computer had. Not a lot, but it had been eight years. Ghosts don't cut their hair either. I thought of that long braid hanging down her back in the moonlight. I thought about the fashionably short cut I'd just seen. And I thought about those eyes, those eyes that I had looked into since I was seven years old.

It was Elizabeth. She was still alive.

I felt the tears come again, but this time I fought them back. Funny thing. I'd always cried easily, but after mourning for Elizabeth it was as though I couldn't cry anymore. Not that I had cried myself out or used up all my tears or any of that nonsense. Or that I'd grown numb from grief, though that might have been a tiny part of it. What I think happened was that I instinctively snapped into a defensive stance. When Elizabeth died, I threw open the doors and let the pain in. I let myself feel it all. And it hurt. It hurt so damn much that now something primordial wouldn't let it happen again.

I don't know how long I sat there. Half an hour maybe. I tried to slow my breath and calm my mind. I wanted to be rational. I needed to be rational. I was supposed to be at Elizabeth's parents' house already, but I couldn't imagine facing them right now.

Then I remembered something else.

Sarah Goodhart.

Sheriff Lowell had asked if I knew anything about the name. I did.

Elizabeth and I used to play a childhood game. Perhaps you did too. You take your middle name and make it your first, then you take your childhood street name and make it your last. For example, my full name is David Craig Beck and I grew up on Darby Road. I would thus be Craig Darby. And Elizabeth would be...

Sarah Goodhart.

What the hell was going on here?

I picked up the phone. First I called Elizabeth's parents. They still lived in that house on Goodhart Road. Her mother answered. I

56

told her I was running late. People accept that from doctors. One of the fringe benefits of the job.

When I called Sheriff Lowell, his voice mail picked up. I told him to beep me when he had a chance. I don't have a cell phone. I realize that puts me in the minority, but my beeper leashes me to the outside world too much as it is.

I sat back, but Homer Simpson knocked me out of my trance with another "The mail is here!" I shot forward and gripped the mouse. The sender's address was unfamiliar, but the subject read Street Cam. Another thud in my chest.

I clicked the little icon and the email came up:

Tomorrow same time plus two hours at Bigfoot.com. A message for you will be left under:
Your user name: Bat Street
Password: Teenage

Beneath this, clinging to the bottom of the screen, just five more words:

They're watching. Tell no one.

Larry Gandle, the man with the bad comb-over, watched Eric Wu quietly handle the cleanup.

Wu, a twenty-six-year-old Korean with a staggering assortment of body pierces and tattoos, was the deadliest man Gandle had ever known. Wu was built like a small army tank, but that alone didn't mean much. Gandle knew plenty of people who had the physique. Too often, show muscles meant useless muscles.

That was not the case with Eric Wu.

The rock brawn was nice, but the real secret of Wu's deadly strength lay in the man's callused hands—two cement blocks with steel-talon fingers. He spent hours on them, punching cinder blocks, exposing them to extreme heat and cold, performing sets of one-finger push-ups. When Wu put those fingers to use, the devastation to bone and tissue was unimaginable.

Dark rumors swirled around men like Wu, most of which were crap, but Larry Gandle had seen him kill a man by digging his fingers into the soft spots of the face and abdomen. He had seen Wu grab a man by both ears and rip them off in a smooth pluck. He had seen him kill four times in four very different ways, never using a weapon.

None of the deaths had been quick.

Nobody knew exactly where Wu came from, but the most accepted tale had something to do with a brutal childhood in North Korea. Gandle had never asked. There were some night paths the mind was better off not traversing; the dark side of Eric Wu—right, like there might be a light side—was one of them.

When Wu finished wrapping up the proto-plasm that had been Vic Letty in the drop cloth, he looked up at Gandle with those eyes of his. Dead eyes, Larry Gandle thought. The eyes of a child in a war newsreel.

Wu had not bothered taking off his headset. His personal stereo did not blare hip hop or rap or even rock 'n' roll. He listened pretty much nonstop to those soothing-sounds CDs you might find at Sharper Image, the ones with names like Ocean Breeze and Running Brook.

"Should I take him to Benny's?" Wu asked. His voice had a slow, odd cadence to it, like a character from a Peanuts cartoon.

Larry Gandle nodded. Benny ran a crematorium. Ashes to ashes. Or, in this case, scum to ashes. "And get rid of this."

Gandle handed Eric Wu the twenty-two. The weapon looked puny and useless in Wu's giant hand. Wu frowned at it, probably disappointed that Gandle had chosen it over Wu's own unique talents, and jammed it in his pocket. With a twenty-two, there were rarely exit wounds. That meant less evidence. The blood had been contained by a vinyl drop cloth. No muss, no fuss.

"Later," Wu said. He picked up the body with one hand as though it were a briefcase and carried it out.

Larry Gandle nodded a good-bye. He took little joy from Vic Letty's pain—but then again, he took little discomfort either. It was a simple matter really. Gandle had to know for absolute certain that Letty was working alone and that he hadn't left evidence around for someone else to find. That meant pushing the man past the breaking point. There was no other way.

In the end, it came down to a clear choice—the Scope family or Vic Letty. The Scopes were good people. They had never done a damn thing to Vic Letty. Vic Letty, on the other hand, had gone out of his way to try to hurt the Scope family. Only one of them could get off unscathed—the innocent, well-meaning victim or the parasite who was trying to feed off another's misery. No choice when you thought about it.

Gandle's cell phone vibrated. He picked it up and said, "Yes."

"They identified the bodies at the lake."

"And?"

"It's them. Jesus Christ, it's Bob and Mel."

Gandle closed his eyes.

"What does it mean, Larry?"

"I don't know."

"So what are we going to do?"

Larry Gandle knew that there was no choice. He'd have to speak with Griffin Scope. It would unearth unpleasant memories. Eight years. After eight years. Gandle shook his head. It would break the old man's heart all over again.

"I'll handle it."

6

Kim Parker, my mother-in-law, is beautiful. She'd always looked so much like Elizabeth that her face had become for me the ultimate what-might-have-been. But Elizabeth's death had slowly sapped her. Her face was drawn now, her features almost brittle. Her eyes had that look of marbles shattered from within.

The Parkers' house had gone through very few changes since the seventies—adhesive wood paneling, wall-to-wall semi-shag carpet of light blue with flecks of white, a faux-stone raised fireplace à la the Brady Bunch. Folded TV trays, the kind with white plastic tops and gold metal legs, lined one wall. There were clown paintings and Rockwell collector plates. The only noticeable update was the television. It had swelled over the years from a bouncing twelve-inch black-and-white to the monstrous full-color fifty-incher that now sat hunched in the corner.

My mother-in-law sat on the same couch where Elizabeth and I had so often made out and then some. I smiled for a moment and thought, ah, if that couch could talk. But then again, that hideous chunk of sitting space with the loud floral design held a lot more than lustful memories. Elizabeth and I had sat there to open our college acceptance letters.

We cuddled to watch *One Flew Over the Cuckoo's Nest* and *The Deer Hunter* and all the old Hitchcock films. We did homework, me sitting upright and Elizabeth lying with her head on my lap. I told Elizabeth I wanted to be a doctor—a big-time surgeon, or so I thought. She told me she wanted to get a law degree and work with kids. Elizabeth couldn't bear the thought of children in pain.

I remember an internship she did during the summer break after our freshman year of college. She worked for Covenant House, rescuing runaway and homeless children from New York's worst streets. I went with her once in the Covenant House van, cruising up and down Forty-second Street pre-Giuliani, sifting through putrid pools of quasi-humanity for children who needed shelter. Elizabeth spotted a fourteen-year-old hooker who was so strung out that she'd soiled herself. I winced in disgust. I'm not proud of that. These people may have been human, but—I'm being honest here—the filth repulsed me. I helped. But I winced.

Elizabeth never winced. That was her gift. She took the children by the hand. She carried them. She cleaned off that girl and nursed her and talked to her all night. She looked them straight in the eye. Elizabeth truly believed that everyone was good and worthy; she was naïve in a way I wish I could be.

I'd always wondered if she'd died that same way—with that naïveté intact—still clinging through the pain to her faith in humanity and all that wonderful nonsense. I hope so, but I suspect that KillRoy probably broke her.

Kim Parker sat primly with her hands in her lap. She'd always liked me well enough, though during our youth both sets of parents had been concerned with our closeness. They wanted us to play with others. They wanted us to make more friends. Natural, I suppose.

Hoyt Parker, Elizabeth's father, wasn't home yet, so Kim and I chatted about nothing—or, to say the same thing a different way, we chatted about everything except Elizabeth. I kept my eyes focused on Kim because I knew that the mantel was chock-full of photographs of Elizabeth and her heart-splitting smile.

She's alive....

I couldn't make myself believe it. The mind, I know from my psychiatric rotation in medical school (not to mention my family history), has incredible distortive powers. I didn't believe I was nuts enough to conjure up her image, but then again, crazy people never do. I thought about my mother and wondered what she realized about her mental health, if she was even capable of engaging in serious introspection.

Probably not.

Kim and I talked about the weather. We talked about my patients. We talked about her new part-time job at Macy's. And then Kim surprised the hell out of me.

"Are you seeing anyone?" she asked.

It was the first truly personal question she

had ever asked me. It knocked me back a step. I wondered what she wanted to hear. "No," I said.

She nodded and looked as though she wanted to say something else. Her hand fluttered up to her face.

"I date," I said.

"Good," she replied with too hearty a nod. "You should."

I stared at my hands and surprised myself by saying, "I still miss her so much." I didn't plan on that. I planned on keeping quiet and following our usual safe track. I glanced up at her face. She looked pained and grateful.

"I know you do, Beck," Kim said. "But you shouldn't feel guilty about seeing other people."

"I don't," I said. "I mean, it's not that."

She uncrossed her legs and leaned toward me. "Then what is it?"

I couldn't speak. I wanted to. For her sake. She looked at me with those shattered eyes, her need to talk about her daughter so surface, so raw. But I couldn't. I shook my head.

I heard a key in the door. We both turned suddenly, straightening up like caught lovers. Hoyt Parker shouldered open the door and called out his wife's name. He stepped into the den and with a hearty sigh, he put down a gym bag. His tie was loosened, his shirt wrinkled, his sleeves rolled up to the elbows. Hoyt had forearms like Popeye. When he saw us sitting on the couch, he let loose another sigh, this one deeper and with more than a hint of disapproval.

"How are you, David?" he said to me.

We shook hands. His grip, as always, was callous-scratchy and too firm. Kim excused herself and hurried out of the room. Hoyt and I exchanged pleasantries, and silence settled in. Hoyt Parker had never been comfortable with me. There might have been some Electra complex here, but I'd always felt that he saw me as a threat. I understood. His little girl had spent all her time with me. Over the years, we'd managed to fight through his resentment and forged something of a friendship. Until Elizabeth's death.

He blames me for what happened.

He has never said that, of course, but I see it in his eyes. Hoyt Parker is a burly, strong man. Rock-solid, honest Americana. He'd always made Elizabeth feel unconditionally safe. Hoyt had that kind of protective aura. No harm would come to his little girl as long as Big Hoyt was by her side.

I don't think I ever made Elizabeth feel safe like that.

"Work good?" Hoyt asked me.

"Fine," I said. "You?"

"A year away from retirement."

I nodded and we again fell into silence. On the ride over here, I decided not to say anything about what I'd seen on the computer. Forget the fact that it sounded loony. Forget the fact that it would open old wounds and hurt them both like all hell. The truth was, I didn't have a clue what was going on. The more time passed, the more the whole episode felt

65

unreal. I also decided to take that last email to heart. *Tell no one.* I couldn't imagine why or what was going on, but whatever connection I'd made felt frighteningly tenuous.

Nonetheless I still found myself making sure Kim was out of earshot. Then I leaned closer to Hoyt and said softly, "Can I ask you something?"

He didn't reply, offering up instead one of his patented skeptical gazes.

"I want to know—" I stopped. "I want to know how you found her."

"Found her?"

"I mean when you first walked into the morgue. I want to know what you saw."

Something happened to his face, like tiny explosions collapsing the foundation. "For the love of Christ, why would you ask me that?"

"I've just been thinking about it," I said lamely. "With the anniversary and all."

He stood suddenly and wiped his palms on the legs of his pants. "You want a drink?"

"Sure."

"Bourbon okay?"

"That would be great."

He walked over to an old bar cart near the mantel and thus the photographs. I kept my gaze on the floor.

"Hoyt?" I tried.

He twisted open a bottle. "You're a doctor," he said, pointing a glass at me. "You've seen dead bodies."

"Yes."

"Then you know."

I did know.

He brought over my drink. I grabbed it a little too quickly and downed a sip. He watched me and then brought his glass to his lips.

"I know I never asked you about the details," I began. More than that, I had studiously avoided them. Other "families of the victims," as the media referred to us, bathed in them. They showed up every day at KillRoy's trial and listened and cried. I didn't. I think it helped them channel their grief. I chose to channel mine back at myself.

"You don't want to know the details, Beck."

"She was beaten?"

Hoyt studied his drink. "Why are you doing this?"

"I need to know."

He peered at me over the glass. His eyes moved along my face. It felt as though they were prodding my skin. I kept my gaze steady.

"There were bruises, yes."

"Where?"

"David—"

"On her face?"

His eyes narrowed, as though he'd spotted something unexpected. "Yes."

"On her body too?"

"I didn't look at her body," he said. "But I know the answer is yes."

"Why didn't you look at her body?"

"I was there as her father, not an investigator—for the purposes of identification only."

"Was that easy?" I asked.

"Was what easy?"

"Making the identification. I mean, you said her face was bruised."

His body stiffened. He put down his drink, and with mounting dread, I realized I'd gone too far. I should have stuck to my plan. I should have just kept my mouth shut.

"You really want to hear all this?"

No, I thought. But I nodded my head.

Hoyt Parker put down his drink, crossed his arms, and leaned back on his heels. "Elizabeth's left eye was swollen closed. Her nose was broken and flattened like wet clay. There was a slash across her forehead, probably made with a box cutter. Her jaw had been ripped out of its hinges, snapping all the tendons." His voice was a total monotone. "The letter K was burnt into her right cheek. The smell of charred skin was still obvious."

My stomach knotted.

Hoyt's eyes settled onto mine hard. "Do you want to know what was the worst part, Beck?"

I looked at him and waited.

"It still took no time at all," he said. "I knew in an instant that it was Elizabeth."

7

Champagne flutes tinkled in harmony with the Mozart sonata. A harp underscored the subdued pitch of the party chatter. Griffin Scope moved serpentine through the black tuxedos and shimmering gowns. People always used the same word to describe Griffin Scope: billionaire. After that, they might call him businessman or power broker or mention that he was tall or a husband or a grandfather or that he was seventy years old. They might comment on his personality or his family tree or his work ethic. But the first word—in the papers, on television, on people's lists—was always the B word. Billionaire. Billionaire Griffin Scope.

Griffin had been born rich. His grandfather was an early industrialist; his father improved the fortune; Griffin multiplied it several-fold. Most family empires fall apart before the third generation. Not the Scopes'. A lot of that had to do with their upbringing. Griffin, for example, did not attend a prestigious prep school like Exeter or Lawrenceville, as so many of his peers did. His father insisted that Griffin not only attend public school but that he do so in the closest major city, Newark. His father had offices there, thus setting up a fake residence was no problem.

Newark's east side wasn't a bad neighbor-

69

hood back then—not like now, when a sane person would barely want to drive through it. It was working class, blue collar—tough rather than dangerous.

Griffin loved it.

His best friends from those high school days were still his friends fifty years later. Loyalty was a rare quality; when Griffin found it, he made sure to reward it. Many of tonight's guests were from those Newark days. Some even worked for him, though he tried to make it a point to never be their day-to-day boss.

Tonight's gala celebrated the cause most dear to Griffin Scope's heart: the Brandon Scope Memorial Charity, named for Griffin's murdered son. Griffin had started the fund with a one-hundred-million-dollar contribution. Friends quickly added to the till. Griffin was not stupid. He knew that many donated to curry his favor. But there was more to it than that. During his too-brief life, Brandon Scope touched people. A boy born with so much luck and talent, Brandon had an almost supernatural charisma. People were drawn to him.

His other son, Randall, was a good boy who had grown up to be a good man. But Brandon... Brandon had been magic.

The pain flooded in again. It was always there, of course. Through the shaking hands and slapping of the backs, the grief stayed by his side, tapping Griffin on the shoulder, whispering in his ear, reminding him that they were partners for life.

"Lovely party, Griff."

70

Griffin said thank you and moved on. The women were well coiffed and wore gowns that highlighted lovely bare shoulders; they fit in nicely with the many ice sculptures—a favorite of Griffin's wife Allison—that slowly melted atop imported linen tablecloths. The Mozart sonata changed over to one by Chopin. White-gloved servers made the rounds with silver trays of Malaysian shrimp and Omaha tenderloin and a potpourri of bizarre finger-food that always seemed to contain sun-dried tomatoes.

He reached Linda Beck, the young lady who headed up Brandon's charitable fund. Linda's father had been an old Newark class-mate too, and she, so like so many others, had become entwined in the massive Scope holdings. She'd started working for various Scope enterprises while still in high school. Both she and her brother had paid for their education with Scope scholarship grants.

"You look smashing," he told her, though in truth he thought she looked tired.

Linda Beck smiled at him. "Thank you, Mr. Scope."

"How many times have I asked you to call me Griff?"

"Several hundred," she said.

"How's Shauna?"

"A little under the weather, I'm afraid."

"Give her my best."

"I will, thank you."

"We should probably meet next week."

"I'll call your secretary."

"Good."

Griffin gave her a peck on the cheek, and that was when he spotted Larry Gandle in the foyer. Larry looked bleary-eyed and disheveled, but then again, he always looked that way. You could slap a custom-cut Joseph Abboud on him, and an hour later he'd still look like someone who'd gotten into a tussle.

Larry Gandle was not supposed to be here.

The two men's eyes met. Larry nodded once and turned away. Griffin waited another moment or two and then followed his young friend down the corridor.

Larry's father, Edward, had also been one of Griffin's classmates from the old Newark days. Edward Gandle died of a sudden heart attack twelve years ago. Damn shame. Edward had been a fine man. Since then, his son had taken over as the Scopes' closest confidant.

The two men entered Griffin's library. At one time, the library had been a wonderful room of oak and mahogany and floor-to-ceiling bookshelves and antique globes. Two years ago, Allison, in a postmodern mood, decided that the room needed a total updating. The old woodwork was torn out and now the room was white and sleek and functional and held all the warmth of a work cubicle. Allison had been so proud of the room that Griffin didn't have the heart to tell her how much he disliked it.

"Was there a problem tonight?" Griffin asked.

"No," Larry said.

Griffin offered Larry a seat. Larry shook him off and started pacing.

"Was it bad?" Griffin asked.

"We had to make certain there were no loose ends."

"Of course."

Someone had attacked Griffin's son Randall—ergo, Griffin attacked back. It was one lesson he never forgot. You don't sit back when you or a loved one is being assaulted. And you don't act like the government with their "proportional responses" and all that nonsense. If someone hurts you, mercy and pity must be put aside. You eliminate the enemy. You scorch the earth. Those who scoffed at this philosophy, who thought it unnecessarily Machiavellian, usually were the ones who caused excess destruction.

In the end, if you eliminate problems swiftly, less blood is shed.

"So what's wrong?" Griffin asked.

Larry kept pacing. He rubbed the front of his bald pate. Griffin didn't like what he was seeing. Larry was not one to get keyed up easily. "I've never lied to you, Griff," he said.

"I know that."

"But there are times for...insulation."

"Insulation?"

"Who I hire, for example. I never tell you names. I never tell them names either."

"Those are details."

"Yes."

"What is it, Larry?"

He stopped pacing. "Eight years ago, you'll

recall that we hired two men to perform a certain task."

The color drained from Griffin's face. He swallowed. "And they performed admirably."

"Yes. Well, perhaps."

"I don't understand."

"They performed their task. Or, at least, part of it. The threat was apparently eliminated."

Even though the house was swept for listening devices on a weekly basis, the two men never used names. A Scope rule. Larry Gandle often wondered if the rule was for the sake of caution or because it helped depersonalize what they were occasionally forced to do. He suspected the latter.

Griffin finally collapsed into a chair, almost as though someone had pushed him. His voice was soft. "Why are you bringing this up now?"

"I know how painful this must be for you."

Griffin did not reply.

"I paid the two men well," Larry continued.

"As I'd have expected."

"Yes." He cleared his throat. "Well, after the incident, they were supposed to lay low for a while. As a precaution."

"Go on."

"We never heard from them again."

"They'd already collected their money, correct?"

"Yes."

"So what's surprising about that? Perhaps they fled with their newfound wealth. Perhaps they moved across the country or changed identities."

"That," Larry said, "was what we'd always assumed."

"But?"

"Their bodies were found last week. They're dead."

"I still don't see the problem. They were violent men. They probably met a violent end."

"The bodies were old."

"Old?"

"They've been dead at least five years. And they were found buried by the lake where... where the incident took place."

Griffin opened his mouth, closed it, tried again. "I don't understand."

"Frankly, neither do I."

Too much. It was all too much. Griffin had been fighting off the tears all night, what with the gala being in Brandon's honor and all. Now the tragedy of Brandon's murder was suddenly resurfacing. It was all he could do not to break down.

Griffin looked up at his confidant. "This can't come back."

"I know, Griff."

"We have to find out what happened. I mean everything."

"I've kept tabs on the men in her life. Especially her husband. Just in case. Now I've put all our resources on it."

"Good," Griffin said. "Whatever it takes, this gets buried. I don't care who gets buried with it."

"I understand."

"And, Larry?"

Gandle waited.

"I know the name of one man you hire." He meant Eric Wu. Griffin Scope wiped his eyes and started back toward his guests. "Use him."

8

Shauna and Linda rent a three-bedroom apartment on Riverside Drive and 116 Street, not far from Columbia University. I'd managed to find a spot within a block, an act that usually accompanies a parting sea or stone tablet.

Shauna buzzed me up. Linda was still out at her formal. Mark was asleep. I tiptoed into his room and kissed his forehead. Mark was still hanging on to the Pokémon craze and it showed. He had Pikachu sheets, and a stuffed Squirtle doll lay nestled in his arms. People criticize the trend, but it reminded me of my own childhood obsession with Batman and Captain America. I watched him a few more seconds. Cliché to say, yes, but it is indeed the little things.

Shauna stood in the doorway and waited. When we finally moved back into the den, I said, "Mind if I have a drink?"

Shauna shrugged. "Suit yourself."

I poured myself two fingers of bourbon. "You'll join me."

She shook her head.

We settled onto the couch. "What time is Linda supposed to be home?" I asked.

"Got me," Shauna said slowly. I didn't like the way she did it.

"Damn," I said.

"It's temporary, Beck. I love Linda, you know that."

"Damn," I said again.

Last year, Linda and Shauna had separated for two months. It hadn't been good, especially for Mark.

"I'm not moving out or anything," Shauna said.

"So what's wrong, then?"

"Same ol' same ol'. I have this glamorous high-profile job. I'm surrounded by beautiful, interesting people all the time. Nothing new, right? We all know this. Anyway, Linda thinks I have a wandering eye."

"You do," I said.

"Yeah, sure, but that's nothing new, is it?"

I didn't reply.

"At the end of the day, Linda is the one I go home to."

"And you never take any detours on the way?"

"If I did, they'd be irrelevant. You know that. I don't do well locked in a cage, Beck. I need the stage."

"Nice mix of metaphors," I said.

"At least it rhymed."

I drank in silence for a few moments.

"Beck?"

"What?"

"Your turn now."

"Meaning?"

She shot me a look and waited.

I thought about the "Tell no one" warning at the end of the email. If the message were indeed from Elizabeth—my mind still had trouble even entertaining such a notion—she would know that I'd tell Shauna. Linda— maybe not. But Shauna? I tell her everything. It would be a given.

"There's a chance," I said, "that Elizabeth is still alive."

Shauna didn't break stride. "She ran off with Elvis, right?" When she saw my face, she stopped and said, "Explain."

I did. I told her about the email. I told her about the street cam. And I told her about seeing Elizabeth on the computer monitor. Shauna kept her eyes on me the whole time. She didn't nod or interrupt. When I finished, she carefully extracted a cigarette from its carton and put it in her mouth. Shauna gave up smoking years ago, but she still liked to fiddle with them. She examined the cancer stick, turning it over in her hand as though she'd never seen one before. I could see the gears churning.

"Okay," she said. "So at eight-fifteen tomorrow night, the next message is supposed to come in, right?"

I nodded.

"So we wait until then."

She put the cigarette back in the pack.

"You don't think it's crazy?"

Shauna shrugged. "Irrelevant," she said.

"Meaning?"

"There are several possibilities that'd explain what you just said."

"Including insanity."

"Yeah, sure, that's a strong one. But what's the point of hypothesizing negatively right now? Let's just assume it's true. Let's just assume you saw what you saw and that Elizabeth is still alive. If we're wrong, hey, we'll learn that soon enough. If we're right..." She knitted her eyebrows, thought about it, shook her head. "Christ, I hope like hell we're right."

I smiled at her. "I love you, you know."

"Yeah," she said. "Everyone does."

When I got home, I poured myself one last quick drink. I took a deep sip and let the warm liquor travel to destinations well known. Yes, I drink. But I'm not a drunk. That's not denial. I know I flirt with being an alcoholic. I also know that flirting with alcoholism is about as safe as flirting with a mobster's underage daughter. But so far, the flirting hasn't led to coupling. I'm smart enough to know that might not last.

Chloe sidled up to me with her customary expression that could be summed up thusly: "Food, walk, food, walk." Dogs are wonderfully consistent. I tossed her a treat and took her for a stroll around the block. The cold air felt good in my lungs, but walking never cleared my head. Walking is, in fact, a tremendous bore. But I liked watching Chloe walk. I know that sounds queer, but a dog derives such pleasure from this simple activity. It made me Zen-happy to watch her.

Back home I moved quietly toward my bedroom. Chloe followed me. Grandpa was asleep. So was his new nurse. She snored with a cartoonlike, high-pitched exhale. I flipped on my computer and wondered why Sheriff Lowell hadn't called me back. I thought about calling him, though the time was nearing midnight. Then I figured: tough.

I picked up the phone and dialed. Lowell had a cell phone. If he was sleeping, he could always turn it off, right?

He answered on the third ring. "Hello, Dr. Beck."

His voice was tight. I also noted that I was no longer Doc.

"Why didn't you call me back?" I asked.

"It was getting late," he said. "I figured I'd catch you in the morning."

"Why did you ask me about Sarah Goodhart?"

"Tomorrow," he said.

"Pardon me?"

"It's late, Dr. Beck. I'm off duty. Besides, I think I'd rather go over this with you in person."

"Can't you at least tell me—?"

"You'll be at your clinic in the morning?"

"Yes."

"I'll call you then."

He bade me a polite but firm good night and then he was gone. I stared at the phone and wondered what the hell that was all about.

Sleep was out of the question. I spent most of the night on the Web, surfing through various city street cams, hoping to stumble across the right one. Talk about the high-tech needle in the worldwide haystack.

At some point, I stopped and slipped under the covers. Part of being a doctor is patience. I constantly give children tests that have life-altering—if not life-ending—implications and tell them and their parents to wait for the results. They have no choice. Perhaps the same could be said for this situation. There were too many variables right now. Tomorrow, when I logged in at Bigfoot under the Bat Street user name and Teenage password, I might learn more.

I stared up at the ceiling for a while. Then I looked to my right—where Elizabeth had slept. I always fell asleep first. I used to lie like this and watch her with a book, her face in profile, totally focused on whatever she was reading. That was the last thing I saw before my eyes closed and I drifted off to sleep.

I rolled over and faced the other way.

At four in the morning, Larry Gandle looked over the bleached-blond locks of Eric Wu. Wu was incredibly disciplined. If he wasn't working on his physical prowess, he was in front of a computer screen. His complexion had turned

81

a sickly blue-white several thousand Web surfs ago, but that physique remained serious cement.

"Well?" Gandle said.

Wu popped the headphones off. Then he folded his marble-column arms across his chest. "I'm confused."

"Tell me."

"Dr. Beck has barely saved any of his emails. Just a few involving patients. Nothing personal. But then he gets two bizarre ones in the last two days." Still not turning from the screen, Eric Wu handed two pieces of paper over his bowling ball of a shoulder. Larry Gandle looked at the emails and frowned.

"What do they mean?"

"I don't know."

Gandle skimmed the message that talked about clicking something at "kiss time." He didn't understand computers—nor did he want to understand them. His eyes traveled back up to the top of the sheet and he read the subject.

E.P.+ D.B. and a bunch of lines.

Gandle thought about it. D.B. David Beck maybe? And E.P....

The meaning landed on him like a dropped piano. He slowly handed the paper back to Wu.

"Who sent this?" Gandle asked.

"I don't know."

"Find out."

"Impossible," Wu said.

"Why?"

"The sender used an anonymous remailer."

82

Wu spoke with a patient, almost unearthly monotone. He used that same tone while discussing a weather report or ripping off a man's cheek. "I won't go into the computer jargon, but there is no way to trace it back."

Gandle turned his attention to the other email, the one with the Bat Street and Teenage. He couldn't make head or tail out of it.

"How about this one? Can you trace it back?"

Wu shook his head. "Also an anonymous remailer."

"Did the same person send both?"

"Your guess would be as good as mine."

"How about the content? Do you understand what either one is talking about?"

Wu hit a few keys and the first email popped up on the monitor. He pointed a thick, veiny finger at the screen. "See that blue lettering there? It's a hyperlink. All Dr. Beck had to do was click it and it would take him someplace, probably a Web site."

"What Web site?"

"It's a broken link. Again, you can't trace it back."

"And Beck was supposed to do this at 'kiss time'?"

"That's what it says."

"Is kiss time some sort of computer term?"

Wu almost grinned. "No."

"So you don't know what time the email refers to?"

"That's correct."

"Or even if we've passed kiss time or not?"

"It's passed," Wu said.

"How do you know?"

"His Web browser is set up to show you the last twenty sites he visited. He clicked the link. Several times, in fact."

"But you can't, uh, follow him there?"

"No. The link is useless."

"What about this other email?"

Wu hit a more few keys. The screen changed and the other email appeared. "This one is easier to figure out. It's very basic, as a matter of fact."

"Okay, I'm listening."

"The anonymous emailer has set up an email account for Dr. Beck," Wu explained. "He's given Dr. Beck a user name and a password and again mentioned kiss time."

"So let me see if I understand," Gandle said. "Beck goes to some Web site. He types in that user name and that password and there'll be a message for him?"

"That's the theory, yes."

"Can we do it too?"

"Sign in using that user name and password?"

"Yes. And read the message."

"I tried it. The account doesn't exist yet."

"Why not?"

Eric Wu shrugged. "The anonymous sender might set up the account later. Closer to kiss time."

"So what can we conclude here?"

"Put simply"—the light from the monitor danced off Wu's blank eyes—"someone is going through a great deal of trouble to stay anonymous."

"So how do we find out who it is?"

Wu held up a small device that looked like something you might find in a transistor radio. "We've installed one of these on his home and work computers."

"What is it?"

"A digital network tracker. The tracker sends digital signals from his computers to mine. If Dr. Beck gets any emails or visits any Web sites or even if he just types up a letter, we'll be able to monitor it all in real time."

"So we wait and watch," Gandle said.

"Yes."

Gandle thought about what Wu had told him—about the lengths someone was going through to remain anonymous—and an awful suspicion started creeping into the pit of his belly.

9

I parked at the lot two blocks from the clinic. I never made it past block one. Sheriff Lowell materialized with two men sporting buzz cuts and gray suits. The two men in suits leaned against a big brown Buick. Physical opposites. One was tall and thin and white, the other short and round and black;

together they looked a little like a bowling ball trying to knock down the last pin. Both men smiled at me. Lowell did not.

"Dr. Beck?" the tall white pin said. He was impeccably groomed—gelled hair, folded hanky in the pocket, tie knotted with supernatural precision, tortoiseshell designer glasses, the kind actors wear when they want to look smart.

I looked at Lowell. He said nothing.

"Yes."

"I'm Special Agent Nick Carlson with the Federal Bureau of Investigation," the impeccably groomed one continued. "This is Special Agent Tom Stone."

They both flashed badges. Stone, the shorter and more rumpled of the two, hitched up his trousers and nodded at me. Then he opened the back door of the Buick.

"Would you mind coming with us?"

"I have patients in fifteen minutes," I said.

"We've already taken care of that." Carlson swept a long arm toward the car door, as though he were displaying a game show prize. "Please."

I got in the back. Carlson drove. Stone squeezed himself into the front passenger seat. Lowell didn't get in. We stayed in Manhattan, but the ride still took close to forty-five minutes. We ended up way downtown on Broadway near Duane Street. Carlson stopped the car in front of an office building marked 26 Federal Plaza.

The interior was basic office building. Men

in suits, surprisingly nice ones, moved about with cups of designer coffee. There were women too, but they were heavily in the minority. We moved into a conference room. I was invited to sit, which I did. I tried crossing my legs, but that didn't feel right.

"Can someone tell me what's going on?" I asked.

White-Pin Carlson took the lead. "Can we get you something?" he asked. "We make the world's worst coffee, if you're interested."

That explained all the designer cups. He smiled at me. I smiled back. "Tempting, but no thanks."

"How about a soft drink? We have soft drinks, Tom?"

"Sure, Nick. Coke, Diet Coke, Sprite, whatever the doctor here wants."

They smiled some more. "I'm fine, thanks," I said.

"Snapple?" Stone tried. He once again hitched up his pants. His stomach was the kind of round that made it hard to find a spot where the waistband wouldn't slide. "We got a bunch of different varieties here."

I almost said yes so that they'd get on with it, but I just gently shook him off. The table, some sort of Formica mix, was bare except for a large manila envelope. I wasn't sure what to do with my hands, so I put them on the table. Stone waddled to the side and stood there. Carlson, still taking the lead, sat on the corner of the table and swiveled to look down at me.

"What can you tell us about Sarah Good-hart?" Carlson asked.

I wasn't sure how to answer. I kept trying to figure out the angles, but nothing was coming to me.

"Doc?"

I looked up at him. "Why do you want to know?"

Carlson and Stone exchanged a quick glance. "The name Sarah Goodhart has surfaced in connection with an ongoing investigation," Carlson said.

"What investigation?" I asked.

"We'd rather not say."

"I don't understand. How am I connected into this?"

Carlson let loose a sigh, taking his time on the exhale. He looked over at his rotund partner and suddenly all smiles were gone. "Am I asking a complicated question here, Tom?"

"No, Nick, I don't think so."

"Me neither." Carlson turned his eyes back at me. "Maybe you object to the form of the question, Doc. That it?"

"That's what they always do on *The Practice*, Nick," Stone chimed in. "Object to the form of the question."

"That they do, Tom, that they do. And then they say, 'I'll rephrase,' right? Something like that."

"Something like that, yeah."

Carlson looked me down. "So let me rephrase: Does the name Sarah Goodhart mean anything to you?"

I didn't like this. I didn't like their attitude or the fact that they had taken over for Lowell or the way I was getting grilled in this conference room. They had to know what the name meant. It wasn't that difficult. All you had to do was casually glance at Elizabeth's name and address. I decided to tread gently.

"My wife's middle name is Sarah," I said.

"My wife's middle name is Gertrude," Carlson said.

"Christ, Nick, that's awful."

"What's your wife's middle name, Tom?"

"McDowd. It's a family name."

"I like when they do that. Use a family name as a middle name. Honor the ancestors like that."

"Me too, Nick."

Both men swung their gazes back in my direction.

"What's your middle name, Doc?"

"Craig," I said.

"Craig," Carlson repeated. "Okay, so if I asked you if the name, say"—he waved his arms theatrically—"Craig Dipwad meant anything to you, would you chirp up, 'Hey, my middle name is Craig'?"

Carlson flashed me the hard eyes again.

"I guess not," I said.

"I guess not. So let's try it again: Have you heard the name Sarah Goodhart, yes or no?"

"You mean ever?"

Stone said, "Jesus Christ."

Carlson's face reddened. "You playing semantic games with us now, Doc?"

He was right. I was being stupid. I was flying blind, and that last line of the email—

Tell no one—kept flashing in my head like something in neon. Confusion took over. They had to know about Sarah Goodhart. This was all a test to see if I was going to cooperate or not. That was it. Maybe. And cooperate about what?

"My wife grew up on Goodhart Road," I said. They both moved back a little, giving me room, folding their arms. They led me to a pool of silence and I foolishly dived in. "See, that's why I said Sarah was my wife's middle name. The Goodhart made me think of her."

"Because she grew up on Goodhart Road?" Carlson said.

"Yes."

"Like the word Goodhart was a catalyst or something?"

"Yes," I said again.

"That makes sense to me." Carlson looked at his partner. "That make sense to you, Tom?"

"Sure," Stone agreed, patting his stomach. "He wasn't being evasive or anything. The word Goodhart was a catalyst."

"Right. That's what got him thinking about his wife."

They both looked at me again. This time I forced myself to keep quiet.

"Did your wife ever use the name Sarah Goodhart?" Carlson asked.

"Use it how?"

"Did she ever say, 'Hi, I'm Sarah Goodhart,' or get an ID with that name or check into some hot-sheets under that name—"

90

"No," I said.

"You sure?"

"Yes."

"That the truth?"

"Yes."

"Don't need another catalyst?"

I straightened up in the chair and decided to show some resolve. "I don't much like your attitude, Agent Carlson."

His toothy, dentist-proud smile returned, but it was like some cruel hybrid of its earlier form. He held up his hand and said, "Excuse me, yeah, okay, that was rude." He looked around as though thinking about what to say next. I waited.

"You ever beat up your wife, Doc?"

The question hit me like a whiplash. "What?"

"That get you off? Smacking around a woman?"

"What...are you insane?"

"How much life insurance did you collect when your wife died?"

I froze. I looked at his face and then at Stone's. Totally opaque. I couldn't believe what I was hearing. "What's going on here?"

"Please just answer the question. Unless, of course, you got something you don't want to tell us."

"It's no secret," I said. "The policy was for two hundred thousand dollars."

Stone whistled. "Two hundred grand for a dead wife. Hey, Nick, where do I get in line?"

"That's a lot of life insurance for a twenty-five-year-old woman."

"Her cousin was starting out with State Farm," I said, my words stumbling over one another. The funny thing is, even though I knew I hadn't done anything wrong—at least not what they thought—I started feeling guilty. It was a weird sensation. Sweat started pouring down my armpits. "She wanted to help him out. So she bought this big policy."

"Nice of her," Carlson said.

"Real nice," Stone added. "Family is so important, don't you think?"

I said nothing. Carlson sat back down on the table's corner. The smile was gone again. "Look at me, Doc."

I did. His eyes bore into mine. I managed to maintain eye contact, but it was a struggle.

"Answer my question this time," he said slowly. "And don't give me shocked or insulted. Did you ever hit your wife?"

"Never," I said.

"Not once?"

"Not once."

"Ever push her?"

"Never."

"Or lash out in anger. Hell, we've all been there, Doc. A quick slap. No real crime in that. Natural when it comes to the affairs of the heart, you know what I mean?"

"I never hit my wife," I said. "I never pushed her or slapped her or lashed out in anger. Never."

Carlson looked over at Stone. "That clear it up for you, Tom?"

"Sure, Nick. He says he never hit her, that's good enough for me."

Carlson scratched his chin. "Unless."

"Unless what, Nick?"

"Well, unless I can provide Dr. Beck here with another one of those catalysts."

All eyes were on me again. My own breaths echoed in my ears, hitched and uneven. I felt light-headed. Carlson waited a beat before he snatched up the large manila envelope. He took his time untying the string flap with long, slender fingers and then he opened the slit. He lifted it high in the air and let the contents fall to the table.

"How's this for a catalyst, huh, Doc?"

They were photographs. Carlson pushed them toward me. I looked down and felt the hole in my heart expand.

"Dr. Beck?"

I stared. My fingers reached out tentatively and touched the surface.

Elizabeth.

They were photographs of Elizabeth. The first one was a close-up of her face. She was in profile, her right hand holding her hair back away from her ear. Her eye was purple and swollen. There was a deep cut and more bruising on her neck, below the ear.

It looked as though she'd been crying.

Another photo was shot from the waist up. Elizabeth stood wearing only a bra, and she was pointing to a large discoloration on her rib cage. Her eyes still had that red-tinged rim. The lighting was strangely harsh, as though the flash itself had sought out the bruise and pulled it closer to the lens.

93

There were three more photographs—all from various angles and of various body parts. All of them highlighted more cuts and bruises.

"Dr. Beck?"

My eyes jerked up. I was almost startled to see them in the room. Their expressions were neutral, patient. I faced Carlson, then Stone, then I went back to Carlson.

"You think I did this?"

Carlson shrugged. "You tell us."

"Of course not."

"Do you know how your wife got those bruises?"

"In a car accident."

They looked at each other as though I'd told them my dog ate my homework.

"She got into a bad fender-bender," I explained.

"When?"

"I'm not sure exactly. Three, four months before"—the words got stuck for a second—"before she died."

"Did she visit a hospital?"

"No, I don't think so."

"You don't *think*?"

"I wasn't around."

"Where were you?"

"I was doing a pediatric workshop in Chicago at the time. She told me about the accident when I got home."

"How long after did she tell you?"

"After the accident?"

"Yeah, Doc, after the accident."

"I don't know. Two, three days maybe."

"You two were married by then?"

"For just a few months."

"Why didn't she tell you right away?"

"She did. I mean, as soon as I got home. I guess she didn't want to worry me."

"I see," Carlson said. He looked at Stone. They didn't bother masking their skepticism. "So did you take these pictures, Doc?"

"No," I said. As soon as I did, I wished I hadn't. They exchanged another glance, smelling blood. Carlson tilted his head and moved closer.

"Have you ever seen these pictures before?"

I said nothing. They waited. I thought about the question. The answer was no, but... where did they get them? Why didn't I know about them? Who took them? I looked at their faces, but they gave away nothing.

It's an amazing thing really, but when you think about it, we learn life's most important lessons from TV. The vast majority of our knowledge about interrogations, Miranda rights, self-incriminations, cross-examinations, witness lists, the jury system, we learn from *NYPD Blue* and *Law & Order* and the like. If I tossed you a gun right now and asked you to fire it, you'd do what you saw on TV. If I told you to look out for a "tail," you'd know what I'm talking about because you'd seen it done on *Mannix* or *Magnum PI*.

I looked up at them and asked the classic question: "Am I a suspect?"

"Suspect for what?"

"For anything," I said. "Do you suspect that I committed any crime?"

"That's a pretty vague question, Doc."

And that was a pretty vague answer. I didn't like the way this was going. I decided to use another line I learned from television.

"I want to call my lawyer," I said.

10

I don't have a criminal lawyer—who does?—so I called Shauna from a pay phone in the corridor and explained the situation. She wasted no time.

"I got just the person," Shauna said. "Sit tight."

I waited in the interrogation room. Carlson and Stone were kind enough to wait with me. They spent the time whispering to each other. Half an hour passed. Again the silence was unnerving. I know that was what they wanted. But I couldn't stop myself. I was innocent, after all. How could I harm myself if I was careful?

"My wife was found branded with the letter K," I said to them.

They both looked up. "Pardon me," Carlson said, craning his long neck back in my direction. "You talking to us?"

"My wife was found branded with the letter K," I repeated. "I was in the hospital after the attack with a concussion. You can't possibly think..." I let it hang.

"Think what?" Carlson said.

In for a penny, in for a pound. "That I had something to do with my wife's death."

That was when the door burst open, and a woman I recognized from television stamped into the room. Carlson jumped back when he saw her. I heard Stone mumble "Holy shit" under his breath.

Hester Crimstein didn't bother with intros. "Didn't my client ask for counsel?" she asked.

Count on Shauna. I had never met my attorney, but I recognized her from her stints as a "legal expert" on talk shows and from her own *Crimstein on Crime* program on Court TV. On the screen Hester Crimstein was quick and cutting and often left guests in tatters. In person, she had the most bizarre aura of power, the kind of person who looks at everyone as though she were a hungry tiger and they were limping gazelles.

"That's right," Carlson said.

"Yet here you are, all nice and cozy, still questioning him."

"He started talking to us."

"Oh, I see." Hester Crimstein snapped open her briefcase, dug out a pen and paper, and tossed them onto the table. "Write down your names."

"Pardon?"

"Your names, handsome. You know how to spell them, right?"

97

It was a rhetorical question, but Crimstein still waited for an answer.

"Yeah," Carlson said.

"Sure," Stone added.

"Good. Write them down. When I mention on my show how you two trampled my client's constitutional rights, I want to make sure I get the names right. Print plainly, please."

She finally looked at me. "Let's go."

"Hold up a second," Carlson said. "We'd like to ask your client a few questions."

"No."

"No? Just like that?"

"Exactly like that. You don't talk to him. He doesn't talk to you. Ever. You two understand?"

"Yes," Carlson said.

She turned her glare to Stone.

"Yes," Stone said.

"Swell, fellas. Now are you arresting Dr. Beck?"

"No."

She turned in my direction. "What are you waiting for?" she snapped at me. "We're out of here."

Hester Crimstein didn't say a word until we were safely ensconced in her limousine.

"Where do you want me to drop you off?" she asked.

I gave the driver the clinic's address.

"Tell me about the interrogation," Crimstein said. "Leave out nothing."

I recounted my conversation with Carlson and Stone as best I could. Hester Crimstein didn't so much as glance in my direction. She took out a day planner thicker than my waist and started leafing through it.

"So these pictures of your wife," she said when I finished. "You didn't take them?"

"No."

"And you told Tweedledee and Tweedledum that?"

I nodded.

She shook her head. "Doctors. They're always the worst clients." She pushed back a stand of hair. "Okay, that was dumb of you, but not crippling. You say you've never seen those pictures before?"

"Never."

"But when they asked you that, you finally shut up."

"Yes."

"Better," she said with a nod. "That story about her getting those bruises in a car accident. Is it the truth?"

"Pardon me?"

Crimstein closed her day planner. "Look... Beck, is it? Shauna says everyone calls you Beck, so you mind if I do the same?"

"No."

"Good. Look, Beck, you're a doctor, right?"

"Right."

"You good at bedside manner?"

"I try to be."

"I don't. Not even a little. You want coddling, go on a diet and hire Richard Sim-

99

mons. So let's skip all the pardon-mes and excuse-mes and all that objectionable crap, okay? Just answer my questions. The car accident story you told them. Is it true?"

"Yes."

"Because the feds will check all the facts. You know that, right?"

"I know."

"Okay, fine, just so we're clear here." Crimstein took a breath. "So maybe your wife had a friend take these pictures," she said, trying it on for size. "For insurance reasons or something. In case she ever wanted to sue. That might make sense, if we need to peddle it."

It didn't make sense to me, but I kept that to myself.

"So question uno: Where have these pictures been, Beck?"

"I don't know."

"Dos and tres: How did the feds get them? Why are they surfacing now?"

I shook my head.

"And most important, what are they trying to nail you on? Your wife's been dead for eight years. It's a little late for a spousal battery charge." She sat back and thought about it a minute or two. Then she looked up and shrugged. "No matter. I'll make some calls, find out what's up. In the meantime, don't be a dimwit. Say nothing to anyone. You understand?"

"Yes."

She sat back and thought about it some more. "I don't like this," she said. "I don't like this even a little bit."

11

On May 12, 1970, Jeremiah Renway and three fellow radicals set off an explosion at Eastern State University's chemistry department. Rumor had it from the Weather Underground that military scientists were using the university labs to make a more powerful form of napalm. The four students, who in a fit of stark originality called themselves Freedom's Cry, decided to make a dramatic albeit showy stand.

At the time, Jeremiah Renway did not know if the rumor was true. Now, more than thirty years later, he doubted it. No matter. The explosion did not damage any of the labs. Two university security guards, however, stumbled across the suspicious package. When one picked it up, the package exploded, killing both men.

Both had children.

One of Jeremiah's fellow "freedom fighters" was captured two days later. He was still in jail. The second died of colon cancer in 1989. The third, Evelyn Cosmeer, was captured in 1996. She was currently serving a seven-year prison sentence.

Jeremiah disappeared into the woods that night and never ventured out. He had rarely seen fellow human beings or listened to the radio or watched television. He had used a telephone only once—and that was in an emergency. His only real connection to the outside world came from newspapers, though they had what happened here eight years ago all wrong.

Born and raised in the foothills of northwest Georgia, Jeremiah's father taught his son all kinds of survival techniques, though his overriding lesson was simply this: You could trust nature but not man. Jeremiah had forgotten that for a little while. Now he lived it.

Fearing they would search near his hometown, Jeremiah took to the woods in Pennsylvania. He hiked around for a while, changing camp every night or two, until he happened upon the relative comfort and security of Lake Charmaine. The lake had old camp bunks that could house a man when the outdoors got a little too nasty. Visitors rarely came to the lake—mostly in the summer, and even then, only on weekends. He could hunt deer here and eat the meat in relative peace. During the few times of the year when the lake was being used, he simply hid or took off for points farther west.

Or he watched.

To the children who used to come here, Jeremiah Renway had been the Boogeyman.

Jeremiah stayed still now and watched the officers move about in their dark windbreakers. FBI windbreakers. The sight of those three letters in big yellow caps still punctured his heart like an icicle.

No one had bothered to yellow-tape the area, probably because it was so remote.

Renway had not been surprised when they found the bodies. Yes, the two men had been buried good and deep, but Renway knew better than most that secrets don't like to stay underground. His former partner in crime, Evelyn Cosmeer, who'd transformed herself into the perfect Ohio suburban mom before her capture, knew that. The irony did not escape Jeremiah.

He stayed hidden in the bush. He knew a lot about camouflage. They would not see him.

He remembered the night eight years ago when the two men had died—the sudden gun blasts, the sounds of the shovels ripping into the earth, the grunts from the deep dig. He'd even debated telling the authorities what happened—all of it.

Anonymously, of course.

But in the end he couldn't risk it. No man, Jeremiah knew, was meant for a cage, though some could live through it. Jeremiah could not. He'd had a cousin named Perry who'd been serving eight years in a federal penitentiary. Perry was locked in a tiny cell for twenty-three hours a day. One morning, Perry tried to kill himself by running headfirst into the cement wall.

That would be Jeremiah.

So he kept his mouth shut and did nothing. For eight years anyway.

But he thought about that night a lot. He thought about the young woman in the nude. He thought about the men in wait. He thought about the scuffle near the car. He thought about the sickening, wet sound of wood against exposed flesh. He thought about the man left to die.

And he thought about the lies. The lies, most of all, haunted him.

12

By the time I returned to the clinic, the waiting room was packed with the sniffing and impatient. A television replayed a video of *The Little Mermaid*, automatically rewinding at the end and starting over, the color frayed and faded from overuse. After my hours with the FBI, my mind sympathized with the tape. I kept rehashing Carlson's words—he was definitely the lead guy—trying to figure out what he was really after, but all that did was make the picture murkier and more surreal. It also gave me a whopping headache.

"Yo, Doc."

Tyrese Barton hopped up. He was wearing butt-plunge baggy pants and what looked like an oversized varsity jacket, all done by some designer I never heard of but soon would.

"Hi, Tyrese," I said.

Tyrese gave me a complicated handshake, which was a bit like a dance routine where he leads and I follow. He and Latisha had a six-year-old son they called TJ. TJ was a hemophiliac. He was also blind. I met him after he was rushed in as an infant and Tyrese was seconds away from being arrested. Tyrese claimed I saved his son's life on that day. That was hyperbole.

But maybe I did save Tyrese.

He thought that made us friends—like he was this lion and I was some mouse who pulled a thorn from his paw. He was wrong.

Tyrese and Latisha were never married, but he was one of the few fathers I saw in here. He finished shaking my hands and slipped me two Ben Franklins as though I were a maître d' at Le Cirque.

He gave me the eye. "You take good care of my boy now."

"Right."

"You the best, Doc." He handed me his business card, which had no name, no address, no job title. Just a cell phone number. "You need anything, you call."

"I'll keep that in mind," I said.

Still with the eye. *Anything,* Doc."

"Right."

I pocketed the bills. We've been going through this same routine for six years now. I knew a lot of drug dealers from working here; I knew none who survived six years.

I didn't keep the money, of course. I gave it to Linda for her charity. Legally debatable, I knew, but the way I figured it, better the money went to charity than to a drug dealer. I had no idea how much money Tyrese had. He always had a new car, though—he favored BMWs with tinted windows—and his kid's wardrobe was worth more than anything that inhabited my closet. But, alas, the child's mother was on Medicaid, so the visits were free.

Maddening, I know.

Tyrese's cell phone sounded something hip-hop.

"Got to take this, Doc. Bidness."

"Right," I said again.

I do get angry sometimes. Who wouldn't? But through that haze, there are real children here. They hurt. I don't claim that all children are wonderful. They are not. I sometimes treat ones that I know—*know*—will amount to no good. But children are, if nothing else, helpless. They are weak and defenseless. Believe me, I've seen examples that would alter your definition of human beings.

So I concentrate on the children.

I was supposed to work only until noon, but to make up for my FBI detour, I saw patients until three. Naturally, I'd been thinking about the interrogation all day. Those pictures of Elizabeth, battered and defeated, kept popping through my brain like the most grotesque sort of strobe light.

Who would know about those pictures?

The answer, when I took the time to think about it, was somewhat obvious. I leaned forward and picked up the phone. I hadn't dialed this number in years, but I still remembered it.

"Schayes Photography," a woman answered.

"Hi, Rebecca."

"Son of a gun. How are you, Beck?"

"Good. How about yourself?"

"Not bad. Busy as all hell."

"You work too hard."

"Not anymore. I got married last year."

"I know. I'm sorry I couldn't make it."

"Bull."

"Yeah. But congrats anyway."

"So what's up?"

"I need to ask you a question," I said.

"Uh-huh."

"About the car accident."

I hear a tinny echo. Then silence.

"Do you remember the car accident? The one before Elizabeth was killed?"

Rebecca Schayes, my wife's closest friend, did not reply.

I cleared my throat. "Who was driving?"

"What?" She did not say that into the phone. "Okay, hold on." Then back at me: "Look, Beck, something just came up here. Can I call you back in a little while?"

"Rebecca—"

But the line was dead.

Here is the truth about tragedy: It's good for the soul.

The fact is, I'm a better person because of the deaths. If every cloud has a silver lining, this one is admittedly pretty flimsy. But there it is. That doesn't mean it's worth it or an even trade or anything like that, but I know I'm a better man than I used to be. I have a finer sense of what's important. I have a keener understanding of people's pain.

There was a time—it's laughable now—when I used to worry about what clubs I belonged to, what car I drove, what college degree I stuck on my wall—all that status crap. I wanted to be a surgeon because that wowed people. I wanted to impress so-called friends. I wanted to be a big man.

Like I said, laughable.

Some might argue that my self-improvement is simply a question of maturity. In part, true. And much of the change is due to the fact I am now on my own. Elizabeth and I were a couple, a single entity. She was so good that I could afford to be not so good, as though her goodness raised us both, was a cosmic equalizer.

Still, death is a great teacher. It's just too harsh.

I wish I could tell you that through the tragedy I mined some undiscovered, life-altering absolute that I could pass on to you. I didn't. The clichés apply—people are what count, life is precious, materialism is overrated, the little things matter, live in the moment—and I can repeat them to you ad nauseam. You might listen, but you won't internalize. Tragedy hammers it home. Tragedy etches it onto your soul. You might not be happier. But you will be better.

What makes this all the more ironic is that

I've often wished that Elizabeth could see me now. Much as I'd like to, I don't believe the dead watch over us or any similar comfort-fantasy we sell ourselves. I believe the dead are gone for good. But I can't help but think: Perhaps now I am worthy of her.

A more religious man might wonder if that is why she's returned.

Rebecca Schayes was a leading freelance photographer. Her work appeared in all the usual glossies, though strangely enough, she specialized in men. Professional athletes who agreed to appear on the cover of, for example, *GQ* often requested her to do the shoot. Rebecca liked to joke that she had a knack for male bodies due to "a lifetime of intense study."

I found her studio on West Thirty-second Street, not far from Penn Station. The building was a butt-ugly semi-warehouse that reeked from the Central Park horse and buggies housed on the ground floor. I skipped the freight elevator and took the stairs.

Rebecca was hurrying down the corridor. Trailing her, a gaunt, black-clad assistant with reedy arms and pencil-sketch facial hair dragged two aluminum suitcases. Rebecca still had the unruly sabra locks, her fiery hair curling angrily and flowing freely. Her eyes were wide apart and green, and if she'd changed in the past eight years, I couldn't see it.

She barely broke stride when she saw me. "It's a bad time, Beck."

"Tough," I said.

"I got a shoot. Can we do this later?"

"No."

She stopped, whispered something to the sulking black-clad assistant, and said, "Okay, follow me."

Her studio had high ceilings and cement walls painted white. There were lots of lighting umbrellas and black screens and extension cords snaking everywhere. Rebecca fiddled with a film cartridge and pretended to be busy.

"Tell me about the car accident," I said.

"I don't get this, Beck." She opened a canister, put it down, put the top back on, then opened it again. "We've barely spoken in, what, eight years? All of a sudden you get all obsessive about an old car accident?"

I crossed my arms and waited.

"Why, Beck? After all this time. Why do you want to know?"

"Tell me."

She kept her eyes averted. The unruly hair fell over half her face, but she didn't bother pushing it back. "I miss her," she said. "And I miss you too."

I didn't reply to that.

"I called," she said.

"I know."

"I tried to stay in touch. I wanted to be there."

"I'm sorry," I said. And I was. Rebecca had been Elizabeth's best friend. They'd shared an apartment near Washington Square Park before we got married. I should have returned her calls or invited her over or made some kind of effort. But I didn't.

Grief can be inordinately selfish.

"Elizabeth told me that you two were in a minor car crash," I went on. "It was her fault, she said. She took her eyes off the road. Is that true?"

"What possible difference does it make now?"

"It makes a difference."

"How?"

"What are you afraid of, Rebecca?"

Now it was her time for silence.

"Was there an accident or not?"

Her shoulders slumped as though something internal had been severed. She took a few deep breaths and kept her face down. "I don't know."

"What do you mean, you don't know?"

"She told me it was a car accident too."

"But you weren't there?"

"No. You were out of town, Beck. I came home one night, and Elizabeth was there. She was bruised up. I asked her what happened. She told me she'd been in a car accident and if anyone asked, we'd been in my car."

"If anyone asked?"

Rebecca finally looked up. "I think she meant you, Beck."

I tried to take this in. "So what really happened?"

"She wouldn't say."

"Did you take her to a doctor?"

"She wouldn't let me." Rebecca gave me a strange look. "I still don't get it. Why are you asking me about this now?"

111

Tell no one.

"I'm just trying to get a little closure."

She nodded, but she didn't believe me. Neither one of us was a particularly adept liar.

"Did you take any pictures of her?" I asked.

"Pictures?"

"Of her injuries. After the accident."

"God, no. Why would I do that?"

An awfully good question. I sat there and thought about it. I don't know how long.

"Beck?"

"Yeah."

"You look like hell."

"You don't," I said.

"I'm in love."

"It becomes you."

"Thanks."

"Is he a good guy?"

"The best."

"Maybe he deserves you, then."

"Maybe." She leaned forward and kissed my cheek. It felt good, comforting. "Something happened, didn't it?"

This time I opted for the truth. "I don't know."

13

Shauna and Hester Crimstein sat in Hester's swanky midtown law office. Hester finished up her phone call and put the receiver back in the cradle.

"No one's doing much talking," Hester said.

"But they didn't arrest him?"

"No. Not yet."

"So what's going on?" Shauna asked.

"Near as I can tell, they think Beck killed his wife."

"That's nuts," Shauna said. "He was in the hospital, for crying out loud. That KillRoy loony tune is on death row."

"Not for her murder," the attorney replied.

"What?"

"Kellerton's suspected of killing at least eighteen women. He confessed to fourteen, but they only had enough hard evidence to prosecute and convict him on twelve. That was enough. I mean, how many death sentences does one man need?"

"But everyone knows he killed Elizabeth."

"Correction: Everyone *knew*."

"I don't get it. How can they possibly think Beck had anything to do with it?"

"I don't know," Hester said. She threw her feet up on her desk and put her hands behind her head. "At least, not yet. But we'll have to be on our guard."

"How's that?"

"For one thing, we have to assume the feds are watching his every step. Phone taps, surveillance, that kind of thing."

"So?"

"What do you mean, so?"

"He's innocent, Hester. Let them watch."

Hester looked up and shook her head. "Don't be naïve."

"What the hell does that mean?"

"It means that if they tape him having eggs for breakfast, it can be something. He has to be careful. But there's something else."

"What?"

"The feds are going to go after Beck."

"How?"

"Got me, but trust me, they will. They got a hard-on for your friend. And it's been eight years. That means they're desperate. Desperate feds are ugly, constitutional-rights-stamping feds."

Shauna sat back and thought about the strange emails from "Elizabeth."

"What?" Hester said.

"Nothing."

"Don't hold back on me, Shauna."

"I'm not the client here."

"You saying Beck isn't telling me everything?"

An idea struck Shauna with something approaching horror. She thought about it some more, ran the idea over some test tracks, let it bounce around for a few moments.

It made sense, and yet Shauna hoped—nay, prayed—that she was wrong. She stood and hurried toward the door. "I have to go."

"What's going on?"

"Ask your client."

Special agents Nick Carlson and Tom Stone positioned themselves on the same couch over which Beck had recently waxed nostalgic. Kim Parker, Elizabeth's mother, sat across from them with her hands primly in her lap. Her face was a frozen, waxy mask. Hoyt Parker paced.

"So what's so important that you couldn't say anything over the phone?" Hoyt asked.

"We want to ask you some questions," Carlson said.

"What about?"

"Your daughter."

That froze them both.

"More specifically, we'd like to ask you about her relationship with her husband, Dr. David Beck."

Hoyt and Kim exchanged a glance. "Why?" Hoyt asked.

"It involves a matter currently under investigation."

"What matter? She's been dead for eight years. Her killer is on death row."

"Please, Detective Parker. We're all on the same side here."

The room was still and dry. Kim Parker's

lips thinned and trembled. Hoyt looked at his wife and then nodded at the two men.

Carlson kept his gaze on Kim. "Mrs. Parker, how would you describe the relationship between your daughter and her husband?"

"They were very close, very much in love."

"No problems?"

"No," she said. "None."

"Would you describe Dr. Beck as a violent man?"

She looked startled. "No, never."

They looked at Hoyt. Hoyt nodded his agreement.

"To your knowledge, did Dr. Beck ever hit your daughter?"

"What?"

Carlson tried a kind smile. "If you could just answer the question."

"Never," Hoyt said. "No one hit my daughter."

"You're certain?"

His voice was firm. "Very."

Carlson looked toward Kim. "Mrs. Parker?"

"He loved her so much."

"I understand that, ma'am. But many wife-beaters profess to loving their wives."

"He never hit her."

Hoyt stopped pacing. "What's going on here?"

Carlson looked at Stone for a moment. "I want to show you some photographs, if I may. They are a bit disturbing, but I think they're important."

Stone handed Carlson the manila envelope. Carlson opened it. One by one, he placed the photographs of the bruised Elizabeth on a coffee table. He watched for a reaction. Kim Parker, as expected, let out a small cry. Hoyt Parker's face seemed at odds with itself, settling into a distant blankness.

"Where did you get these?" Hoyt asked softly.

"Have you seen them before?"

"Never," he said. He looked at his wife. She shook her head.

"But I remember the bruises," Kim Parker offered.

"When?"

"I can't remember exactly. Not long before she died. But when I saw them, they were less"—she searched for the word—"pronounced."

"Did your daughter tell you how she got them?"

"She said she was in a car accident."

"Mrs. Parker, we've checked with your wife's insurance company. She never reported a car accident. We checked police files. No one ever made a claim against her. No policeman ever filled out a report."

"So what are you saying?" Hoyt came in.

"Simply this: If your daughter wasn't in a car accident, how did she get these bruises?"

"You think her husband gave them to her?"

"It's a theory we're working on."

"Based on what?"

The two men hesitated. The hesitation said one of two things: not in front of the lady or not in front of the civilian. Hoyt picked up on it. "Kim, do you mind if I talk to the agents alone for moment?"

"Not at all." She stood on wobbly legs and teetered toward the stairs. "I'll be in the bedroom."

When she was out of sight, Hoyt said, "Okay, I'm listening."

"We don't think Dr. Beck just beat your daughter," Carlson said. "We think he murdered her."

Hoyt looked from Carlson to Stone and back to Carlson, as though waiting for the punch line. When none came, he moved to the chair. "You better start explaining."

14

What else had Elizabeth been keeping from me?

As I headed down Tenth Avenue toward the Quick-n-Park, I again tried to dismiss those photographs as merely a record of her car accident injuries. I remembered how nonchalant Elizabeth had been about the whole thing at the time. Just a fender-bender, she said. No big deal. When I asked for details, she had pretty much brushed me off.

Now I knew that she'd lied to me about it.

I could tell you that Elizabeth never lied to

me, but that would be, in light of this recent discovery, a pretty unconvincing argument. This was, however, the first lie I was aware of. I guess we both had our secrets.

When I reached the Quick-n-Park, I spotted something strange—or perhaps, I should say, someone strange. There, on the corner, was a man in a tan overcoat.

He was looking at me.

And he was oddly familiar. No one I knew, but there was still the unease of déjà vu. I'd seen this man before. This morning even. Where? I ran through my morning and spotted him in my mind's eye:

When I pulled over for coffee at eight A.M. The man with the tan overcoat had been there. In the parking lot of Starbucks.

Was I sure?

No, of course not. I diverted my eyes and hurried over to the attendant's booth. The parking attendant—his name tag read Carlo—was watching television and eating a sandwich. He kept his eyes on the screen for half a minute before sliding his gaze toward me. Then he slowly brushed the crumbs off his hands, took my ticket, and stamped it. I quickly paid the man and he handed me my key.

The man in the tan overcoat was still there.

I tried very hard not to look in his direction as I walked to my car. I got in, started it up, and when I hit Tenth Avenue, I checked the rearview mirror.

The man with the tan overcoat didn't so much

as glance at me. I kept watching him until I turned toward the West Side Highway. He never looked in my direction. Paranoid. I was going nutsy paranoid.

So why had Elizabeth lied to me?

I thought about it and came up with nothing.

There were still three hours until my Bat Street message came in. Three hours. Man, I needed to distract myself. Thinking too hard about what might be on the other end of that cyber-connection shredded my stomach lining.

I knew what I had to do. I was just trying to delay the inevitable.

When I got home, Grandpa was in his customary chair, alone. The television was off. The nurse was yakking on the phone in Russian. She wasn't going to work out. I'd have to call the agency and get her replaced.

Small particles of egg were stuck to the corners of Grandpa's mouth, so I took out a handkerchief and gently scraped them away. Our eyes met, but his gaze was locked on something far beyond me. I saw us all up at the lake. Grandpa would be doing his beloved weight-loss before-and-after pose. He'd turn profile, slump, let his elastic gut hang out, and shout "Before!" and then suck it up and flex and yell "After!" He did it brilliantly. My father would howl. Dad had the greatest, most infectious laugh. It was a total body release. I used to have it too. It died with him. I could never laugh like that again. Somehow it seemed obscene.

Hearing me, the nurse hurried off the phone and hightailed it into the room with a bright smile. I didn't return it.

I eyed the basement door. I was still delaying the inevitable.

No more stalling.

"Stay with him," I said.

The nurse bowed her head and sat down.

The basement had been finished in the days before people finished basements, and it showed. The once-brown shag carpet was pockmarked and water-buckled. Faux white brick made from some sort of bizarre synthetic had been glued to asphalt walls. Some sheets had fallen to the shag; others stopped mid-topple, like columns of the Acropolis.

In the center of the room, the Ping-Pong table's green had been washed to an almost in-vogue spearmint. The torn net looked like the barricades after the French troops stormed. The paddles were stripped down to the splintery wood.

Some cardboard boxes, many sprouting mold, sat on top of the Ping-Pong table. Others were piled in the corner. Old clothes were in wardrobe boxes. Not Elizabeth's. Shauna and Linda had cleared those out for me. Goodwill got them, I think. But some of the other boxes held old items. *Her* items. I couldn't throw them away, and I couldn't let other people have them. I'm not sure why. Some things we pack away, stick in the back of the closet, never expect to see again—but we can't quite make ourselves discard them. Like dreams, I guess.

I wasn't sure where I had put it, but I knew it was there. I started going through old photographs, once again averting my gaze. I was pretty good at that, though as time went on, the photographs hurt less and less. When I saw Elizabeth and me together in some greening Polaroid, it was as though I were looking at strangers.

I hated doing this.

I dug deeper into the box. My fingertips hit something made of felt, and I pulled out her tennis varsity letter from high school. With a sad smirk, I remembered her tan legs and the way her braid bounced as she hopped toward the net. On the court, her face was locked in pure concentration. That was how Elizabeth would beat you. She had decent enough ground strokes and a pretty good serve, but what lifted her above her classmates was that focus.

I put the letter down gingerly and started digging again. I found what I was looking for at the bottom.

Her daily planner.

The police had wanted it after the abduction. Or so I was told. Rebecca came by the apartment and helped them find it. I assume they searched for clues in it—the same thing I was about to do—but when the body popped up with the K branding, they probably stopped.

I thought about that some more—about how everything had been neatly pinned on KillRoy—and another thought scurried through my brain. I ran upstairs to my computer and got online. I found the Web site for the New York City Department of Correction. Tons of stuff on it, including the name and phone number I needed.

I signed off and called Briggs Penitentiary. That's the prison that holds KillRoy.

When the recording came on, I pressed in the proper extension and was put through. Three rings later, a man said, "Deputy Superintendent Brown speaking."

I told him that I wanted to visit Elroy Kellerton.

"And you are?" he said.

"Dr. David Beck. My wife, Elizabeth Beck, was one of his victims."

"I see." Brown hesitated. "May I ask the purpose of your visit?"

"No."

There was more silence on the line.

"I have the right to visit him if he's willing to see me," I said.

"Yes, of course, but this is a highly unusual request."

"I'm still making it."

"The normal procedure is to have your attorney go through his—"

"But I don't have to," I interrupted. I learned this at a victim's rights Web site—that I could make the request myself. If Kellerton was willing to see me, I was in. "I just want

123

to talk to Kellerton. You have visiting hours tomorrow, don't you?"

"Yes, we do."

"Then if Kellerton agrees, I'll be up tomorrow. Is there a problem with that?"

"No, sir. If he agrees, there's no problem."

I thanked him and hung up the phone. I was taking action. It felt damn good.

The day planner sat on the desk next to me. I was avoiding it again, because as painful as a photograph or recording might be, hand-writing was somehow worse, somehow more personal. Elizabeth's soaring capital letters, the firmly crossed ts, the too many loops between letters, the way it all tilted to the right...

I spent an hour going through it. Elizabeth was detailed. She didn't shorthand much. What surprised me was how well I'd known my wife. Everything was clear, and there were no surprises. In fact, there was only one appointment I couldn't account for.

Three weeks before her death, there was an entry that read simply: *PF*.

And a phone number without an area code.

In light of how specific she'd been else-where, I found this entry a little unsettling. I didn't have a clue what the area code would be. The call was made eight years ago. Area codes had split and changed several different ways since then.

I tried 201 and got a disconnect. I tried 973. An old lady answered. I told her she'd won a free subscription to the *New York Post*. She gave me her name. Neither initial matched. I tried

212, which was the city. And that was where I hit bingo.

"Peter Flannery, attorney at law," a woman said mid-yawn.

"May I speak to Mr. Flannery, please."

"He's in court."

She could have sounded more bored but not without a quality prescription. I heard a lot of noise in the background.

"I'd like to make an appointment to see Mr. Flannery."

"You answering the billboard ad?"

"Billboard ad?"

"You injured?"

"Yes," I said. "But I didn't see an ad. A friend recommended him. It's a medical malpractice case. I came in with a broken arm and now I can't move it. I lost my job. The pain is non-stop."

She set me up for an appointment tomorrow afternoon.

I put the phone back into the cradle and frowned. What would Elizabeth be doing with a probable ambulance-chaser like Flannery?

The sound of the phone made me jump. I snatched it up mid-ring.

"Hello," I said.

It was Shauna. "Where are you?" she asked.

"Home."

"You need to get over here right away," she said.

15

Agent Carlson looked Hoyt Parker straight in the eye. "As you know, we recently found two bodies in the vicinity of Lake Charmaine."

Hoyt nodded.

A cell phone chirped. Stone managed to hoist himself up and said "Excuse me" before lumbering into the kitchen. Hoyt turned back to Carlson and waited.

"We know the official account of your daughter's death," Carlson said. "She and her husband, David Beck, visited the lake for an annual ritual. They went swimming in the dark. KillRoy lay in wait. He assaulted Dr. Beck and kidnapped your daughter. End of story."

"And you don't think that's what happened?"

"No, Hoyt—can I call you Hoyt?"

Hoyt nodded.

"No, Hoyt, we don't."

"So how do you see it?"

"I think David Beck murdered your daughter and pinned it on a serial killer."

Hoyt, a twenty-eight-year veteran of the NYPD, knew how to keep a straight face, but he still leaned back as though the words were jabs at his chin. "Let's hear it."

"Okay, let's start from the beginning. Beck

126

takes your daughter up to a secluded lake, right?"

"Right."

"You've been there?"

"Many times."

"Oh?"

"We were all friends. Kim and I were close to David's parents. We used to visit all the time."

"Then you know how secluded it is."

"Yes."

"Dirt road, a sign that you'd only see if you knew to look for it. It's as hidden as hidden can be. No signs of life."

"What's your point?"

"What are the odds of KillRoy pulling up that road?"

Hoyt raised his palms to the sky. "What are the odds of anyone meeting up with a serial killer?"

"True, okay, but in other cases, there was a logic to it. Kellerton abducted somebody off a city street, he carjacked a victim, even broke into a house. But think about it. He sees this dirt road and somehow decides to search for a victim up there? I'm not saying it's impossible, but it's highly unlikely."

Hoyt said, "Go on."

"You'll admit that there are plenty of logic holes in the accepted scenario."

"All cases have logic holes."

"Right, okay, but let me try an alternate theory on you. Let's just say that Dr. Beck wanted to kill your daughter."

"Why?"

"For one thing, a two-hundred-thousand-dollar life insurance policy."

"He doesn't need money."

"Everyone needs money, Hoyt. You know that."

"I don't buy it."

"Look, we're still digging here. We don't know all the motivations yet. But let me just go through our scenario, okay?"

Hoyt gave him a suit-yourself shrug.

"We have evidence here that Dr. Beck beat her."

"What evidence? You have some photographs. She told my wife she'd been in a car accident."

"Come on, Hoyt." Carlson swept his hand at the photographs. "Look at the expression on your daughter's face. That look like the face of a woman in a car accident?"

No, Hoyt thought, it didn't. "Where did you find these pictures?"

"I'll get to that in a second, but let's go back to my scenario, okay? Let's assume for the moment that Dr. Beck beat your daughter and that he had a hell of an inheritance coming his way."

"Lot of assuming."

"True, but stay with me. Think of the accepted scenario and all those holes. Now compare it with this one: Dr. Beck brings your daughter up to a secluded spot where he knows there will be no witnesses. He hires two thugs to grab her. He knows about KillRoy. It's in all the papers. Plus your brother worked on the case. Did he ever discuss it with you or Beck?"

Hoyt sat still for a moment. "Go on."

"The two hired thugs abduct and kill your daughter. Naturally, the first suspect will be the husband—always is in a case like this, right? But the two thugs brand her cheek with the letter K. Next thing we know, it's all blamed on KillRoy."

"But Beck was assaulted. His head injury was real."

"Sure, but we both know that's not inconsistent with him being behind it. How would Beck explain coming out of the abduction healthy? 'Hi, guess what, someone kidnapped my wife, but I'm fine'? It'd never play. Getting whacked on the head gave his story credibility."

"He took a hell of a shot."

"He was dealing with thugs, Hoyt. They probably miscalculated. And what about his injury anyway? He tells some bizarre story about miraculously crawling out of the water and dialing 911. I gave several doctors Beck's old medical chart. They claim his account of what he did defies medical logic. It would have been pretty much impossible, given his injuries."

Hoyt considered that. He had often wondered about that himself. How had Beck survived and called for help? "What else?" Hoyt said.

"There's strong evidence that suggests the two thugs, not KillRoy, assaulted Beck."

"What evidence?"

"Buried with the bodies, we found a baseball bat with blood on it. The full DNA match will take a while, but the preliminary results strongly suggest that the blood is Beck's."

Agent Stone plodded back in the room and sat down hard. Hoyt once again said, "Go on."

"The rest is pretty obvious. The two thugs do the job. They kill your daughter and pin it on KillRoy. Then they come back to get the rest of their payment—or maybe they decide to extort more money from Dr. Beck. I don't know. Whatever, Beck has to get rid of them. He sets up a meet in the secluded woods near Lake Charmaine. The two thugs probably thought they were dealing with a wimpy doctor or maybe he caught them unprepared. Either way Beck shoots them and buries the bodies along with the baseball bat and whatever evidence might haunt him later on. The perfect crime now. Nothing to tie him with the murder. Let's face it. If we didn't get enormously lucky, the bodies would have never been found."

Hoyt shook his head. "Hell of a theory."

"There's more."

"Like?"

Carlson looked at Stone. Stone pointed to his cell phone. "I just got a strange phone call from someone at Briggs Penitentiary," Stone said. "It seems your son-in-law called there today and demanded a meeting with KillRoy."

Hoyt now looked openly stunned. "Why the hell would he do that?"

"You tell us," Stone responded. "But keep in mind that Beck knows we're onto him. All of a sudden, he has this overwhelming desire to visit the man he set up as your daughter's killer."

"Hell of a coincidence," Carlson added.

"You think he's trying to cover his tracks?"

"You have a better explanation?"

Hoyt sat back and tried to let all of this settle. "You left something out."

"What?"

He pointed to the photographs on the table. "Who gave you those?"

"In a way," Carlson said, "I think your daughter did."

Hoyt's face looked drained.

"More specifically, her alias did. One Sarah Goodhart. Your daughter's middle name and the name of this street."

"I don't understand."

"At the crime scene," Carlson said. "One of the two thugs—Melvin Bartola—had a small key in his shoe." Carlson held up the key. Hoyt took it from his hand, peering at it as though it held some mystical answer. "See the *UCB* on the flip side?"

Hoyt nodded.

"That stands for United Central Bank. We finally traced this key down to their branch at 1772 Broadway in the city. The key opens Box 174, which is registered to one Sarah Goodhart. We got a search warrant for it."

Hoyt looked up. "The photographs were in there?"

Carlson and Stone glanced at each other. They had already made the decision not to tell Hoyt everything about that box—not until all the tests came back and they knew for sure—but both men nodded now.

"Think about it, Hoyt. Your daughter kept these pictures hidden in a safety-deposit box. The reasons are obvious. Want more? We questioned Dr. Beck. He admitted knowing nothing about the pictures. He'd never seen them before. Why would your daughter hide them from him?"

"You talked to Beck?"

"Yes."

"What else did he say?"

"Not much because he demanded a lawyer." Carlson waited a beat. Then he leaned forward. "He not only lawyered up, he called Hester Crimstein. That sound like the act of an innocent man to you?"

Hoyt actually gripped the sides of the chair, trying to steady himself. "You can't prove any of this."

"Not yet, no. But we know. That's half the battle sometimes."

"So what are you going to do?"

"Only one thing we can do." Carlson smiled at him. "Apply pressure until something breaks."

Larry Gandle looked over the day's developments and mumbled to himself, "Not good."

One, the FBI picks up Beck and questions him.

Two, Beck calls a photographer named Rebecca Schayes. He asks her about an old car accident involving his wife. Then he visits her studio.

A photographer no less.

Three, Beck calls Briggs Penitentiary and says he wants to meet Elroy Kellerton.

Fourth, Beck calls Peter Flannery's office.

All of this was puzzling. None of it was good.

Eric Wu hung up the phone and said, "You're not going to like this."

"What?"

"Our source with the FBI says that they suspect Beck killed his wife."

Gandle nearly fell over. "Explain."

"That's all the source knows. Somehow, they've tied the two dead bodies by the lake to Beck."

Very puzzling.

"Let me see those emails again," Gandle said.

Eric Wu handed them to him. When Gandle thought about who could have sent them, the creeping feeling in the pit of his stomach started to claw and grow. He tried to add the pieces together. He'd always wondered how Beck had survived that night. Now he wondered something else.

Had anyone else survived it?

"What time is it?" Gandle asked.

"Six-thirty."

"Beck still hasn't looked up that Bat-whatever address?"

"Bat Street. And no, he hasn't."

"Anything more on Rebecca Schayes?"

"Just what we already know. Close friend of Elizabeth Parker's. They shared an apartment before Parker married Beck. I checked old phone records. Beck hasn't called her in years."

"So why would he contact her now?"

Wu shrugged. "Ms. Schayes must know something."

Griffin Scope had been very clear. Learn what you can, then bury it.

And use Wu.

"We need to have a chat with her," Gandle said.

16

Shauna met me on the ground floor of a high-rise at 462 Park Avenue in Manhattan.

"Come on," she said without preamble. "I have something to show you upstairs."

I checked my watch. A little under two hours until the Bat Street message came in. We entered an elevator. Shauna hit the button for the twenty-third floor. The lights climbed and the blind-person-counter beeped.

"Hester got me thinking," Shauna said.

"What about?"

"She said the feds would be desperate. That they'd do anything to get you."

"So?"

The elevator sounded its final ding.

"Hang on, you'll see."

The door slid open on a massive cubicle-divided floor. The norm in the city nowadays. Rip off the ceiling and view from above and you'd have a very hard time telling the difference between this floor and a rat maze. From down here too, when you thought about it.

Shauna marched between countless cloth-lined dividers. I trailed in her wake. Halfway down she turned left and then right and then left again.

"Maybe I should drop bread crumbs," I said.

Her voice was flat. "Good one."

"Thank you, I'm here all week."

She wasn't laughing.

"What is this place anyway?" I asked.

"A company called DigiCom. The agency works with them sometimes."

"Doing what?"

"You'll see."

We made a final turn into a cluttered cubbyhole occupied by a young man with a long head and the slender fingers of a concert pianist.

"This is Farrell Lynch. Farrell, this is David Beck."

I shook the slender hand briefly. Farrell said, "Hi."

I nodded.

"Okay," Shauna said. "Key it up."

Farrell Lynch swiveled his chair so that he was facing the computer. Shauna and I watched over his shoulders. He started typing with those slender fingers.

"Keyed up," he said.

"Run it."

He hit the return button. The screen went black and then Humphrey Bogart appeared. He wore a fedora and a trench coat. I recognized the scene right away. The fog, the plane in the background. The finale of *Casablanca*.

I looked at Shauna.

"Wait," she said.

The camera was on Bogie. He was telling Ingrid Bergman that she was getting on that plane with Laszlo and that the problems of three little people didn't amount to a hill of beans in this world. And then, when the camera went back to Ingrid Bergman...

...it wasn't Ingrid Bergman.

I blinked. There, beneath the famed hat, gazing up at Bogie and bathed in the gray glow, was Shauna.

"I can't go with you, Rick," the computer Shauna said dramatically, "because I'm madly in love with Ava Gardner."

I turned to Shauna. My eyes asked the question. She nodded yes. I said it anyway.

"You think..." I stammered. "You think I was fooled by trick photography?"

Farrell took that one. "Digital photography," he corrected me. "Far simpler to

136

manipulate." He spun his chair toward me. "See, computer images aren't film. They're really just pixels in files. Not unlike your word processing document. You know how easy it is to change a word processing document, right? To alter content or fonts or spacing?"

I nodded.

"Well, for someone with even a rudimentary understanding of digital imaging, that's how easy it is to manipulate a computer's streaming images. These aren't pictures, nor are they films or tapes. Computer video streams are simply a bunch of pixels. Anyone can manipulate them. Simply cut and paste and then you run a blend program."

I looked at Shauna. "But she looked older in the video," I insisted. "Different."

Shauna said, "Farrell?"

He hit another button. Bogie returned. When they went to Ingrid Bergman this time, Shauna looked seventy years old.

"Age progression software," Farrell explained. "It's mostly used to age missing children, but nowadays they sell a home version at any software store. I can also change any part of Shauna's image—her hairstyle, her eye color, the size of her nose. I can make her lips thinner or thicker, give her a tattoo, whatever."

"Thank you, Farrell," Shauna said.

She gave him a look of dismissal a blind man could read. "Excuse me," Farrell said before making himself scarce.

I couldn't think.

When Farrell was out of earshot, Shauna said,

"I remembered a photo shoot I did last month. One picture came out perfectly—the sponsor loved it—except my earring had slipped down. We brought the image over here. Farrell did a quick cut-and-paste and *voilà,* my earring was back in the right place."

I shook my head.

"Think about it, Beck. The feds think you killed Elizabeth, but they have no way to prove it. Hester explained how desperate they've become. I started thinking: Maybe they'd play mind games with you. What better mind game than sending you these emails?"

"But kiss time...?"

"What about it?"

"How would they know about kiss time?"

"I know about it. Linda knows about it. I bet Rebecca knows too, maybe Elizabeth's parents. They could have found out."

I felt tears rush up to the surface. I tried to work my voice and managed to croak out, "It's a hoax?"

"I don't know, Beck. I really don't. But let's be rational here. If Elizabeth was alive, where has she been for eight years? Why choose now of all times to come back from the grave—the same time, by coincidence, that the FBI starts suspecting you of killing her? And come on, do you really believe she's still alive? I know you want to. Hell, I want to. But let's try to look at this rationally. When you really think about it, which scenario makes more sense?"

I stumbled back and fell into a chair. My heart

started crumbling. I felt the hope start to shrivel up.

A hoax. Has this all been nothing but a hoax?

17

Once he was settled inside Rebecca Schayes's studio, Larry Gandle called his wife on the cell phone. "I'll be home late," he said.

"Don't forget to take your pill," Patty told him.

Gandle had a mild case of diabetes, controlled through diet and a pill. No insulin.

"I will."

Eric Wu, still plugged into his Walkman, carefully laid down a vinyl drop cloth near the door.

Gandle hung up the phone and snapped on a pair of latex gloves. The search was both thorough and time-consuming. Like most photographers, Rebecca Schayes saved tons of negatives. There were four metal file cabinets jammed full of them. They'd checked Rebecca Schayes's schedule. She was finishing up a shoot. She'd be back here to work the darkroom in about an hour. Not enough time.

"You know what would help," Wu said.

"What?"

"Having some idea what the hell we're looking for."

"Beck gets these cryptic emails," Gandle said. "And what does he do? For the first time in eight years, he rushes over to see his wife's oldest friend. We need to know why."

Wu looked through him some more. "Why don't we just wait and ask her?"

"We will, Eric."

Wu nodded slowly and turned away.

Gandle spotted a long metal desk in the darkroom. He tested it. Strong. The size was about right too. You could lay someone on it and tape a limb to each table leg.

"How much duct tape did we bring?"

"Enough," Wu said.

"Do me a favor, then," Gandle said. "Move the drop cloth under the table."

Half an hour until I picked up the Bat Street message.

Shauna's demonstration had hit me like a surprise left hook. I felt groggy, and I took the full count. But a funny thing happened. I got my ass off the canvas. I stood back up and shook off the cobwebs and started circling.

We were in my car. Shauna had insisted on coming back to the house with me. A limousine would take her back in a few hours. I know that she wanted to comfort me, but it was equally clear that she didn't want to go home yet.

"Something I don't get," I said.

Shauna turned to me.

"The feds think I killed Elizabeth, right?"

"Right."

"So why would they send me emails pretending she's alive?"

Shauna had no quick answer.

"Think about it," I said. "You claim that this is some sort of elaborate plot to get me to reveal my guilt. But if I killed Elizabeth, I'd know that it was a trick."

"It's a mind game," Shauna said.

"But that doesn't make sense. If you want to play a mind game with me, send me emails and pretend to be—I don't know—someone who witnessed the murder or something."

Shauna thought about it. "I think they're just trying to keep you off balance, Beck."

"Yeah, but still. It doesn't add up."

"Okay, how long until the next message comes in?"

I checked the clock. "Twenty minutes."

Shauna sat back in her seat. "We'll wait and see what it says."

Eric Wu set up his laptop on the floor in a corner of Rebecca Schayes's studio.

He checked Beck's office computer first. Still idle. The clock read a little past eight o'clock. The clinic was long closed. He switched over to the home computer. For a few seconds there was nothing. And then:

"Beck just signed on," Wu said.

Larry Gandle hurried over. "Can we get on and see the message before him?"

"It wouldn't be a good idea."

"Why not?"

"If we sign in and then he tries to, it will tell him that someone is currently using that screen name."

"He'll know he's being watched?"

"Yes. But it doesn't matter. We're watching him in real time. The moment he reads the message, we'll see it too."

"Okay, let me know when."

Wu squinted at the screen. "He just brought up the Bigfoot site. It should be any second now."

I typed in bigfoot.com and hit the return button.

My right leg started jackhammering. It does that when I'm nervous. Shauna put her hand on my knee. My knee slowed to a stop. She took the hand off. My knee stayed still for a minute, and then it started up again. Shauna put her hand back on my knee. The cycle began again.

Shauna was playing it cool, but I know that she kept sneaking glances at me. She was my best friend. She'd support me to the end. But only an idiot wouldn't be wondering at this juncture if my elevator was stopping at every floor. They say that insanity, like heart disease or intelligence, is hereditary. The thought had been running through my mind since I'd first seen Elizabeth on the street cam. It wasn't a comforting one.

My father died in a car crash when I was twenty. His car toppled over an embankment. According to an eyewitness—a truck driver from Wyoming—my father's Buick drove straight off it. It had been a cold night. The road, while well plowed, was slick.

Many suggested—well, suggested in whispers anyway—that he committed suicide. I don't believe it. Yes, he had been more withdrawn and quiet in his last few months. And yes, I often wonder if all that made him more susceptible to an accident. But suicide? No way.

My mother, always a fragile person of seemingly gentle neuroses, reacted by slowly losing her mind. She literally shrank into herself. Linda tried to nurse her for three years, until even she agreed that Mom needed to be committed. Linda visits her all the time. I don't.

After a few more moments, the Bigfoot home page came up. I found the user name box and typed in Bat Street.

I hit the tab key and in the password text box I typed Teenage. I hit return.

Nothing happened.

"You forgot to click the Sign In icon," Shauna said.

I looked at her. She shrugged. I clicked the icon.

The screen went white. Then an ad for a CD store came up. The bar on the bottom went back and forth in a slow wave. The percentage climbed slowly. When it hit about eighteen percent, it vanished and then several seconds later a message appeared.

ERROR—Either the user name or password you entered is not in our database.

"Try again," Shauna said.

I did. The same error message came up. The computer was telling me the account didn't even exist.

What did that mean?

I had no idea. I tried to think of a reason that the account wouldn't exist.

I checked the time: 8:13.34 P.M.

Kiss time.

Could that be the answer? Could it be that the account, like the link yesterday, simply didn't exist yet? I mulled that one over. It was possible, of course, but unlikely.

As though reading my mind, Shauna said, "Maybe we should wait until eight-fifteen."

So I tried again at eight-fifteen. At eight-eighteen. At eight-twenty.

Nothing but the same error message.

"The feds must have pulled the plug," Shauna said.

I shook my head, not willing yet to give up.

My leg started shaking again. Shauna used one hand to stop it and one hand to answer her cell phone. She started barking at someone on the other end. I checked the clock. I tried again. Nothing. Twice more. Nothing.

It was after eight-thirty now.

"She, uh, could be late," Shauna said.

I frowned.

"When you saw her yesterday," Shauna tried, "you didn't know where she was, right?"

"Right."

"So maybe she's in a different time zone," Shauna said. "Maybe that's why she's late."

"A different time zone?" I frowned some more. Shauna shrugged.

We waited another hour. Shauna, to her credit, never said I told you so. After a while she put a hand on my back and said, "Hey, I got an idea."

I turned to her.

"I'm going to wait in the other room," Shauna said. "I think that might help."

"How do you figure?"

"See, if this were a movie, this would be the part where I get all fed up by your craziness and storm out and then bingo, the message appears, you know, so only you see it and everyone still thinks you're crazy. Like on Scooby-Doo when only he and Shaggy see the ghost and no one believes them?"

I thought about it. "Worth a try," I said.

"Good. So why don't I go wait in the kitchen for a while? Take your time. When the message comes in, just give a little shout."

She stood.

"You're just humoring me, aren't you?" I said.

Shauna thought about it. "Yeah, probably."

She left then. I turned and faced the screen. And I waited.

18

Nothing's happening," Eric Wu said. "Beck keeps trying to sign on, but all he gets is an error message."

Larry Gandle was about to ask a follow-up question, when he heard the elevator rev up. He checked the clock.

Rebecca Schayes was right on time.

Eric Wu turned away from his computer. He looked at Larry Gandle with the kind of eyes that make a man take a step back. Gandle took out his gun—a nine-millimeter this time. Just in case. Wu frowned. He moved his bulk to the door and flipped off the light.

They waited in the dark.

Twenty seconds later, the elevator stopped on their floor.

Rebecca Schayes rarely thought about Elizabeth and Beck anymore. It had, after all, been eight years. But this morning events had stirred up some long-dormant sensations. Nagging sensations.

About the "car accident."

After all these years, Beck had finally asked her about it.

Eight years ago, Rebecca had been prepared to tell him all about it. But Beck hadn't returned her calls. As time went by—and after an arrest had been made—she saw no point in dredging up the past. It would only hurt Beck. And after KillRoy's arrest, it seemed irrelevant.

But the nagging sensation—the sensation that Elizabeth's bruises from the "car accident" were somehow a precursor to her murder—lingered, even though it made no sense. More than that, the nagging sensation taunted her, making her wonder if she, Rebecca, had insisted, *really* insisted, on finding out the truth about the "car accident," maybe, just maybe, she could have saved her friend.

The lingering, however, faded away over time. At the end of the day, Elizabeth had been her friend, and no matter how close you are, you get over a friend's death. Gary Lamont had come into her life three years ago and changed everything. Yes, Rebecca Schayes, the bohemian photographer from Greenwich Village, had fallen in love with a money-grubbing Wall Street bond trader. They'd gotten married and moved into a trendy high-rise on the Upper West Side.

Funny how life worked.

Rebecca stepped into the freight elevator and slid the gate down. The lights were out, which was hardly unusual in this building. The elevator started heading up to her floor, the churning sound reverberating off the stone. Sometimes at night, she could hear the horses whinny, but they were silent now. The smell of hay and something probably fouler mingled in the air.

147

She liked being here at night. The way the solitude blended with the city's night noises made her feel her most "artsy."

Her mind started drifting back to the conversation she'd had last night with Gary. He wanted to move out of New York City, preferably to a spacious home on Long Island, at Sands Point, where he'd been raised. The idea of moving to the 'burbs horrified her. More than her love of the city, she knew that it would be the final betrayal of her bohemian roots. She would become what she swore she would never become: her mother and her mother's mother.

The elevator stopped. She lifted the gate and stepped down the corridor. All the lights were off up here. She pulled back her hair and tied it into a thick ponytail. She peered at her watch. Almost nine o'clock. The building would be empty. Of human beings at least.

Her shoes clacked against the cool cement. The truth was—and Rebecca was having a hard time accepting it, she being a bohemian and all—that the more she thought about it, the more she realized that yes, she wanted children, and that the city was a lousy place to raise them. Children need a backyard and swings and fresh air and...

Rebecca Schayes was just reaching a decision—a decision that would have no doubt thrilled her broker husband, Gary—when she stuck her key in the door and opened her studio. She went inside and flipped the light switch.

That was when she saw the weirdly shaped Asian man.

For a moment or two the man simply stared at her. Rebecca stood frozen in his gaze. Then the Asian man stepped to the side, almost behind her, and blasted a fist into the small of her back.

It was like a sledgehammer hit her kidney.

Rebecca crumbled to her knees. The man grabbed her neck with two fingers. He squeezed a pressure point. Rebecca saw bright lights. With his free hand, the man dug with fingers like ice picks under her rib cage. When they reached her liver, her eyes bulged. The pain was beyond anything she'd ever imagined. She tried to scream, but only a choking grunt escaped her mouth.

From across the room, a man's voice sliced through the haze.

"Where is Elizabeth?" the voice asked.

For the first time.

But not the last.

19

I stayed in front of that damn computer and started drinking pretty heavily. I tried logging on to the site a dozen different ways. I used Explorer and then I used Netscape. I cleared my cache and reloaded the pages and signed off my provider and signed back on again.

It didn't matter. I still got the error message.

At ten o'clock, Shauna headed back into the den. Her cheeks were glowing from drink. Mine too, I imagined. "No luck?"

"Go home," I said.

She nodded. "Yeah, I think I'd better."

The limousine was there in five minutes. Shauna wobbled to the curb, fairly wasted on bourbon and Rolling Rock. Me too.

Shauna opened the door and turned back to me. "Were you ever tempted to cheat? I mean, when you two were married."

"No," I said.

Shauna shook her head, disappointed. "You know nothing about how to mess up your life."

I kissed her good-bye and went back inside. I continued to gaze at the screen as though it were something holy. Nothing changed.

Chloe slowly approached a few minutes later. She nudged my hand with her wet nose. Through her forest of hair, our eyes met and I swear that Chloe understood what I was feeling. I'm not one of those who give human characteristics to dogs—for one thing, I think that it might demean them—but I do believe they have a base understanding of what their anthropological counterparts are feeling. They say that dogs can smell fear. Is it such a stretch to believe that they also smell joy or anger or sadness?

I smiled down at Chloe and petted her head. She put a paw on my arm in a comforting gesture. "You want to go for a walk, girl?" I said.

Chloe's reply was to bound about like a circus freak on speed. Like I told you before, it's the little things.

The night air tingled in my lungs. I tried to concentrate on Chloe—her frolicking step, her wagging tail—but I was, well, crestfallen. Crestfallen. That is not a word I use very often. But I thought it fit.

I hadn't fully bought Shauna's too-neat digital-trick hypothesis. Yes, someone could manipulate a photograph and make it part of a video. And yes, someone could have known about kiss time. And yes, someone could have even made the lips whisper "I'm sorry." And yes, my hunger probably helped make the illusion real and made me susceptible to such trickery.

And the biggest yes: Shauna's hypothesis made a hell of a lot more sense than a return from the grave.

But there were two things that overrode a lot of that. First off, I'm not one for flights of fancy. I'm frighteningly boring and more grounded than most. Second, the hunger could have clouded my reasoning, and digital photography could do a lot of things.

But not those eyes...

Her eyes. Elizabeth's eyes. There was no way, I thought, that they could be old photographs manipulated into a digital video. Those eyes belonged to my wife. Was my rational mind sure of it? No, of course not. I'm not a fool. But between what I saw and all the questions I'd raised, I had semi-dismissed Shauna's video demonstration. I had come home still believing that I was to receive a message from Elizabeth.

Now I didn't know what to think. The booze was probably helping in that respect.

Chloe stopped to do some prolonged sniffing. I waited under a streetlight and stared at my elongated shadow.

Kiss time.

Chloe barked at a movement in the bush. A squirrel sprinted across the street. Chloe growled and feigned a chase. The squirrel stopped and turned back toward us. Chloe barked a boy-you're-lucky-I'm-on-a-leash sound. She didn't mean it. Chloe was a pure thoroughbred wimp.

Kiss time.

I tilted my head the way Chloe does when she hears a strange sound. I thought again about what I had seen yesterday on my computer— and I thought about the pains someone had gone through to keep this whole thing secret. The unsigned email telling me to click the hyperlink at "kiss time." The second email setting up a new account in my name.

They're watching....

Someone was working hard to keep these communications under wraps.

Kiss time...

If someone—okay, if Elizabeth—had simply wanted to give me a message, why hadn't she just called or written it in an email? Why make me jump through all these hoops?

The answer was obvious: secrecy. Someone—

I won't say Elizabeth again—wanted to keep it all a secret.

And if you have a secret, it naturally follows that you have someone you want to keep it secret from. And maybe that someone is watching or searching or trying to find you. Either that or you're paranoid. Normally I'd side with paranoid but...

They're watching....

What did that mean exactly? Who was watching? The feds? And if the feds were behind the emails in the first place, why would they warn me that way? The feds wanted me to act.

Kiss time...

I froze. Chloe's head snapped in my direction.

Oh my God, how could I have been so stupid?

They hadn't bothered to use the duct tape.

Rebecca Schayes lay upon the table now, whimpering like a dying dog on the side of the road. Sometimes, she uttered words, two or even three at a time, but they never formed a coherent chain. She was too far gone to cry anymore. The begging had stopped. Her eyes were still wide and uncomprehending; they saw nothing now. Her mind had shattered midscream fifteen minutes ago.

Amazingly, Wu had left no marks. No marks, but she looked twenty years older.

Rebecca Schayes had known nothing. Dr.

Beck had visited her because of an old car accident that wasn't really a car accident. There were pictures too. Beck had assumed she had taken them. She hadn't.

The creeping feeling in his stomach—the one that had started as a mere tickle when Larry Gandle first heard about the bodies being found at the lake—kept growing. Something had gone wrong that night. That much was certain. But now Larry Gandle feared that maybe everything had gone wrong.

It was time to flush out the truth.

He had checked with his surveillance man. Beck was taking his dog for a walk. Alone. In light of the evidence Wu would plant, that would be a terrible alibi. The feds would shred it for laughs.

Larry Gandle approached the table. Rebecca Schayes looked up and made an unearthly noise, a cross between a high-pitched groan and a wounded laugh.

He pressed the gun against her forehead. She made that sound again. He fired twice and all the world fell silent.

I started heading back to the house, but I thought about the warning.

They're watching.

Why take the chance? There was a Kinko's three blocks away. They stay open twenty-four hours a day. When I reached the door, I saw why. It was midnight, and the place was packed. Lots of exhausted businesspeople carrying papers and slides and poster boards.

I stood in a maze line formed by crushed-velvet ropes and waited my turn. It reminded me of visiting a bank in the days before ATMs. The woman in front of me sported a business suit—at midnight—and big enough bags under her eyes to be mistaken for a bellhop. Behind me, a man with curly hair and dark sweats whipped out a cell phone and started pressing buttons.

"Sir?"

Someone with a Kinko's smock pointed at Chloe.

"You can't come in here with a dog."

I was about to tell him I already had but thought better of it. The woman in the business suit didn't react. The curly-haired guy with the dark sweats gave me a what-are-you-gonna-do shrug. I rushed outside, tied Chloe to a parking meter, headed back inside. The curly-haired man let me have my place back in line. Manners.

Ten minutes later, I was at the front of the line. This Kinko's clerk was young and overly exuberant. He showed me to a computer terminal and explained too slowly their per-minute pricing plan.

I nodded through his little speech and signed on to the Web.

Kiss time.

That, I realized, was the key. The first email had said kiss time, not 6:15 P.M. Why? The answer was obvious. That had been code—in case the wrong people got their hands on the email. Whoever had sent it had realized that the possibility of interception existed. Whoever had sent it had known that only I would know what kiss time meant.

That was when it came to me.

First off, the account name Bat Street. When Elizabeth and I were growing up, we used to ride our bikes down Morewood Street on the way to the Little League field. There was this creepy old woman who lived in a faded yellow house. She lived alone and scowled at passing kids. Every town has one of those creepy old ladies. She usually has a nickname. In our case, we'd called her:

Bat Lady.

I brought up Bigfoot again. I typed Morewood into the user name box.

Next to me, the young and exuberant Kinko's clerk was repeating his Web spiel to the curly-haired man with the dark sweat suit. I hit the tab button and moved into the text box for the password.

The clue Teenage was easier. In our junior year of high school, we'd gone to Jordan Goldman's house late one Friday night. There were maybe ten of us. Jordan had found out where his father hid a porn video. None of us had ever seen one before. We all watched, laughing uncomfortably, making the usual snide remarks and feeling deliciously naughty. When we needed a name for our intramural softball team, Jordan suggested we use the movie's stupid title:

Teenage Sex Poodles.

156

I typed in Sex Poodles under the password.
I swallowed hard and clicked the Sign In
icon.

I glanced over at the curly-haired man. He
was focused on a Yahoo! search. I looked
back toward the front desk. The woman in the
business suit was frowning at another too-
happy-at-midnight Kinko's staff member.

I waited for the error message. But that
didn't happen this time. A welcome screen
rolled into view. On the top, it read:

Hi, Morewood!

Underneath that it said:

You have 1 email in your box.

My heart felt like a bird banging against my
rib cage.

I clicked on the New Mail icon and did the
leg shake again. No Shauna around to stop it.
Through the store window I could see my
tethered Chloe. She spotted me and started
barking. I put a finger to my lips and signaled for her to hush up.

The email message appeared:

Washington Square Park. Meet me at
the southeast corner.
Five o'clock tomorrow.
You'll be followed.

And on the bottom:

157

No matter what, I love you.

Hope, that caged bird that just won't die, broke free. I leaned back. Tears flooded my eyes, but for the first time in a long while, I let loose a real smile.

Elizabeth. She was still the smartest person I knew.

20

At two A.M., I crawled into bed and rolled onto my back. The ceiling started doing the too-many-drinks spins. I grabbed the sides of the bed and hung on.

Shauna had earlier asked if I had ever been tempted to cheat after getting married. She'd added that last part—the "after getting married" part—because she already knew about the other incident.

Technically, I did cheat on Elizabeth once, though cheating doesn't really fit. Cheating denotes doing harm to another. It didn't harm Elizabeth—I'm sure of that—but during my freshman year of college, I partook in a rather pitiful rite of passage known as the collegiate one-night stand. Out of curiosity, I guess. Purely experimental and strictly physical. I didn't like it much. I'll spare you the corny sex-without-love-is-meaningless cliché.

It's not. But while I think it's fairly easy to have sex with someone you don't particularly know or like, it's hard to stay the night. The attraction, as it were, was strictly hormonal. Once the, uh, release took place, I wanted out. Sex is for anyone; the aftermath is for lovers.

Pretty nice rationalization, don't you think?

If it matters, I suspect Elizabeth probably did something similar. We both agreed that we would try to "see"—"see" being such a vague, all-encompassing term—other people when we first got to college. Any indiscretion could thus be chalked up to yet another commitment test. Whenever the subject was raised, Elizabeth denied that there had ever been anyone else. But then again, so did I.

The bed continued to spin as I wondered: What do I do now?

For one thing, I wait for five o'clock tomorrow. But I couldn't just sit back until then. I'd done enough of that already, thank you very much. The truth was—a truth I didn't like to admit even to myself—I hesitated at the lake. Because I was scared. I climbed out of the water and paused. That gave whomever a chance to hit me. And I didn't fight back after that first strike. I didn't dive for my assailant. I didn't tackle him or even make a fist. I simply went down. I covered up and surrendered and let the stronger man take away my wife.

Not again.

I considered approaching my father-in-law again—it hadn't escaped my attention that Hoyt might have been less than forthcoming during my previous visit—but what good would that do? Hoyt was either lying or...or I don't know what. But the message had been clear. *Tell no one.* The only way I could maybe get him to talk would be by telling him what I saw on that street cam. But I wasn't ready to do that yet.

I got out of bed and hopped on the computer. I started surfing again. By morning, I had something of a plan.

Gary Lamont, Rebecca Schayes's husband, didn't panic right away. His wife often worked late, very late, sometimes spending the night on an old cot in the far right corner of her studio. So when four in the morning rolled around and Rebecca still wasn't home, he grew only concerned, not panicked.

At least, that's what he told himself.

Gary called her studio, but the answering machine picked up. Again that wasn't rare. When Rebecca was working, she hated interruptions. She didn't even keep a phone extension in the darkroom. He left a message and settled back into their bed.

Sleep came in fits and spurts. Gary contemplated doing something more, but that would only piss off Rebecca. She was a free spirit, and if there was a tension in their otherwise fulfilling relationship, it had to do with his relatively "traditional" lifestyle "clipping" her creative wings. Her terms.

So he gave her space. To unclip her wings or whatever.

By seven in the morning, concern had segued into something closer to genuine fear. Gary's call woke up Arturo Ramirez, Rebecca's gaunt, black-clad assistant.

"I just got in," Arturo complained groggily.

Gary explained the situation. Arturo, who had fallen asleep in his clothes, did not bother changing. He ran out the door. Gary promised to meet him at the studio. He hopped on the downtown A.

Arturo arrived first and found the studio door ajar. He pushed it open.

"Rebecca?"

No answer. Arturo called her name again. Still no answer. He entered and scanned the studio. She wasn't there. He opened the dark-room door. The usual harsh smell of film-development acids still dominated, but there was something else, something faint and below the surface that still had the ability to make his hair stand on end.

Something distinctly human.

Gary rounded the corner in time to hear the scream.

21

In the morning, I grabbed a bagel and headed west on Route 80 for forty-five minutes. Route 80 in New Jersey is a fairly nondescript strip of pavement. Once you get past Saddle Brook or so, the buildings pretty much vanish and you're faced with identical lines of trees on either side of the road. Only the interstate signs break up the monotony.

As I veered off exit 163 at a town called Gardensville, I slowed the car and looked out at the high grass. My heart started thumping. I had never been here before—I'd purposely avoided this stretch of interstate for the past eight years—but it was here, less than a hundred yards from where I now drove, that they found Elizabeth's body.

I checked the directions I'd printed off last night. The Sussex County coroner's office was on Mapquest.com, so I knew to the tenth of a kilometer how to get there. The building was a blinds-closed storefront with no sign or window lettering, a plain brick rectangle with no frills, but then again, did you want any at a morgue? I arrived a few minutes before eight-thirty and pulled around back. The office was still locked up. Good.

A canary-yellow Cadillac Seville pulled into a spot marked Timothy Harper, County Medical Examiner. The man in the car stubbed out a cigarette—it never ceases to amaze me how many M.E.'s smoke—before he stepped out. Harper was my height, a shade under six feet, with olive skin and wispy gray hair. He saw me standing by the door and set his face. People didn't visit morgues first thing in the morning to hear good news.

He took his time approaching me. "Can I help you?" he said.

"Dr. Harper?"

"Yes, that's right."

"I'm Dr. David Beck." Doctor. So we were colleagues. "I'd like a moment of your time."

He didn't react to the name. He took out a key and unlocked the door. "Why don't we sit in my office?"

"Thank you."

I followed him down a corridor. Harper flicked light switches. The ceiling fluorescents popped on grudgingly and one at a time. The floor was scratched linoleum. The place looked less like a house of death than a faceless DMV office, but maybe that was the point. Our footsteps echoed, mixing with the buzzing from the lights as though keeping the beat. Harper picked up a stack of mail and quick-sorted it as we walked.

Harper's private office, too, was no-frills. There was the same metal desk you might find a teacher using in an elementary school. The chairs were overvarnished wood, strictly functional. Several diplomas spotted one wall. He'd gone to medical school at Columbia, too, I saw, though he'd graduated almost twenty years before me. No family photographs, no golf trophy, no Lucite announcements, nothing personal. Visitors to this office were not in for pleasant chitchat. The last thing they needed to see was someone's smiling grandkids.

Harper folded his hands and put them on the desk. "What can I do for you, Dr. Beck?"

"Eight years ago," I began, "my wife was brought here. She was the victim of a serial killer known as KillRoy."

I'm not particularly good at reading faces. Eye contact has never been my forte. Body language means little to me. But as I watched Harper, I couldn't help but wonder what would make a practiced medical examiner, a man who oft dwelled in the world of the dead, blanch so.

"I remember," he said softly.

"You did the autopsy?"

"Yes. Well, in part."

"In part?"

"Yes. The federal authorities were involved too. We worked on the case in tandem, though the FBI doesn't have coroners, so we took the lead."

"Back up a minute," I said. "Tell me what you saw when they first brought the body in."

Harper shifted in his seat. "May I ask why you want to know this?"

"I'm a grieving husband."

"It was eight years ago."

"We all grieve in our own way, Doctor."

164

"Yes, I'm sure that's true, but—"

"But what?"

"But I'd like to know what you want here."

I decided to take the direct route. "You take pictures of every corpse brought in here, right?"

He hesitated. I saw it. He saw me seeing it and cleared his throat. "Yes. Currently, we use digital technology. A digital camera, in other words. It allows us to store photographs and various images on a computer. We find it helpful for both diagnosis and cataloguing."

I nodded, not caring. He was chattering. When he didn't continue, I said, "Did you take pictures of my wife's autopsy?"

"Yes, of course. But—how long ago did you say again?"

"Eight years."

"We would have taken Polaroids."

"And where would those Polaroids be right now, Doctor?"

"In the file."

I looked at the tall filing cabinet standing in the corner like a sentinel.

"Not in there," he added quickly. "Your wife's case is closed. Her killer was caught and convicted. Plus it was more than five years ago."

"So where would it be?"

"In a storage facility. In Layton."

"I'd like to see the photographs, if I could."

He jotted something down and nodded at the scrap of paper. "I'll look into it."

"Doctor?"

He looked up.

"You said you remember my wife."

"Well, yes, I mean, somewhat. We don't have many murders here, especially ones so high profile."

"Do you remember the condition of her body?"

"Not really. I mean, not details or anything."

"Do you remember who identified her?"

"You didn't?"

"No."

Harper scratched his temple. "Her father, wasn't it?"

"Do you remember how long it took for him to make an identification?"

"How long?"

"Was it immediate? Did it take a few minutes? Five minutes, ten minutes?"

"I really couldn't say."

"You don't remember if it was immediate or not?"

"I'm sorry, I don't."

"You just said this was a big case."

"Yes."

"Maybe your biggest?"

"We had that pizza delivery thrill kill a few years ago," he said. "But, yes, I'd say it was one of the biggest."

"And yet you don't remember if her father had trouble identifying the body?"

He didn't like that. "Dr. Beck, with all due respect, I don't see what you're getting at."

"I'm a grieving husband. I'm asking some simple questions."

"Your tone," he said. "It seems hostile."

"Should it be?"

"What on earth does that mean?"

"How did you know she was a victim of KillRoy's?"

"I didn't."

"So how did the feds get involved?"

"There were identifying marks—"

"You mean that she was branded with the letter K?"

"Yes."

I was on a roll now, and it felt oddly right. "So the police brought her in. You started examining her. You spotted the letter K—"

"No, they were here right away. The federal authorities, I mean."

"Before the body got here?"

He looked up, either remembering or fabricating. "Or immediately thereafter. I don't remember."

"How did they know about the body so quickly?"

"I don't know."

"You have no idea?"

Harper folded his arms across his chest. "I might surmise that one of the officers on the scene spotted the branding and called the FBI. But that would only be an educated guess."

My beeper vibrated against my hip. I checked it. The clinic with an emergency.

"I'm sorry for your loss," he said in a practiced tone. "I understand the pain you must be going through, but I have a very busy schedule today. Perhaps you can make an appointment at a later date—"

"How long will it take you to get my wife's file?" I asked.

"I'm not even sure I can do that. I mean, I'll have to check—"

"The Freedom of Information Act."

"Pardon me?"

"I looked it up this morning. My wife's case is closed now. I have the right to view her file."

Harper had to know that—I wasn't the first person to ask for an autopsy file—and he started nodding a little too vigorously. "Still, there are proper channels you have to go through, forms to fill out."

"Are you stalling?" I said.

"Excuse me?"

"My wife was the victim of a terrible crime."

"I understand that."

"And I have the right to view my wife's file. If you drag your feet on this, I'm going to wonder why. I've never spoken to the media about my wife or her killer. I'll gladly do so now. And we'll all be wondering why the local M.E. gave me such a hard time over such a simple request."

"That sounds like a threat, Dr. Beck."

I got to my feet. "I'll be back here tomorrow morning," I said. "Please have my wife's file ready."

I was taking action. It felt damn good.

22

Detectives Roland Dimonte and Kevin Krinsky of the NYPD's homicide division arrived first on the scene, even before the uniforms. Dimonte, a greasy-haired man who favored hideous snakeskin boots and an overchewed toothpick, took the lead. He barked orders. The crime scene was immediately sealed. A few minutes later, lab technicians from the Crime Scene Unit skulked in and spread out.

"Isolate the witnesses," Dimonte said.

There were only two: the husband and the fey weirdo in black. Dimonte noted that the husband appeared distraught, though that could be an act. But first things first.

Dimonte, still chewing on the toothpick, took the fey weirdo—his name, figures, was Arturo—to the side. The kid looked pale. Normally, Dimonte would guess drugs, but the guy had tossed his cookies when he found the body.

"You okay?" Dimonte asked. Like he cared.

Arturo nodded.

Dimonte asked him if anything unusual had happened involving the victim lately. Yes, Arturo replied. What would that be? Rebecca got a phone call yesterday that disturbed her. Who called? Arturo was not sure, but an hour later—maybe less, Arturo couldn't

169

be sure—a man stopped by to see Rebecca. When the man left, Rebecca was a wreck.

Do you remember the man's name?

"Beck," Arturo said. "She called the guy Beck."

Shauna put Mark's sheets in the dryer. Linda came up behind her.

"He's wetting his bed again," Linda said.

"God, you're perceptive."

"Don't be mean." Linda walked away. Shauna opened her mouth to apologize, but nothing came out. When she had moved out the first time—the *only* time—Mark had reacted badly. It started with bed-wetting. When she and Linda reunited, the bed-wetting stopped. Until now.

"He knows what's going on," Linda said. "He can feel the tension."

"What do you want me to do about that, Linda?"

"Whatever we have to."

"I'm not moving out again. I promised."

"Clearly, that's not enough."

Shauna tossed a sheet of fabric softener into the dryer. Exhaustion lined her face. She didn't need this. She was a big-money model. She couldn't arrive at work with bags under her eyes or a lack of sheen in her hair. She didn't need this shit.

She was tired of it all. Tired of a domesticity that didn't sit well with her. Tired of the pressure from damn do-gooders. Forget the bigotry, that was easy. But the pressure on a lesbian couple with a child—applied by supposedly well-meaning supporters—was beyond suffocating. If the relationship failed, it was a failure for all lesbianism or some such crap, as though hetero couples never break up. Shauna was not a crusader. She knew that. Selfish or not, her happiness would not be sacrificed on the altar of "greater good."

She wondered if Linda felt the same way.

"I love you," Linda said.

"I love you too."

They looked at each other. Mark was wetting his bed again. Shauna wouldn't sacrifice herself for the greater good. But she would for Mark.

"So what do we do?" Linda asked.

"We work it out."

"You think we can?"

"You love me?"

"You know I do," Linda said.

"Do you still think I'm the most exciting, wonderful creature on God's green earth?"

"Oh, yeah," Linda said.

"Me too." Shauna smiled at her. "I'm a narcissistic pain in the ass."

"Oh, yeah."

"But I'm your narcissistic pain in the ass."

"Damn straight."

Shauna moved closer. "I'm not destined for a life of easy relationships. I'm volatile."

"You're sexy as hell when you're volatile," Linda said.

"And even when I'm not."

"Shut up and kiss me."

The downstairs door buzzer sounded. Linda looked at Shauna. Shauna shrugged. Linda pressed the intercom and said, "Yes?"

"Is this Linda Beck?"

"Who is this?"

"I'm Special Agent Kimberly Green with the Federal Bureau of Investigation. I'm with my partner, Special Agent Rick Peck. We'd like to come up and ask you some questions."

Shauna leaned over before Linda could respond. "Our attorney's name is Hester Crimstein," she shouted into the intercom. "You can call her."

"You're not suspects in any crime. We just want to ask you some questions—"

"Hester Crimstein," Shauna interrupted. "I'm sure you have her number. Have a really special day."

Shauna released the button. Linda looked at her. "What the hell was that?"

"Your brother's in trouble."

"What?"

"Sit down," Shauna said. "We need to talk."

Raisa Markov, a nurse who cared for Dr. Beck's grandfather, answered the firm knock. Special agents Carlson and Stone, now working in conjunction with NYPD detectives Dimonte and Krinsky, handed her the document.

"Federal warrant," Carlson announced.

Raisa stepped aside without reacting. She

had grown up in the Soviet Union. Police aggression did not faze her.

Eight of Carlson's men flooded into the Beck abode and fanned out.

"I want everything videotaped," Carlson called out. "No mistakes."

They were moving fast in the hope of staying a half-step ahead of Hester Crimstein. Carlson knew that Crimstein, like many a natty defense attorney in this post-OJ era, clung to the claims of police incompetence and/or misconduct like a desperate suitor. Carlson, a rather natty law enforcement officer in his own right, would not let that happen here. Every step/movement/breath would be documented and corroborated.

When Carlson and Stone first burst into Rebecca Schayes's studio, Dimonte had not been happy to see him. There had been the usual local-cops-versus-feds macho-turf posturing. Few things unify the FBI and the local authorities, especially in a big city like New York.

But Hester Crimstein was one of those things.

Both sides knew that Crimstein was a master obscurer and publicity hound. The world would be watching. No one wanted to screw up. That was the driving force here. So they forged an alliance with all the trust of a Palestinian-Israeli handshake, because in the end, both sides knew that they needed to gather and nail down the evidence fast— before Crimstein mucked up the waters.

The feds had gotten the search warrant. For them, it was a simple matter of walking across Federal Plaza to the southern district federal court. If Dimonte and the NYPD had wanted to get one, they'd have had to go to the county courthouse in New Jersey—too much time with Hester Crimstein lurking at their heels.

"Agent Carlson!"

The shout came from the street corner. Carlson sprinted outside, Stone waddling behind him. Dimonte and Krinsky followed. At the curb, a young federal agent stood next to an open trash canister.

"What is it?" Carlson asked.

"Might be nothing, sir, but..." The young federal agent pointed down to what looked like a hastily discarded pair of latex gloves.

"Bag them," Carlson said. "I want a gun residue test done right away." Carlson looked over to Dimonte. Time for more cooperation—this time, via competition. "How long will it take to get done at your lab?"

"A day," Dimonte said. He had a fresh toothpick in his mouth now and was working it over pretty well. "Maybe two."

"No good. We'll have to fly the samples down to our lab at Quantico."

"Like hell you will," Dimonte snapped. "We agreed to go with what's fastest."

"Staying here is fastest," Dimonte said. "I'll see to that."

Carlson nodded. It was as he expected. If you wanted the local cops to make the case a

174

big-time priority, threaten to take it away from them. Competition. It was a good thing.

Half an hour later, they heard another cry, this time coming from the garage. Again they sprinted in that direction.

Stone whistled low. Dimonte stared. Carlson bent down for a better look.

There, under the newspapers in a recycle bin, sat a nine-millimeter handgun. A quick sniff told them the gun had recently been fired.

Stone turned to Carlson. He made sure that his smile was off camera.

"Got him," Stone said softly.

Carlson said nothing. He watched the technician bag the weapon. Then, thinking it all through, he began to frown.

23

The emergency call on my beeper involved TJ. He scraped his arm on a doorjamb. For most kids, that meant a stinging spray of Bactine; for TJ, it meant a night in the hospital. By the time I got there, they had already hooked him up to an IV. You treat hemophilia by administering blood products such as cryoprecipitate or frozen plasma. I had a nurse start him up right away.

As I mentioned earlier, I first met Tyrese six years ago when he was in handcuffs and screaming obscenities. An hour earlier, he had rushed his then nine-month-old son, TJ, into the emergency room. I was there, but I wasn't working the acute side. The attending physician handled TJ.

TJ was unresponsive and lethargic. His breathing was shallow. Tyrese, who behaved, according to the chart, "erratically" (how, I wondered, was a father who rushes an infant to an emergency room supposed to act?), told the attending physician that the boy had been getting worse all day. The attending physician gave his nurse a knowing glance. The nurse nodded and went to make the call. Just in case.

A fundoscopic examination revealed that the infant had multiple retinal hemorrhages bilaterally—that is, the blood vessels in the back of both eyes had exploded. When the physician put the pieces together—retinal bleeding, heavy lethargy, and, well, the father—he made a diagnosis:

Shaken baby syndrome.

Armed security guards arrived in force. They handcuffed Tyrese, and that was when I heard the screamed obscenities. I rounded the corner to see what was up. Two uniformed members of the NYPD arrived. So did a weary woman from ACS—aka the Administration for Children Services. Tyrese tried to plead his case. Everybody shook their heads in that what's-this-world-coming-to way.

I'd witnessed scenes like this a dozen times at the hospital. In fact, I'd seen a lot worse.

I'd treated three-year-old girls with venereal diseases. I once ran a rape kit on a four-year-old boy with internal bleeding. In both cases—and in all similar abuse cases I'd been involved with—the perpetrator was either a family member or the mother's most recent boyfriend.

The Bad Man isn't lurking in playgrounds, kiddies. He lives in your house.

I also knew—and this statistic never failed to stagger me—that more than ninety-five percent of serious intracranial injuries in infants were due to child abuse. That made it pretty damn good—or bad, depending on your vantage point—odds that Tyrese had abused his son.

In this emergency room, we've heard all the excuses. The baby fell off the couch. The oven door landed on the baby's head. His older brother dropped a toy on him. You work here long enough, you grow more cynical than the most weathered city cop. The truth is, healthy children tolerate those sorts of accidental blows well. It is very rare that, say, a fall off a couch alone causes retinal hemorrhaging.

I had no problem with the child abuse diagnosis. Not at first blush anyway.

But something about the way Tyrese pleaded his case struck me odd. It was not that I thought he was innocent. I'm not above making quick judgments based on appearance—or, to use a more politically current term, racial profiling. We all do it. If you cross the street to avoid a gang of black teens, you're racial profiling; if you don't cross because you're afraid you'll look like a racist, you're racial profiling; if you see the gang and think nothing whatsoever, you're from some planet I've never visited.

What made me pause here was the pure dichotomy. I had seen a frighteningly similar case during my recent rotation out in the wealthy suburb of Short Hills, New Jersey. A white mother and father, both impeccably dressed and driving a well-equipped Range Rover, rushed their six-month-old daughter into the emergency room. The daughter, their third child, presented the same as TJ.

Nobody shackled the father.

So I moved toward Tyrese. He gave me the ghetto glare. On the street, it fazed me; in here, it was like the big bad wolf blowing at the brick house. "Was your son born at this hospital?" I asked.

Tyrese didn't reply.

"Was your son born here, yes or no?"

He calmed down enough to say "Yeah."

"Is he circumcised?"

Tyrese relit the glare. "You some kind of faggot?"

"You mean there's more than one kind?' I countered. "Was he circumcised here, yes or no?"

Grudgingly, Tyrese said, "Yeah."

I found TJ's social security number and plugged it into the computer. His records came up. I checked under the circumcision. Normal. Damn. But then I saw another entry.

This was not TJ's first visit to the hospital. At the age of two weeks, his father brought him in because of a bleeding umbilicus—bleeding from the umbilical cord.

Curious.

We ran some blood tests then, though the police insisted on keeping Tyrese in custody. Tyrese didn't argue. He just wanted the tests done. I tried to have them rushed, but I have no power in this bureaucracy. Few do. Still the lab was able to ascertain through the blood samples that the partial thromboplastin time was prolonged, yet both the prothrombin time and platelet count were normal. Yeah, yeah, but bear with me.

The best—and worst—was confirmed. The boy had not been abused by his ghetto-garbed father. Hemophilia caused the retinal hemorrhages. They had also left the boy blind.

The security guards sighed and uncuffed Tyrese and walked away without a word. Tyrese rubbed his wrists. Nobody apologized or offered a word of sympathy to this man who had been falsely accused of abusing his now-blind son.

Imagine that in the wealthy 'burbs.

TJ has been my patient ever since.

Now, in his hospital room, I stroked TJ's head and looked into his unseeing eyes. Kids usually look at me with undiluted awe, a heady cross between fear and worship. My colleagues believe that children have a deeper understanding than adults of what is happening to them. I think the answer is probably

179

simpler. Children view their parents as both intrepid and omnipotent—yet here their parents are, gazing up at me, the doctor, with a fear-filled longing normally reserved for religious rapture.

What could be more terrifying to a small child?

A few minutes later, TJ's eyes closed. He drifted off to sleep.

"He just bumped into the side of the door," Tyrese said. "That was all. He's blind. Gonna happen, right?"

"We'll need to keep him overnight," I said. "But he'll be fine."

"How?" Tyrese looked at me. "How will he ever be all right when he can't stop bleeding?"

I had no answer.

"I gotta get him out of here."

He didn't mean the hospital.

Tyrese reached into his pocket and started peeling off bills. I wasn't in the mood. I held up a hand and said, "I'll check back later."

"Thanks for coming, Doc. I appreciate it."

I was about to remind him that I had come for his son, not him, but I opted for silence.

Careful, Carlson thought, while his pulse raced. Be oh so careful.

The four of them—Carlson, Stone, Krinsky, and Dimonte—sat at a conference table with Assistant District Attorney Lance Fein. Fein, an ambitious weasel with constantly undulating eyebrows and a face so waxy that it looked ready to melt in extreme heat, strapped on his game face.

Dimonte said, "Let's bust his sorry ass."

"One more time," Lance Fein said. "Put it together for me so that even Alan Dershowitz would want him locked up."

Dimonte nodded at his partner. "Go ahead, Krinsky. Make me wet."

Krinsky took out his pad and started reading:

"Rebecca Schayes was shot twice in the head at very close range with a nine-millimeter automatic pistol. Under a federally issued warrant, a nine-millimeter was located in Dr. David Beck's garage."

"Fingerprints on the gun?" Fein asked.

"None. But a ballistic test confirmed that the nine-millimeter found in Dr. Beck's garage is the murder weapon."

Dimonte smiled and raised his eyebrows. "Anybody else getting hard nipples?"

Fein's eyebrows knitted and dropped. "Please continue," he said.

"Under the same federally issued warrant, a pair of latex gloves was retrieved from a trash canister at Dr. David Beck's residence. Gunpowder residue was found on the right glove. Dr. Beck is right-handed."

Dimonte put up his snakeskin boots and moved the toothpick across his mouth. "Oh, yeah, baby, harder, harder. I like it like that."

Fein frowned. Krinsky, his eyes never leaving the pad, licked a finger and turned the page.

"On the same right-hand latex glove, the lab

discovered a hair that has been positively color matched to Rebecca Schayes."

"Oh God! Oh God!" Dimonte started screaming in fake orgasm. Or maybe it was real.

"A conclusive DNA test will take more time," Krinsky went on. "Moreover, fingerprints belonging to Dr. David Beck were found at the murder scene, though not in the darkroom where her body was found."

Krinsky closed up his notebook. All eyes turned to Lance Fein.

Fein stood and rubbed his chin. Dimonte's behavior notwithstanding, they were all suppressing a bit of giddiness. The room crackled with pre-arrest sparks, that heady, addictive high that came with the really infamous cases. There would be press conferences and calls from politicians and pictures in the paper.

Only Nick Carlson remained the tiniest bit apprehensive. He sat twisting and untwisting and retwisting a paper clip. He couldn't stop. Something had crawled into his periphery, hanging on the edges, still out of sight, but there, and irksome as all hell. For one thing, there were the listening devices in Dr. Beck's home. Someone had been bugging him. Tapping his phone too. Nobody seemed to know or care why.

"Lance?" It was Dimonte.

Lance Fein cleared his throat. "Do you know where Dr. Beck is right now?" he asked.

"At his clinic," Dimonte said. "I got two uniforms keeping an eye on him."

Fein nodded.

"Come on, Lance," Dimonte said. "Give it to me, big boy."

"Let's call Ms. Crimstein first," Fein said. "As a courtesy."

Shauna told Linda most of it. She left out the part about Beck's "seeing" Elizabeth on the computer. Not because she gave the story any credence. She'd pretty much proven that it was a digital hoax. But Beck had been adamant. Tell no one. She didn't like having secrets from Linda, but that was preferable to betraying Beck's confidence.

Linda watched Shauna's eyes the whole time. She didn't nod or speak or even move. When Shauna finished, Linda asked, "Did you see the pictures?"

"No."

"Where did the police get them?"

"I don't know."

Linda stood. "David would never hurt Elizabeth."

"I know that."

Linda wrapped her arms around herself. She started sucking in deep breaths. Her face drained of color.

"You okay?" Shauna said.

"What aren't you telling me?"

"What makes you think I'm not telling you something?"

Linda just looked at her.

"Ask your brother," Shauna said.

"Why?"

"It's not my place to tell."

The door buzzed again. Shauna took it this time.

"Yeah?"

Through the speaker: "It's Hester Crimstein."

Shauna hit the release button and left their door open. Two minutes later, Hester hurried into the room.

"Do you two know a photographer named Rebecca Schayes?"

"Sure," Shauna said. "I mean, I haven't seen her in a long time. Linda?"

"It's been years," Linda agreed. "She and Elizabeth shared an apartment downtown. Why?"

"She was murdered last night," Hester said. "They think Beck killed her."

Both women froze as though someone had just slapped them. Shauna recovered first.

"But I was with Beck last night," she said. "At his house."

"Till what time?"

"Till what time do you need?"

Hester frowned. "Don't play games with me, Shauna. What time did you leave the house?"

"Ten, ten-thirty. What time was she killed?"

"I don't know yet. But I have a source inside. He said they have a very solid case against him."

"That's nuts."

A cell phone sounded. Hester Crimstein snatched hers up and pressed it against her ear. "What?"

The person on the other end spoke for what seemed a long time. Hester listened in silence.

Her features started softening in something like defeat. A minute or two later, without saying good-bye, she closed the phone with a vicious snap.

"A courtesy call," she mumbled.

"What?"

"They're arresting your brother. We have an hour to surrender him to authorities."

24

All I could think about was Washington Square Park. True, I wasn't supposed to be there for another four hours. But emergencies notwithstanding, today was my day off. Free as a bird, as Lynyrd Skynyrd would sing—and this bird wanted to flock down to Washington Square Park.

I was on my way out of the clinic when my beeper once again sang its miserable song. I sighed and checked the number. It was Hester Crimstein's cell phone. And it was coded for an emergency.

This couldn't be good news.

For a moment or two, I debated not calling back—just continuing to flock—but what would be the point in that? I backpedaled to my examining room. The door was closed, and the red lever was slid into place. That meant another doctor was using the room.

I headed down the corridor, turned left, and found an empty room in the ob-gyn section of the clinic. I felt like a spy in enemy camp. The room gleamed with too much metal. Surrounded by stirrups and other devices that looked frighteningly medieval, I dialed the number.

Hester Crimstein did not bother with hello: "Beck, we got a big problem. Where are you?"

"I'm at the clinic. What's going on?"

"Answer a question for me," Hester Crimstein said. "When was the last time you saw Rebecca Schayes?"

My heart started doing a deep, slow thud. "Yesterday. Why?"

"And before that?"

"Eight years ago."

Crimstein let loose a low curse.

"What's going on?" I asked.

"Rebecca Schayes was murdered last night in her studio. Somebody shot her twice in the head."

A plunging feeling, the one you get moments before you fall asleep. My legs wobbled. I landed with a thump on a stool. "Oh Christ..."

"Beck, listen to me. Listen closely."

I remembered how Rebecca looked yesterday.

"Where were you last night?"

I pulled the phone away and sucked in some air. Dead. Rebecca was dead. Oddly I kept flashing to the sheen in her beautiful hair. I thought about her husband. I thought about what the nights would bring, lying in that bed, thinking about how that hair used to fan across the pillow.

"Beck?"

"Home," I said. "I was home with Shauna."

"And after that?"

"I took a walk."

"Where?"

"Around."

"Where around?"

I did not reply.

"Listen to me, Beck, okay? They found the murder weapon at your house."

I heard the words, but their meaning was having trouble reaching the cerebrum. The room suddenly felt cramped. There were no windows. It was hard to breathe.

"Do you hear me?"

"Yes," I said. Then, sort of understanding, I said, "That's not possible."

"Look, we don't have time for that now. You're about to be arrested. I spoke to the D.A. in charge. He's a prick and a half, but he agreed to let you surrender."

"Arrested?"

"Stay with me here, Beck."

"I didn't do anything."

"That's irrelevant right now. They're going to arrest you. They're going to arraign you. Then we're going to get you bail. I'm on my way over to the clinic now. To pick you up. Sit tight. Don't say anything to anyone, you hear me? Not to the cops, not to the feds, not to your new buddy in lockup. You understand?"

My gaze got snagged on the clock above the examining table. It was a few minutes after two. Washington Square. I thought about Washington Square. "I can't be arrested, Hester."

"It'll be all right."

"How long?" I said.

"How long what?"

"Until I get bail."

"Can't say for sure. I don't think bail per se will be a problem. You have no record. You're an upstanding member of the community with roots and ties. You'll probably have to surrender your passport—"

"But how long?"

"How long until what, Beck? I don't understand."

"Until I get out."

"Look, I'll try to push them, okay? But even if they rush it—and I'm not saying they will—they still have to send your fingerprints to Albany. That's the rule. If we're lucky—I mean very lucky—we can get you arraigned by midnight."

Midnight?

Fear wrapped itself around my chest like steel bands. Jail meant missing the meet at Washington Square Park. My connection with Elizabeth was so damn fragile, like strands of Venetian glass. If I'm not at Washington Square at five o'clock...

"No good," I said.

"What?"

"You have to stall them, Hester. Have them arrest me tomorrow."

"You're kidding, right? Look, they're probably there already, watching you."

I leaned my head out the door and looked down the corridor. I could see only part of the reception desk from my angle, the corner near the right, but it was enough.

There were two cops, maybe more.

"Oh Christ," I said, falling back into the room.

"Beck?"

"I can't go to jail," I said again. "Not today."

"Don't freak out on me here, Beck, okay? Just stay there. Don't move, don't talk, don't do anything. Sit in your office and wait. I'm on my way."

She hung up.

Rebecca was dead. They thought I killed her. Ridiculous, of course, but there had to be a connection. I visited her yesterday for the first time in eight years. That very night she ended up dead.

What the hell was going on here?

I opened the door and peeked my head out. The cops weren't looking my way. I slid out and started down the corridor. There was a back emergency exit. I could sneak out that way. I could make my way down to Washington Square Park.

Was this for real? Was I really going to run away from the police?

I didn't know. But when I reached the door, I risked a look behind me. One of the cops spotted me. He pointed and hurried toward me.

I pushed open the door and ran.

189

I couldn't believe this. I was running from the police.

The exit door banged into a dark street directly behind the clinic. The street was unfamiliar to me. That might sound strange, but this neighborhood was not mine. I came, I worked, I left. I stayed locked inside a windowless environment, sickened by the lack of sunshine like some dour owl. One parallel block from where I worked and I was in totally alien territory.

I veered right for no particular reason. Behind me I heard the door fling open.

"Stop! Police!"

They actually yelled that. I didn't let up. Would they shoot? I doubted it. Not with all the repercussions in shooting an unarmed man who was in the midst of fleeing. Not impossible—not in this neighborhood anyway—but unlikely.

There weren't many people on this block, but those who were there regarded me with little more than passing, channel-surfing interest. I kept running. The world passed by in a blur. I sprinted past a dangerous-looking man with a dangerous-looking rottweiler. Old men sat at the corner and whined about the day. Women carried too many bags. Kids who probably should have been in school leaned against whatever was available, one cooler than the next.

Me, I was running away from the police.

My mind was having difficulty wrapping itself around that one. My legs were already feeling tingly, but the image of Elizabeth looking into that camera kept shoving me forward, pumping me up.

I was breathing too fast.

You hear about adrenaline, how it spurs you on and gives you uncanny strength, but there's a flip side. The feeling is heady, out of control. It heightens your senses to the point of paralysis. You have to harness the power or it'll choke you down.

I dove down an alleyway—that was what they always do on TV—but it dead-ended into a group of the foulest Dumpsters on the planet. The stench made me draw up like a horse. At one time, maybe when LaGuardia was mayor, the Dumpsters might have been green. All that remained was rust. In many places the rust ate through the metal, facilitating the many rats that poured through like sludge through a pipe.

I looked for some outlet, a door or something, but there was nothing. No back exit at all. I considered smashing a window to gain access, but all the lower ones were barred.

The only way out was the way I'd come in—where the police undoubtedly would see me.

I was trapped.

I looked left, right, and then, oddly enough, I looked up.

Fire escapes.

There were several above my head. Still mining my internal adrenaline drip, I leapt with all my might, stretched high with both hands, and fell flat on my ass. I tried again. Not even close. The ladders were far too high.

Now what?

Maybe I could somehow drag over a Dumpster, stand on it, and leap again. But the tops of the Dumpsters had been totally eaten away. Even if I could get footing on the piles of trash, it would still be too low.

I sucked in air and tried to think. The stench was getting to me; it crawled into my nose and seemed to nest there. I moved back toward the mouth of the alley.

Radio static. Like something you might hear coming from a police radio.

I threw my back against the wall and listened.

Hide. Had to hide.

The static grew louder. I heard voices. The cops were coming closer. I was totally exposed. I flattened myself closer to the wall, like that would help. Like they might turn the corner and mistake me for a mural.

Sirens shattered the still air.

Sirens for me.

Footsteps. They were definitely coming closer. There was only one place to hide.

I quickly discerned which Dumpster might be the least foul, closed my eyes, and dove in.

Sour milk. *Very* sour milk. That was the first smell that hit me. But it wasn't the only one. Something approaching vomit and worse. I was sitting in it. Something wet and putrid. It was sticking to me. My throat decided to do the gag reflex. My stomach heaved.

I heard someone run by the mouth of the alley. I stayed low.

A rat scrambled over my leg.

I almost screamed, but something in the subconscious kept it in the voice box. God, this was surreal. I held my breath. That lasted only so long. I tried to breathe through my mouth, but I started gagging again. I pressed my shirt against my nose and mouth. That helped, but not much.

The radio static was gone. So, too, were the footsteps. Did I fool them? If so, not for long. More police sirens joined in, harmonizing with the others, a true rhapsody in blue. The cops would have backup now. Someone would return soon. They would check the alley. Then what?

I grabbed hold of the Dumpster's edge to hoist myself out. The rust cut my palm. My hand flew toward my mouth. Bleeding. The pediatrician in me immediately scolded about the dangers of tetanus; the rest of me noted that tetanus would be the least of my worries.

I listened.

No footsteps. No blasts of radio static. Sirens wailed, but what had I expected? More backup. A murderer was on the loose in our fair city. The good guys would come out in force. They'd seal the area and throw a dragnet around it.

How far had I run?

I couldn't say. But I knew one thing. I had

to keep moving. I had to put distance between the clinic and my person.

That meant getting out of this alley.

I crept toward the mouth again. Still no footsteps or radio. Good sign. I tried to think for a moment. Fleeing was a great plan, but a destination would make it even better. Keep heading east, I decided, even though it meant less safe neighborhoods. I remember seeing train tracks aboveground.

The subway.

That would get me out of here. All I had to do was get on a train, make a few sudden switches, and I could probably manage to disappear. But where was the closest entrance?

I was trying to conjure up my internal subway map, when a policeman turned into the alley.

He looked so young, so clean-cut and fresh-scrubbed and pink-faced. His blue shirt-sleeves were neatly rolled up, two tourniquets on his bloated biceps. He started when he saw me—as surprised to see me as I was to see him.

We both froze. But he froze for a split second longer.

If I had approached him like a boxer or kung-fu expert, I'd probably have ended up picking my teeth out of my skull like so many splinters. But I didn't. I panicked. I worked on pure fear.

I launched myself straight at him.

With my chin tucked tight, I lowered my head and aimed for his center, rocketlike. Elizabeth played tennis. She told me once that when your opponent was at the net, it was often best to slam the ball right at their gut because he or she wouldn't know which way to move. You slow down their reaction time.

That was what happened here.

My body slammed into his. I grabbed hold of his shoulders like a monkey hanging on to a fence. We toppled over. I scrunched up my knees and dug them into his chest. My chin stayed tucked, the top of my head under the young cop's jaw.

We landed with an awful thud.

I heard a cracking noise. A shooting pain ricocheted down from where my skull had connected with his jaw. The young cop made a quiet "pluuu" noise. The air went out of his lungs. His jaw, I think, was broken. The flee panic took total control now. I scrambled off him as though he were a stun gun.

I had assaulted a police officer.

No time to dwell on it. I just wanted to be away from him. I managed to get to my feet and was about to turn and run, when I felt his hand on my ankle. I looked down and our eyes met.

He was in pain. Pain I had caused.

I kept my balance and unleashed a kick. It connected with his ribs. He made a wet "pluuu" sound this time. Blood trickled from his mouth. I couldn't believe what I was doing. I kicked him again. Just hard enough to loosen his grip. I pulled free.

And then I ran.

25

Hester and Shauna took a taxi to the clinic. Linda had taken the number 1 train down to their financial consultant at the World Financial Center to see about liquidating assets for bail.

A dozen police cars were angled in front of Beck's clinic, all pointing in various directions like darts thrown by a drunk. Their lights whirled at full red-blue alert. Sirens whined. More police cars pulled up.

"What the hell is going on?" Shauna asked.

Hester spotted Assistant District Attorney Lance Fein, but not before he spotted her. He stormed toward them. His face was scarlet and the vein in his forehead was pulsing.

"The son of a bitch ran," Fein spat out without preamble.

Hester took the hit and countered: "Your men must have spooked him."

Two more police cars pulled up. So did the Channel 7 news van. Fein cursed under his breath. "The press. Goddammit, Hester. You know how this is going to make me look?"

"Look, Lance—"

"Like a goddamn hack who gives special treatment to the rich, that's how. How could you do this to me, Hester? You know what the mayor is going to do to me? He's going to chew on my ass for jollies. And Tucker"—Tucker was the Manhattan district attorney—"Jesus Christ, can you imagine what he'll do?"

"Mr. Fein!"

One of the police officers was calling him. Fein eyed both of them one more time before turning away with a snap.

Hester quickly spun on Shauna. "Is Beck out of his mind?"

"He's scared," Shauna said.

"He's running away from the police," Hester shouted. "Do you get that? Do you get what that means?" She pointed toward the news van. "The media is here, for Chrissake. They're going to talk about the killer on the run. It's dangerous. It makes him look guilty. Taints the jury pool."

"Calm down," Shauna said.

"Calm down? Do you understand what he's done?"

"He's run away. That's all. Like OJ, right? Didn't seem to hurt him with the jury."

"We're not talking about OJ here, Shauna. We're talking about a rich white doctor."

"Beck's not rich."

"That's not the point, dammit. Everyone is going to want to nail his ass to a wall after this. Forget bail. Forget a fair trial." She took a breath, crossed her arms. "And Fein isn't the only one whose reputation is going to be compromised."

"Meaning?"

"Meaning me!" Hester shrieked. "In one bold stroke, Beck's destroyed my credibility with the D.A.'s office. If I promise to deliver a guy, I have to deliver him."

"Hester?"

"What?"

"I don't give a rat's ass about your reputation right now."

A sudden eruption of noise jolted them both. They turned and saw an ambulance hurry down the block. Somebody cried out. Then another cry. Cops started bouncing around like too many balls released at the same time into a pinball machine.

The ambulance skidded to a stop. The EMTs—one male, one female—jumped out of the cab. Fast. Too fast. They unsnapped the back door and pulled out a stretcher.

"This way!" someone shouted. "He's over here!"

Shauna felt her heart skip a beat. She ran over to Lance Fein. Hester followed. "What's wrong?" Hester asked. "What's happened?"

Fein ignored her.

"Lance?"

He finally faced them. The muscles in his face quaked in rage. "Your client."

"What about him? Is he hurt?"

"He just assaulted a police officer."

This was nuts.

I had crossed a line by running, but attacking that young cop... No going back now. So I ran. I sprinted with all I had.

"Officer down!"

Someone actually shouted that. More shouts followed. More radio static. More sirens.

198

They all swirled toward me. My heart leapt into my throat. I kept pumping my legs. They started feeling stiff and heavy, as though the muscles and ligaments were hardening to stone. I was out of shape. Mucus started flowing out of my nose. It mixed with whatever dirt I'd accumulated on my upper lip and snaked into my mouth.

I kept veering from block to block as though that would fool the police. I didn't turn around to see if they were following. I knew they were. The sirens and radio static told me so.

I had no chance.

I dashed through neighborhoods I wouldn't even drive through. I hopped a fence and sprinted through the high grass of what might have once been a playground. People talked about the rising price of Manhattan real estate. But here, not far from the Harlem River Drive, there were vacant lots littered with broken glass and rusted ruins of what might have once been swing sets and jungle gyms and probably cars.

In front of a cluster of low-income high-rises, a group of black teens, all with the gangsta strut and coordinated ensemble, eyed me like a tasty leftover. They were about to do something—I didn't know what—when they realized that the police were chasing me.

They started cheering me on.

"Go, white boy!"

I sort of nodded as I dashed past them, a marathoner grateful for the little boost from the crowd. One of them yelled out, "Diallo!" I kept running, but I knew, of course, who Amadou Diallo was. Everyone in New York did. He'd been shot forty-one times by police officers—and he'd been unarmed. For a moment, I thought it was some kind of warning that the police might fire upon me.

But that wasn't it at all.

The defense in the Amadou Diallo trial claimed that when Diallo reached for his wallet, the officers thought it was a gun. Since then, people had been protesting by quickly reaching into their pockets, withdrawing their wallets, and yelling "Diallo!" Street officers reported that every time someone's hand went into their pockets like that, they still felt the thump of fear.

It happened now. My new allies—allies built on the fact that they probably thought I was a murderer—whipped out their wallets. The two cops on my tail hesitated. It was enough to increase my lead.

But so what?

My throat burned. I was sucking in way too much air. My hightops felt like lead boots. I got lazy. My toe dragged, tripping me up. I lost my balance, skidding across the pavement, scraping my palms and my face and my knees.

I managed to get back up, but my legs were trembling.

Closing in now.

Sweat pasted my shirt to my skin. My ears had that surf rush whooshing through them.

I'd always hated running. Born-again joggers described how they got addicted to the rapture of running, how they achieved a nirvana known as runner's high. Right. I'd always firmly believed that—much like the high of auto-asphyxiation—the bliss came more from a lack of oxygen to the brain than any sort of endorphin rush.

Trust me, this was not blissful.

Tired. Too tired. I couldn't keep running forever. I glanced behind me. No cops. The street was abandoned. I tried a door. No go. I tried another. The radio crackle started up again. I ran. Toward the end of the block I spotted a street cellar door slightly ajar. Also rusted. Everything was rusted in this place.

I bent down and pulled at the metal handle. The door gave with an unhappy creak. I peered down into the blackness.

A cop shouted, "Cut him off the other side!"

I didn't bother looking back. I stepped down quickly into the hole. I reached the first step. Shaky. I put my foot out for the second step. But there was none.

I stayed suspended for a second, like Wile E. Coyote after running off a cliff, before I plunged helplessly into the dark pit.

The fall was probably no more than ten feet, but I seemed to take a long time to hit ground. I flailed my arms. It didn't help. My body landed on cement, the impact rattling my teeth.

I was on my back now, looking up. The

door slammed closed above me. A good thing, I suppose, but the darkness was now pretty much total. I did a quick survey of my being, the doctor doing an internal exam. Everything hurt.

I heard the cops again. The sirens had not let up, or maybe now the sound was just ringing in my ears. Lots of voices. Lots of radio static.

They were closing in on me.

I rolled onto my side. My right hand pressed down, stinging the cuts in my palms, and my body started to rise. I let the head trail; it screamed in protest when I got to my feet. I almost fell down again.

Now what?

Should I just hide here? No, that wouldn't work. Eventually, they'd start going house to house. I'd be caught. And even if they didn't, I hadn't run with the intention of hiding in a dank basement. I ran so that I could keep my appointment with Elizabeth in Washington Square.

Had to move.

But where?

My eyes started adjusting to the dark, enough to see shadowy shapes anyway. Boxes were stacked haphazardly. There were piles of rags, a few barstools, a broken mirror. I caught my reflection in the glass and almost jumped back at the sight. There was a gash on my forehead. My pants were ripped in both knees. My shirt was tattered like the Incredible Hulk's. I was smeared with enough soot to work as a chimney sweep.

Where to go?

A staircase. There had to be a staircase down here somewhere. I felt my way forward, moving in a sort of spastic dance, leading with my left leg as though it were a white cane. My foot crunched over some broken glass. I kept moving.

I heard what I thought was a mumbling noise, and a giant rag pile rose in my path. What could have been a hand reached out to me like something from a grave. I bit back a scream.

"Himmler likes tuna steaks!" he shouted at me.

The man—yes, I could see now it was clearly a man—started to stand. He was tall and black and he had a beard so white-gray and woolly it looked as though he might be eating a sheep.

"You hear me?" the man shouted. "You hear what I'm telling you?"

He stepped toward me. I shrunk back.

"Himmler! He likes tuna steaks!"

The bearded man was clearly displeased about something. He made a fist and aimed it at me. I stepped to the side without thought. His fist traveled past me with enough momentum—or maybe enough drink—to make him topple over. He fell on his face. I didn't bother to wait. I found the staircase and ran up.

The door was locked.

"Himmler!"

He was loud, too loud. I pressed against the door. No go.

"You hear me? You hear what I'm saying?"

I heard a creak. I glanced behind me and saw something that struck fear straight into my heart.

Sunlight.

Someone had pulled open the same storm door I'd come in from.

"Who's down there?"

A voice of authority. A flashlight started dancing around the floor. It reached the bearded man.

"Himmler likes tuna steaks!"

"That you yelling, old man?"

"You hear me?"

I used my shoulder against the door, putting everything I had behind it. The doorjamb started to crack. Elizabeth's image popped up— the one I'd seen on the computer—her arm raised, her eyes beckoning. I pushed a little harder.

The door gave way.

I fell out onto the ground floor, not far from the building's front door.

Now what?

Other cops were close by—I could still hear the radio static—and one of them was still interviewing Himmler's biographer. I didn't have much time. I needed help.

But from where?

I couldn't call Shauna. The police would be all over her. Same with Linda. Hester would insist I surrender.

Someone was opening the front door.

I ran down the corridor. The floor was

linoleum and filthy. The doors were all metal and closed. The motif was chipped paint. I banged open a fire door and headed up the stairwell. At the third floor, I got out.

An old woman stood in the corridor.

She was, I was surprised to see, white. My guess was that she'd probably heard the commotion and stepped out to see what was going on. I stopped short. She stood far enough away from her open door that I could get past her....

Would I? Would I go that length to get away?

I looked at her. She looked at me. Then she took out a gun.

Oh, Christ...

"What do you want?" she asked.

And I found myself answering: "May I please use your phone?"

She didn't miss a beat. "Twenty bucks."

I reached into my wallet and plucked out the cash. The old lady nodded and let me in. The apartment was tiny and well kept. There was lace on all the upholstery and on the dark wood tables.

"Over there," she said.

The phone was rotary dial. I jammed my finger into the little holes. Funny thing. I had never called this number before—had never wanted to—but I knew it by heart. Psychiatrists would probably have a field day with that one. I finished dialing and waited.

Two rings later, a voice said, "Yo."

"Tyrese? It's Dr. Beck. I need your help."

26

Shauna shook her head. "Beck hurt someone? That's not possible."

Assistant D.A. Fein's vein started fluttering again. He stepped toward her until his face was right up against hers. "He attacked a police officer in an alley. He probably broke the man's jaw and a couple of ribs." Fein leaned a little closer, his spittle landing on Shauna's cheeks. "You hear what I'm telling you?"

"I hear you," Shauna said. "Now step back, Breath Boy, or I'll knee your balls into your throat."

Fein stayed in place for a screw-you second before turning away. Hester Crimstein did likewise. She started heading back toward Broadway. Shauna chased her.

"Where are you going?"

"I quit," Hester said.

"What?"

"Find him another lawyer, Shauna."

"You can't be serious."

"I am."

"You can't just walk out on him."

"Watch me."

"It's prejudicial."

"I gave them my word he'd surrender," she said.

"Screw your word. Beck's the priority here, not you."

"To you maybe."

"You're putting yourself before a client?"

"I won't work with a man who'd do something like that."

"Who are you kidding? You've defended serial rapists."

She waved a hand. "I'm out of here."

"You're just a goddamn media-hound hypocrite."

"Ouch, Shauna."

"I'll go to them."

"What?"

"I'll go to the media."

Hester stopped. "And say what? That I walked away from a dishonest murderer? Great, go ahead. I'll leak so much shit about Beck, he'll make Jeffrey Dahmer look like a good dating prospect."

"You have nothing to leak," Shauna said.

Hester shrugged. "Never stopped me before."

The two women glared. Neither looked away.

"You may think my reputation is irrelevant," Hester said, her voice suddenly soft. "But it's not. If the D.A.'s office can't rely on my word, I'm useless to my other clients. I'm also useless to Beck. It's that simple. I won't let my practice—and my clients—go down the tubes because your boy acted erratically."

Shauna shook her head. "Just get out my face."

"One more thing."

"What?"

"Innocent men don't run, Shauna. Your boy

Beck? Hundred to one he killed Rebecca Schayes."

"You're on," Shauna said. "And one more thing for you too, Hester. You say one word against Beck, and they'll need a soup ladle to bury your remains. We clear?"

Hester didn't reply. She took another step away from Shauna. And that was when the gunfire ripped through the air.

I was in mid-crouch, crawling down a rusted fire escape, when the sound of the gunfire nearly made me topple over. I flattened myself on the grated walk and waited.

More gunfire.

I heard shouts. I should have expected this, but it still packed a wallop. Tyrese told me to climb out here and wait for him. I had wondered how he planned on getting me out. Now I was getting some idea.

A diversion.

In the distance, I heard someone shouting, "White boy shooting up the place!" Then another voice: "White boy with a gun! White boy with a gun!"

More gunfire. But—and I strained my ears— no more police radio static. I stayed low and tried not to think much. My brain, it seemed, had short-circuited. Three days ago, I was a dedicated doctor sleepwalking through my own life. Since then, I had seen a ghost, gotten emails from the dead, had become a suspect in not one but two murders, was on the run from the law, had assaulted a police officer, and had enlisted the aid of a known drug dealer.

Heck of a seventy-two hours.

I almost laughed.

"Yo, Doc."

I looked down. Tyrese was there. So was another black man, early twenties, only slightly smaller than this building. The big man peered up at me with those sleek up-yours sunglasses that fit perfectly with his deadened facial expression.

"Come on, Doc. Let's roll."

I ran down the fire escape stairs. Tyrese kept glancing left and right. The big guy stood perfectly still, his arms folded across his chest in what we used to call the buffalo stance. I hesitated before the last ladder, trying to figure out how to release it so I could reach the ground.

"Yo, Doc, lever on the left."

I found it, pulled, and the ladder slid down. When I reached the bottom, Tyrese made a face and waved his hand in front of his nose. "You ripe, Doc."

"I didn't have a chance to shower, sorry."

"This way."

Tyrese did a quick-walk through the back lot. I followed, having to do a little run to keep up. The big man glided behind us in silence. He never moved his head left or right, but I still got the impression he didn't miss much.

A black BMW with tinted windows, a complicated antenna, and a chain frame on the back license plate was running. The doors were all closed, but I could feel the rap music. The bass vibrated in my chest like a tuning fork.

"The car," I said with a frown. "Isn't it kind of conspicuous?"

"If you five-oh and you looking for a lily-white doctor, where would be the last place you look?"

He had a point.

The big guy opened the back door. The music blared at the volume of a Black Sabbath concert. Tyrese extended his arm doorman-style. I got in. He slid next to me. The big guy bent into the driver's seat.

I couldn't understand much of what the rapper on the CD was saying, but he was clearly pissed off with "da man." I suddenly understood.

"This here is Brutus," Tyrese said.

He meant the big-guy driver. I tried to catch his eye in the rearview mirror, but I couldn't see them through the sunglasses.

"Nice to meet you," I said.

Brutus didn't respond.

I turned my attention back to Tyrese. "How did you pull this off?"

"Coupla my boys are doing some shooting down a Hundred Forty-seventh Street."

"Won't the cops find them?"

Tyrese snorted. "Yeah, right."

"It's that easy?"

"From there, yeah, it's easy. We got this place, see, in Building Five at Hobart Houses. I give the tenants ten bucks a month to stick their garbage in front of the back doors. Blocks it up, see. Cops can't get through. Good place to conduct bidness. So my boys, they pop off some shots from the windows, you know what I'm saying. By the time the cops get through, poof, they gone."

"And who was yelling about a white man with a gun?"

"Couple other of my boys. They just running down the street yelling about a crazy white man."

"Theoretically, me," I said.

"Theoretically," Tyrese repeated with a smile. "That's a nice big word, Doc."

I laid my head back. Fatigue settled down hard on my bones. Brutus drove east. He crossed that blue bridge by Yankee Stadium— I'd never learned the bridge's name—and that meant we were in the Bronx. For a while I slumped down in case someone peered into the car, but then I remembered that the windows were tinted. I looked out.

The area was ugly as all hell, like one of those scenes you see in apocalyptic movies after the bomb detonates. There were patches of what might have once been buildings, all in various states of decay. Structures had crumbled, yes, but as though from within, as though the supporting innards had been eaten away.

We drove a little while. I tried to get a grip on what was going on, but my brain kept throwing up roadblocks. Part of me recognized that I was in something approaching shock; the rest of me wouldn't allow me even to consider it. I concentrated on my surroundings. As we drove a little more—as we dove deeper into the decay—the habitable dwellings dwindled. Though we were probably less than a couple of miles from the clinic, I had no idea where we were. Still the Bronx, I guessed. South Bronx probably.

Worn tires and ripped mattresses lay like war wounded in the middle of the road. Big chunks of cement peeked out from the high grass. There were stripped cars and while there were no fires burning, maybe there should have been.

"You come here much, Doc?" Tyrese said with a small chuckle.

I didn't bother responding.

Brutus pulled the car to a stop in front of yet another condemned building. A chain-link fence encircled the sad edifice. The windows had been boarded over with plywood. I could see a piece of paper glued to the door, probably a demolition warning. The door, too, was plywood. I saw it open. A man stumbled out, raising both hands to shield his eyes from the sun, staggering like Dracula under its onslaught.

My world kept swirling.

"Let's go," Tyrese said.

Brutus was out of the car first. He opened the door for me. I thanked him. Brutus stuck with the stoic. He had the kind of cigar-store-Indian face you couldn't imagine—and probably wouldn't ever want to see—smiling.

On the right, the chain-link had been clipped and pulled back. We crouched through. The stumbling man approached Tyrese. Brutus stiffened, but Tyrese waved him down. The stumbling man and Tyrese greeted each other warmly and performed a complicated handshake. Then they went their separate ways.

"Come in," Tyrese said to me.

I ducked inside, my mind still numb. The stench came first, the acid smells of urine and the never-mistaken stink of fecal matter. Something was burning—I think I knew what—and the damp yellow odor of sweat seemed to be coming from the walls. But there was something else here. The smell, not of death, but of predeath, like gangrene, like something dying and decomposing while still breathing.

The stifling heat was of the blast furnace variety. Human beings—maybe fifty of them, maybe a hundred—littered the floor like losing stubs at an OTB. It was dark inside. There seemed to be no electricity, no running water, no furniture of any sort. Wood planks blocked out most of the sun, the only illumination coming through cracks where the sun sliced through like a reaper's scythe. You could make out shadows and shapes and little more.

I admit to being naïve about the drug scene. In the emergency room, I'd seen the results plenty of times. But drugs never interested me personally. Booze was my poison of choice, I guess. Still, enough stimuli were getting through that even I could deduce that we were in a crack house.

"This way," Tyrese said.

We started walking through the wounded. Brutus led. The dearly reclined parted for him as though he were Moses. I fell in behind Tyrese. The ends of pipes would light up, popping through the darkness. It reminded me of going to the Barnum and Bailey circus as a kid and twirling those tiny flashlights around in the dark. That was what this looked liked. I saw dark. I saw shadows. I saw the flashes of light.

No music played. No one seemed to talk much either. I heard a hum. I heard the wet sucking sound of the pipes. Shrieks pierced the air every once in a while, the sound not quite human.

I also heard groaning. People were performing the lewdest of sex acts, out in the open, no shame, no attempt at privacy.

One particular sight—I'll spare you the details—made me pull up in horror. Tyrese watched my expression with something close to amusement.

"They run out of money, they trade this"— Tyrese pointed—"for hits."

The bile worked its way into my mouth. I turned to him. He shrugged.

"Commerce, Doc. Makes the world go round."

Tyrese and Brutus kept walking. I staggered alongside. Most of the interior walls had crumbled to the ground. People—old, young, black, white, men, women—hung everywhere, spineless, flopped over like Dali clocks.

"Are you a crackhead, Tyrese?" I said.

"Used to be. Got hooked when I was sixteen."

"How did you stop?"

Tyrese smiled. "You see my man Brutus?"

"Hard to miss him."

"I told him I'd give him a thousand dollars for every week I stayed clean. Brutus moved in with me."

I nodded. That sounded far more effective than a week with Betty Ford.

Brutus opened a door. This room, while not exactly well appointed, at least had tables and chairs, even lights and a refrigerator. I noticed a portable generator in the corner.

Tyrese and I stepped inside. Brutus closed the door and stayed in the corridor. We were left alone.

"Welcome to my office," Tyrese said.

"Does Brutus still help you stay off the junk?"

He shook his head. "Nah, TJ does that now. You know what I'm saying?"

I did. "And you don't have a problem with what you do here?"

"I got lots of problems, Doc." Tyrese sat down and invited me to do the same. His eyes flashed at me, and I didn't like what I saw in them. "I ain't one of the good guys."

I didn't know what to say to that, so I changed subjects. "I have to get down to Washington Square Park by five o'clock."

He leaned back. "Tell me what's up."

"It's a long story."

Tyrese took out a blunt blade and started

cleaning his nails. "My kid gets sick, I go to the expert, right?"

I nodded.

"You in trouble with the law, you should do likewise."

"That's some analogy."

"Something bad's happening with you, Doc." He spread his arms. "Bad is my world. I'm the best tour guide there is."

So I told him the story. Almost all of it. He nodded a lot, but I doubted he believed me when I said I had nothing to do with the murders. I doubted he cared either.

"Okay," he said when I finished, "let's get you ready. Then we need to talk about something else."

"What?"

Tyrese did not answer. He moved to what looked like a reinforced metal locker in the corner. He unlocked it with a key, leaned inside, and withdrew a gun.

"Glock, baby, Glock," he said, handing me the gun. I stiffened. An image of black and blood flashed in my mind and quickly fled; I didn't chase it. It had been a long time. I reached out and plucked the gun with two fingers, as though it might be hot. "Gun of champions," he added.

I was going to refuse it, but that would be stupid. They already had me on suspicion of two murders, assaulting a police officer, resisting arrest, and probably a bunch of stuff for fleeing from the law. What's a concealed-weapon charge on top of all that?

"It's loaded," he said.

"Is there a safety or something?"

"Not anymore."

"Oh," I said. I slowly turned it over and over, remembering the last time I held a weapon in my hand. It felt good, holding a gun again. Something about the weight, I guessed. I liked the texture, the cold of the steel, the way it fit perfectly in my palm, the heft. I didn't like that I liked it.

"Take this too." He handed me what looked like a cell phone.

"What's this?" I asked.

Tyrese frowned. "What it look like? A cell phone. But it's got a stolen number. Can't be traced back to you, see?"

I nodded, feeling very much out of my element.

"Got a bathroom behind that door," Tyrese said, gesturing to my right. "No shower but there's a bath. Wash your smelly ass off. I'll get you some fresh clothes. Then Brutus and me, we'll get you down to Washington Square."

"You said you had something you wanted to talk to me about."

"After you get dressed," Tyrese said. "We'll talk then."

27

Eric Wu stared at the sprawling tree. His face was serene, his chin tilted up slightly.

"Eric?" The voice belonged to Larry Gandle.

Wu did not turn around. "Do you know what this tree is called?" he asked.

"No."

"The Hangman's Elm."

"Charming."

Wu smiled. "Some historians believe that during the eighteenth century, this park was used for public executions."

"That's great, Eric."

"Yeah."

Two shirtless men whipped by on Rollerblades. A boom box played Jefferson Airplane. Washington Square Park—named, not surprisingly, for George Washington—was one of those places that tried to cling to the sixties though the grip kept slipping. There were usually protestors of some sort, but they looked more like actors in a nostalgic revival than genuine revolutionaries. Street performers took the stage with a little too much finesse. The homeless were the type of colorful that felt somehow contrived.

"You sure we have this place covered?" Gandle asked.

Wu nodded, still facing the tree. "Six men. Plus the two in the van."

Gandle looked behind him. The van was white with a magnetic sign reading B&T Paint and a phone number and a cute logo of a guy who looked a lot like the Monopoly man holding a ladder and a paintbrush. If asked to describe the van, witnesses would remember, if anything at all, the name of the paint company and maybe the phone number.

Neither existed.

The van was double-parked. In Manhattan, a legally parked work van would be more apt to draw suspicion than one that was double-parked. Still, they kept their eye out. If a police officer approached, they would drive away. They would take the van to a lot on Lafayette Street. They would change license plates and magnetic signs. They would then return.

"You should go back to the van," Wu said.

"Do you think Beck will even make it?"

"Doubt it," Wu said.

"I figured getting him arrested would draw her out," Gandle said. "I didn't figure that he'd have a meet set up."

One of their operatives—the curly-haired man who'd worn sweat pants at Kinko's last night—had seen the message pop up on the Kinko's computer. But by the time he relayed the message, Wu had already planted the evidence at Beck's house.

No matter. It would work out.

"We have to grab them both, but she's the priority," Gandle said. "Worse comes to worst, we kill them. But it would be best to have them alive. So we can find out what they know."

Wu did not respond. He was still staring at the tree.

"Eric?"

"They hung my mother from a tree like this," Wu said.

Gandle wasn't sure how to respond, so he settled for "I'm sorry."

"They thought she was a spy. Six men stripped her naked and took a bullwhip to her. They lashed her for hours. Everywhere. Even the flesh on her face was ripped open. She was conscious the whole time. She kept screaming. It took a long time for her to die."

"Jesus Christ," Gandle said softly.

"When they were done, they hung her on a huge tree." He pointed to the Hangman's Elm. "One just like this. It was supposed to be a lesson, of course. So no one else would spy. But birds and animals got to her. Two days later, there were only bones left on that tree."

Wu put the Walkman back on his ears. He turned away from the tree. "You really should get out of sight," he told Gandle.

Larry had trouble wresting his eyes from the massive elm, but he managed to nod and go on his way.

28

I put on a pair of black jeans with a waist the approximate circumference of a truck tire. I folded over the slack and tightened the belt. The black White Sox's uniform shirt fit like a muumuu. The black baseball cap—it had some logo on it I didn't recognize—already had the bill broken in for me. Tyrese also gave me a pair of the same up-yours sunglasses Brutus favored.

Tyrese almost laughed when I came out of the bathroom. "You look good, Doc."

"I think the word you're looking for is *phat*."

He chuckled and shook his head. "White people." Then his face grew serious. He slid some stapled sheets of paper toward me. I picked it up. On top it read Last Will and Testament. I looked the question at him.

"Been meaning to talk to you about this," Tyrese said.

"About your will?"

"I got two more years on my plan."

"What plan?"

"I do this two more years, I got enough money to get TJ out of here. I figure I got maybe sixty-forty chance of making it."

"What do you mean, making it?"

Tyrese's eyes locked on mine. "You know."

I did know. He meant surviving. "Where will you go?"

He handed me a postcard. The scene was sun, blue water, palm trees. The postcard was crinkled from too much handling. "Down in Florida," he said with a soft lilt in his voice. "I know this place. It's quiet. Gotta pool and good schools. Nobody to start wondering where I got my money, you know what I'm saying?"

I handed him back the picture. "I don't understand what I have to do with this."

"This"—he held up the photograph—"is the plan if the sixty percent happens. That"—he pointed to the will—"that's if the forty plays out."

I told him that I still didn't understand.

"I went downtown six months ago, you know what I'm saying. Got a fancy lawyer. Cost me two grand for a coupla hours with him. His name is Joel Marcus. If I die, you have to go see him. You the executor of my will. I got some papers locked up. They'll tell you where the money is."

"Why me?"

"You care about my boy."

"What about Latisha?"

He scoffed. "She a woman, Doc. Soon as I hit the pavement, she be looking for another cock, you know what I'm saying? Probably get knocked up again. Maybe get back on the stuff." He sat back and folded his arms. "Can't trust women, Doc. You should know that."

"She's TJ's mother."

"Right."

"She loves him."

"Yeah, I know that. But she just a woman, you know what I'm saying? You give her this kind of cash, she'll blow it in a day. That's why I set up some trust funds and shit. You the executor. She want money for TJ, you have to approve it. You and this Joel Marcus."

I would have argued that it was sexist and that he was a Neanderthal, but this hardly seemed the time. I shifted in the chair and looked at him. Tyrese was maybe twenty-five years old. I had seen so many like him. I had always lumped them into a single entity, blurring their faces into a dark mass of bad. "Tyrese?"

He looked at me.

"Leave now."

He frowned.

"Use the money you have. Get a job down in Florida. I'll lend you more if you need it. But take your family and go now."

He shook his head.

"Tyrese?"

He stood up. "Come on, Doc. We best get going."

"We're still looking for him."

Lance Fein fumed, his waxy face almost dripping. Dimonte chewed. Krinsky took notes. Stone hitched up his pants.

Carlson was distracted, bent over a fax that had just come through in the car.

"What about the gunshots?" Lance Fein snapped.

The uniformed officer—Agent Carlson hadn't bothered learning his name—shrugged. "Nobody knows anything. I think they were probably unrelated."

"Unrelated?" Fein shrieked. "What kind of incompetent idiot are you, Benny? They were running down the street yelling about a white guy."

"Well, no one knows nothing now."

"Lean on them," Fein said. "Lean on them hard. I mean, for crying out loud, how the hell does a guy like this escape, huh?"

"We'll get him."

Stone tapped Carlson on the shoulder. "What's up, Nick?"

Carlson frowned at the printout. He didn't speak. He was a neat man, orderly to the point of obsessive-compulsive. He washed his hands too much. He often locked and unlocked his door a dozen times before leaving the house. He stared some more because something here just did not mesh.

"Nick?"

Carlson turned toward him. "The thirty-eight we found in Sarah Goodhart's safety-deposit box."

"The one the key on the body led us to?"

"Right."

"What about it?" Stone asked.

Carlson kept frowning. "There's lots of holes here."

"Holes?"

"First off," Carlson continued, "we assume the Sarah Goodhart safety-deposit box was Elizabeth Beck's, right?"

"Right."

"But someone's paid the bill for the box every year for the past eight years," Carlson said. "Elizabeth Beck is dead. Dead women pay no tabs."

"Her father maybe. I think he knows more than he's letting on."

Carlson didn't like it. "How about those listening devices we found at Beck's house? What's the deal there?"

"I don't know," Stone replied with a shrug. "Maybe someone else in the department suspected him too."

"We'd have heard by now. And this report on that thirty-eight we found in the box." He motioned toward it. "You see what the ATF came back with?"

"No."

"Bulletproof had no hits, but that's not surprising since the data doesn't go back eight years anyway." Bulletproof, a bullet-analyzing module used by the Bureau of Alcohol, Tobacco and Firearms, was used to link data from past crimes with more recently discovered firearms. "But the NTC got a hit." NTC stood for the National Tracing Center. "Guess who the last registered owner was."

He handed Stone the printout. Stone scanned down and found it. "Stephen Beck?"

"David Beck's father."

"He died, right?"

"Right."

Stone handed it back to him. "So his son probably inherited the weapon," he said. "It was Beck's gun."

"So why would his wife keep it locked in a safety-deposit box with those photographs?"

Stone considered that one a minute. "Maybe she feared he'd use it on her."

Carlson frowned some more. "We're missing something."

"Look, Nick, let's not make this more complicated than we have to. We got Beck nailed good on the Schayes murder. It'll be a righteous collar. Let's just forget about Elizabeth Beck, okay?"

Carlson looked at him. "Forget about her?"

Stone cleared his throat and spread his hands. "Let's face it. Nailing Beck on Schayes, that'll be a piece of pie. But his wife—Christ, that case is eight years old. We got some scraps, okay, but we're not going to get him for it. It's too late. Maybe"—he gave too dramatic a shrug—"maybe it's best to let sleeping dogs lie."

"What the hell are you talking about?"

Stone moved closer and beckoned Carlson to bend down. "Some people at the Bureau would rather we didn't dig this all up."

"Who doesn't want us digging what up?"

"It's not important, Nick. We're all on the same side, right? If we find out KillRoy didn't kill Elizabeth Beck, it just opens a can of worms, right? His lawyer will probably ask for a new trial—"

"They never tried him for Elizabeth Beck."

"But we wrote her off as KillRoy's handiwork. It would add doubt, that's all. It's neater this way."

"I don't want neat," Carlson said. "I want the truth."

"We all want that, Nick. But we want justice even more, right? Beck will get a life sentence for Rebecca Schayes. KillRoy will stay in jail. That's how it should be."

"There are holes, Tom."

"You keep saying that, but I don't see any. You were the one who first came up with Beck being good for his wife's murder."

"Exactly," Carlson said. "For his wife's murder. Not Rebecca Schayes's."

"I don't get what you mean."

"The Schayes murder doesn't fit."

"You kidding me? It makes it more solid. Schayes knew something. We started closing in. Beck had to shut her up."

Carlson frowned again.

"What?" Stone continued. "You think Beck's visit to her studio yesterday—right after we pressured him—was just a coincidence?"

"No," Carlson said.

"Then what, Nick? Don't you see? Schayes's murder fits in beautifully."

"A little too beautifully," Carlson said.

"Ah, don't start with that crap."

"Let me ask you something, Tom. How well did Beck plan and execute his wife's murder?"

"Pretty damn well."

"Exactly. He killed every witness. He got rid of the bodies. If it wasn't for the rainfall and that bear, we'd have nothing. And let's face it. Even with that, we still don't have enough to indict, much less convict."

"So?"

"So why is Beck suddenly so stupid? He knows we're after him. He knows that Schayes's assistant will be able to testify that he saw Rebecca Schayes the day of the murder. So why would he be stupid enough to keep the gun in his garage? Why would he be stupid enough to leave those gloves in his own trash can?"

"Easy," Stone said. "He rushed this time. With his wife, he had plenty of time to plan."

"Did you see this?"

He handed Stone the surveillance report.

"Beck visited the medical examiner this morning," Carlson said. "Why?"

"I don't know. Maybe he wanted to know if there was anything incriminating in the autopsy file."

Carlson frowned yet again. His hands were itching for another wash. "We're missing something, Tom."

"I don't see what, but hey, either way, we got to get him into custody. Then we can sort it out, okay?"

Stone headed over to Fein. Carlson let the doubts sink in. He thought again about Beck's visit to the medical examiner's office. He took out his phone, wiped it down with a handkerchief, and pressed the digits. When someone answered, he said, "Get me the Sussex County medical examiner."

29

In the old days—ten years ago anyway—she had friends living at the Chelsea Hotel on West Twenty-third Street. The hotel was half tourist, half residential, all-around kooky. Artists, writers, students, methadone addicts of every stripe and persuasion. Black fingernails, goth-white face paint, bloodred lipstick, hair without a trace of curl—all in the days before it was mainstream.

Little had changed. It was a good place to remain anonymous.

After grabbing a slice of pizza across the street, she'd checked in and had not ventured out of her room. New York. She'd once called this city home, but this was only her second visit in the past eight years.

She missed it.

With too practiced a hand, she tucked her hair under the wig. Today's color would be blond with dark roots. She put on a pair of wire-rim glasses and jammed the implants into her mouth. They changed the shape of her face.

Her hands were shaking.

Two airplane tickets sat on the kitchen table. Tonight, they would take British Airways Flight 174 from JFK to London's Heathrow Airport, where her contact would meet them with new identities. Then they would take the train to Gatwick and take the afternoon flight to Nairobi, Kenya. A jeep would take them near the foothills of Mount Meru in Tanzania, and a three-day hike would follow.

Once they were there—in one of the few spots on this planet with no radio, no television, no electricity—they would be free.

The names on the tickets were Lisa Sherman. And David Beck.

She gave her wig one more tug and stared at her reflection. Her eyes blurred, and for a moment, she was back at the lake. Hope ignited in her chest, and for once she did nothing to extinguish it. She managed a smile and turned away.

She took the elevator to the lobby and made a right on Twenty-third Street.

Washington Square Park was a nice walk from here.

Tyrese and Brutus dropped me on the corner of West Fourth and Lafayette streets, about four blocks east of the park. I knew the area well enough. Elizabeth and Rebecca had shared an apartment on Washington Square, feeling deliciously avant garde in their West Village digs—the photographer and the social-working attorney, striving for Bohemia as they mingled with their fellow suburban-

raised wanna-bes and trust-fund revolutionaries. Frankly I never quite bought it, but
that was okay.

I was attending Columbia Medical School
at the time, and technically, I lived uptown on
Haven Avenue near the hospital now known
as New York-Presbyterian. But naturally I
spent a lot of time down here.

Those were good years.

Half an hour until the meet time.

I headed down West Fourth Street past
the Tower Records and into a region of the city
heavily occupied by New York University.
NYU wanted you to know this. They staked
claim to this land with garish purple NYU-logo
flags everywhere. Ugly as hell, this garish
purple set against Greenwich Village's subdued brick. Very possessive and territorial
too, thought I, for such a liberal enclave. But
there you go.

My heart pounded on my chest wall as
though it wanted to break free.

Would she be there already?

I didn't run. I kept cool and tried to distract
myself from what the next hour or so could
bring. The wounds from my recent ordeal
were in that state between burn and itch. I
caught my reflection in a building window and
couldn't help but notice that I looked utterly
ridiculous in my borrowed garb. Gangsta
Prep. Yo, word.

My pants kept sliding down. I hitched them
up with one hand and tried to keep pace.

Elizabeth might be at the park.

I could see the square now. The southeast corner was only a block away. There seemed to be a rustle in the air, the onset of a storm maybe, but that was probably my imagination shifting into high gear. I kept my head lowered. Had my picture reached the television yet? Had the anchors broken in with a be-on-the-lookout announcement? I doubted it. But my eyes still stayed on the pavement.

I hurried my step. Washington Square had always been too intense for me during the summer months. It was trying too hard—too much happening with just a little too much desperation. Manufactured edge, I called it. My favorite spot was the large clutter of humanity near the cement game tables. I played chess there sometimes. I was pretty good, but in this park, chess was the great equalizer. Rich, poor, white, black, homeless, high-rised, rental, co-oped—all harmonized over the age-old black and white figurines. The best player I'd ever seen down here was a black man who spent most of his pre-Giuliani afternoons harassing motorists for change with his squeegee.

Elizabeth wasn't there yet.

I took a seat on a bench.

Fifteen more minutes.

The tightness in my chest increased fourfold. I had never been so scared in my entire life. I thought about Shauna's technological demonstration. A hoax? I wondered again. What if this was all a hoax? What if Elizabeth was indeed dead? What would I do then?

232

Useless speculation, I told myself. A waste of energy.

She had to be alive. There was no other choice.

I sat back and waited.

"He's here," Eric Wu said into his cell phone.

Larry Gandle looked out the van's tinted window. David Beck was indeed where he was supposed to be, dressed like a street punk. His face was covered with scrapes and flowering bruises.

Gandle shook his head. "How the hell did he pull it off?"

"Well," Eric Wu said in that singsong voice, "we can always ask him."

"We need this to go smoothly, Eric."

"Yes indeed."

"Is everybody in place?"

"Of course."

Gandle checked his watch. "She should be here any minute now."

Located between Sullivan and Thompson streets, Washington Square's most striking edifice was a high tower of washed-brown brick on the south side of the park. Most believed that the tower was still part of the Judson Memorial Church. It wasn't. For the past two decades, the tower held NYU student dorm rooms and offices. The top of the tower was easily accessible to anyone who looked as though she knew where she was going.

From up here, she could look down at the whole park. And when she did, she started to cry.

Beck had come. He wore the most bizarre disguise, but then again, the email had warned him that he might be followed. She could see him sitting on that bench, all alone, waiting, his right leg shaking up and down. His leg always did that when he was nervous.

"Ah, Beck..."

She could hear the pain, the bitter agony, in her own voice. She kept staring at him.

What had she done?

So stupid.

She forced herself to turn away. Her legs folded and she slid with her back against the wall until she reached the floor. Beck had come for her.

But so had they.

She was sure of it. She had spotted three of them, at the very least. Probably more. She had also spotted the B&T Paint van. She'd dialed the number on the van's sign, but it was out of service. She checked with directory assistance. There was no B&T Paint.

They'd found them. Despite all her pre-cautions, they were here.

She closed her eyes. Stupid. So stupid. To think that she could pull this off. How could she have allowed it to happen? Yearning had clouded her judgment. She knew that now. Somehow, she had fooled herself into believing that she could turn a devastating catastrophe—the two bodies being discovered near the lake—into some sort of divine windfall.

Stupid.

She sat up and risked another look at Beck. Her heart plummeted like a stone down a well. He looked so alone down there, so small and fragile and helpless. Had Beck adjusted to her death? Probably. Had he fought through what happened and made a life for himself? Again probably. Had he recovered from the blow only to have her stupidity whack him over the head again?

Definitely.

The tears returned.

She took out the two airplane tickets. Preparation. That had always been the key to her survival. Prepare for every eventuality. That was why she had planned the meet here, at a public park she knew so well, where she would have this advantage. She hadn't admitted it to herself, but she'd known that this possibility—no, this likelihood—existed.

It was over.

The small opening, if there had ever been one, had been slammed shut.

Time to go. By herself. And this time for good.

She wondered how he'd react to her not showing up. Would he keep scouring his computer for emails that would never come? Would he search the faces of strangers and imagine he saw hers? Would he just forget and go on—and, when she really mined her true feelings, did she want him to?

No matter. Survival first. His anyway. She had no choice. She had to go.

With great effort, she tore her gaze away and hurried down the stairs. There was a back exit that led out to West Third Street, so she'd never even had to enter the park. She pushed the heavy metal door and stepped outside. Down Sullivan Street, she found a taxi on the corner of Bleecker.

She leaned back and closed her eyes.

"Where to?" the driver asked.

"JFK Airport," she said.

30

Too much time passed.

I stayed on the bench and waited. In the distance I could see the park's famed marble arch. Stanford White, the famous turn-of-the-century architect who murdered a man in a jealous fit over a fifteen-year-old girl, had purportedly "designed" it. I didn't get that. How do you design something that is a replica of someone else's work? The fact that the Washington Arch was a direct rip-off of the Arc de Triomphe in Paris was no secret. New Yorkers got excited over what was in effect a facsimile. I had no idea why.

You couldn't touch the arch anymore. A chain-link fence, not unlike the ones I'd just seen in the South Bronx, encircled it so as to discourage "graffiti artists." The park was big on fences. Almost all grassy areas were lined with loose fencing—double fencing in most places.

Where was she?

Pigeons waddled with the type of possessiveness usually associated with politicians. Many flocked in my direction. They pecked my sneakers and then looked up as though disappointed they weren't edible.

"Ty usually sits there."

The voice came from a homeless guy wearing a pinwheel hat and Spock ears. He sat across from me.

"Oh," I said.

"Ty feeds them. They like Ty."

"Oh," I said again.

"That's why they're all over you like that. They don't like you or nothing. They think maybe you're Ty. Or a friend of Ty's."

"Uh-huh."

I checked my watch. I had been sitting here the better part of two hours. She wasn't coming. Something had gone wrong. Again I wondered if it had all been a hoax, but I quickly pushed it away. Better to continue assuming that the messages were from Elizabeth. If it's all a hoax, well, I'd learn that eventually.

No matter what, I love you....

That was what the message said. No matter what. As though something might go wrong. As though something could happen. As though I should just forget about it and go on.

To hell with that.

It felt strange. Yes, I was crushed. The police were after me. I was exhausted and beaten up and near the edge sanity-wise. And yet I felt stronger than I had in years. I didn't know why. But I knew I was not going to let it go. Only Elizabeth knew all those things—kiss time, the Bat Lady, the Teenage Sex Poodles. Ergo, it was Elizabeth who had sent the emails. Or someone who was making Elizabeth send them. Either way, she was alive. I had to pursue this. There was no other way.

So, what next?

I took out my new cell phone. I rubbed my chin for a minute and then came up with an idea. I pressed in the digits. A man sitting across the way—he'd been reading a newspaper for a very long time there—sneaked a glance at me. I didn't like that. Better safe than sorry. I stood and moved out of hearing distance.

Shauna answered the phone. "Hello?"

"Old man Teddy's phone," I said.

"Beck? What the hell—?"

"Three minutes."

I hung up. I figured that Shauna and Linda's phone would be tapped. The police would be able to hear every word we said. But one floor below them lived an old widower named Theodore Malone. Shauna and Linda looked in on him from time to time. They had a key to his apartment. I'd call there. The feds or cops or whoever wouldn't have a tap on that phone. Not in time anyway.

I pressed the number.

Shauna sounded out of breath. "Hello?"

"I need your help."

"Do you have any idea what's going on?"

"I assume there's a massive manhunt for me." I still felt oddly calm—in the eye, I guess.

"Beck, you have to turn yourself in."

"I didn't kill anyone."

"I know that, but if you stay out there—"

"Do you want to help me or not?" I interrupted.

"Tell me," she said.

"Have they established a time for the murder yet?"

"Around midnight. Their timetable is a little tight, but they figure you took off right after I left."

"Okay," I said. "I need you to do something for me."

"Name it."

"First off, you have to pick up Chloe."

"Your dog?"

"Yes."

"Why?"

"For one thing," I said, "she needs a walk."

Eric Wu spoke on his cell phone. "He's on the phone, but my man can't get close enough."

"Did he make your guy?"

"Possibly."

"Maybe he's calling off the meet then."

Wu did not reply. He watched as Dr. Beck pocketed his cell phone and started crossing through the park.

"We have a problem," Wu said.

"What?"

"It appears as though he's leaving the park."

There was silence on the other end of the line. Wu waited.

"We lost him before," Gandle said.

Wu did not reply.

"We can't risk it, Eric. Grab him. Grab him now, find out what he knows, and end it."

Eric nodded a signal in the direction of the van. He started walking toward Beck. "Done."

I headed past the park's statue of Garibaldi unsheathing his sword. Strangely enough, I had a destination in mind. Forget visiting KillRoy, that was out for now. But the PF from Elizabeth's diary, aka Peter Flannery, ambulance-chaser-at-law, was another matter. I could still get to his office and have a chat with him. I had no idea what I would learn. But I'd be doing something. That would be a start.

A playground was nestled up on my right, but there were fewer than a dozen children in there. On my left, "George's Dog Park," a glorified doggy run, was chock-full of bandanna-clad canines and their parental alternatives. On the park's stage, two men juggled. I walked past a group of poncho-sheathed students sitting in a semi-circle. A dyed-blond Asian man built like the Thing from the Fantastic Four glided to my right. I glanced behind me. The man who'd been reading the newspaper was gone.

I wondered about that.

He had been there almost the whole time I was. Now, after several hours, he decided to leave at the exact time I did. Coincidence? Probably.

You'll be followed....

That was what the email had said. It didn't say maybe. It seemed, in hindsight, pretty sure of itself. I kept walking and thought about it a little more. No way. The best tail in the world wouldn't have stuck with me after what I'd just been through today.

The guy with the newspaper couldn't have been following me. At least, I couldn't imagine it.

Could they have intercepted the email?

I couldn't see how. I'd erased it. It had never even been on my own computer.

I crossed Washington Square West. When I reached the curb, I felt a hand on my shoulder. Gentle at first. Like an old friend sneaking up behind me. I turned and had enough time to see it was the Asian guy with the dyed hair.

Then he squeezed my shoulder.

31

His fingers bore into the joint's crevice like spearheads.

Pain—crippling pain—slashed down my left side. My legs gave out. I tried to scream or fight, but I couldn't move. A white van swung up next to us. The side door slid open. The Asian guy moved his hand onto my neck. He squeezed the pressure points on either side, and my eyes started rolling back. With his other hand, he toyed with my spine and I bent forward. I felt myself folding up.

He shoved me toward the van. Hands reached from inside the back and dragged me in. I landed on the cool metal floor. No seats in here. The door closed. The van pulled back into the traffic.

The whole episode—from the hand touching my shoulder to the van starting up—took maybe five seconds.

The Glock, I thought.

I tried to reach for it, but someone leapt on my back. My hands were pinned down. I heard a snap, and my right arm was cuffed at the wrist to the floorboard. They flipped me over, nearly ripping my shoulder out of the socket. Two of them. I could see them now. Two men, both white, maybe thirty years old. I could see them clearly. Too clearly. I could identify them. They would have to know that.

This wasn't good.

They cuffed my other hand so I was spread-eagle on the floorboard. Then they sat on my legs. I was chained down now and totally exposed.

"What do you want?" I asked.

No one answered. The van pulled to a quick stop around the corner. The big Asian guy slid in, and the van started up again. He bent down, gazing at me with what looked like mild curiosity.

"Why were you at the park?" he asked me.

His voice threw me. I had expected something growling or menacing, but his tone was gentle, high-pitched, and creepily childlike.

"Who are you?" I asked.

He slammed his fist in my gut. He punched me so hard, I was sure his knuckles scraped the van floor. I tried to bend or crumple into a ball, but the restraints and the men sitting on my legs made that impossible. Air. All I wanted was air. I thought that I might throw up.

You'll be followed...

All the precautions—the unsigned emails, the code words, the warnings—they all made sense now. Elizabeth was afraid. I didn't have all the answers yet—hell, I barely had any of them—but I finally understood that her cryptic communications were a result of fear. Fear of being found.

Found by these guys.

I was suffocating. Every cell in my body craved oxygen. Finally, the Asian nodded at the other two men. They got off my legs. I snapped my knees toward my chest. I tried to gather some air, thrashing around like an epileptic. After a while, my breath came back. The Asian man slowly kneeled closer to me. I kept my eyes steady on his. Or, at least, I tried to. It wasn't like staring into the eyes of a fellow human being or even an animal. These were the eyes of something inanimate. If you could look into the eyes of a file cabinet, this would be what it felt like.

But I did not blink.

He was young too, my captor—no more than twenty, twenty-five tops. He put his hand on the inside of my arm, right above the elbow. "Why were you in the park?" he asked again in his singsong way.

"I like the park," I said.

He pressed down hard. With just two fingers. I gasped. The fingers knifed through my flesh and into a bundle of nerves. My eyes started to bulge. I had never known pain like this. It shut down everything. I flailed like a dying fish on the end of a hook. I tried to kick, but my legs landed like rubber bands. I couldn't breathe.

He wouldn't let go.

I kept expecting him to release the grip or let up a bit. He didn't. I started making small whimpering sounds. But he held on, his expression one of boredom.

The van kept going. I tried to ride out the pain, to break it down into intervals or something. But that didn't work. I needed relief.

Just for a second. I needed him to let go. But he remained stonelike. He kept looking at me with those empty eyes. The pressure built in my head. I couldn't speak—even if I wanted to tell him what he wanted to know, my throat had shut down. And he knew that.

Escape the pain. That was all I could think about. How could I escape the pain? My entire being seemed to focus and converge on that nerve bundle in my arm. My body felt on fire, the pressure in my skull building.

With my head seconds from exploding, he suddenly released his grip. I gasped again, this time in relief. But it was short-lived. His hand began to snake down to my lower abdomen and stopped.

"Why were you in the park?"

I tried to think, to conjure up a decent lie. But he didn't give me time. He pinched deeply, and the pain was back, somehow worse than before. His finger pierced my liver like a bayonet. I started bucking against the restraints. My mouth opened in a silent scream.

I whipped my head back and forth. And there, in mid-whip, I saw the back of the driver's head. The van had stopped, probably for a traffic light. The driver was looking straight ahead—at the road, I guess. Then everything happened very fast.

I saw the driver's head swivel toward his door window as though he'd heard a noise. But he was too late. Something hit him in the side of the skull. He went down like a shooting gallery mallard. The van's front doors opened.

"Hands up now!"

Guns appeared. Two of them. Aimed in the back. The Asian guy let go. I flopped back, unable to move.

Behind the guns I saw two familiar faces, and I almost cried out in joy.

Tyrese and Brutus.

One of the white guys made a move. Tyrese casually fired his weapon. The man's chest . exploded. He fell back with his eyes open. Dead. No doubt about that. In the front, the driver groaned, starting to come to. Brutus elbowed him hard in the face. The driver went quiet again.

The other white guy had his hands up. My Asian tormenter never changed his expression. He looked on as though from a distance, and he didn't raise or lower his hands. Brutus took the driver's seat and shifted into gear. Tyrese kept his weapon pointed straight at the Asian guy.

"Uncuff him," Tyrese said.

The white guy looked at the Asian. The Asian nodded his consent. The white guy uncuffed me. I tried to sit up. It felt as if something inside me had shattered and the shards were digging into tissue.

"You okay?" Tyrese asked.

I managed a nod.

"You want me to waste them?"

I turned to the still-breathing white guy. "Who hired you?"

The white guy slid his eyes toward the young Asian. I did the same.

"Who hired you?" I asked him.

The Asian finally smiled, but it didn't change his eyes. And then, once again, everything happened too fast.

I never saw his hand shoot out, but next thing I knew the Asian guy had me by the scruff of my neck. He hurled me effortlessly at Tyrese. I was actually airborne, my legs kicking out as though that might slow me down. Tyrese saw me coming, but he couldn't duck out of the way. I landed on him. I tried to roll off quickly, but by the time we righted ourselves, the Asian had gotten out via the van's side door.

He was gone.

"Fucking Bruce Lee on steroids," Tyrese said.

I nodded.

The driver was stirring again. Brutus prepared a fist, but Tyrese shook him off. "These two won't know dick," he said to me.

"I know."

"We can kill them or let them go." Like it was no big deal either way, a coin toss.

"Let them go," I said.

Brutus found a quiet block, probably someplace in the Bronx, I can't be sure. The still-breathing white guy got out on his own. Brutus heaved the driver and the dead guy out like yesterday's refuse. We started driving again. For a few minutes, nobody spoke.

Tyrese laced his hands behind his neck and settled back. "Good thing we hung around, huh, Doc?"

I nodded at what I thought might be the understatement of the millennium.

32

The old autopsy files were kept in a U-Store-'Em in Layton, New Jersey, not far from the Pennsylvania border. Special Agent Nick Carlson arrived on his own. He didn't like storage facilities much. They gave him the black-cat creeps. Open twenty-four hours a day, no guard, a token security camera at the entrance... God only knows what lay padlocked in these houses of cement. Carlson knew that many were loaded with drugs, money, and contraband of all sorts. That didn't bother him much. But he remembered a few years back when an oil executive had been kidnapped and crate-stored in one. The executive had suffocated to death. Carlson had been there when they found him. Ever since, he imagined *living* people in here too, right now, the inexplicably missing, just yards from where he stood, chained in the dark, straining against mouth gags.

People often note that it's a sick world. They had no idea.

Timothy Harper, the county medical examiner, came out of a garagelike facility, holding a large manila envelope closed with a wraparound string. He handed Carlson an autopsy file with Elizabeth Beck's name on it.

"You have to sign for it," Harper said.

Carlson signed the form.

"Beck never told you why he wanted to see it?" Carlson asked.

"He talked about being a grieving husband and something about closure, but outside of that..." Harper shrugged.

"Did he ask you anything else about the case?"

"Nothing that sticks out."

"How about something that doesn't stick out?"

Harper thought about it a moment. "He asked if I remembered who identified the body."

"Did you?"

"Not at first, no."

"Who did identify her?"

"Her father. Then he asked me how long it took."

"How long what took?"

"The identification."

"I don't understand."

"Neither did I, quite frankly. He wanted to know if her father had made the ID immediately or if it took a few minutes."

"Why would he want to know that?"

"I have no idea."

Carlson tried to find an angle on that one, but nothing came to him. "How did you answer him?"

"With the truth actually. I don't remember. I assume he did it in a timely fashion or I'd remember it better."

"Anything else?"

"Not really, no," he said. "Look, if we're done

here, I got two kids who smashed a Civic into a telephone pole waiting for me."

Carlson gripped the file in his hand. "Yeah," he said. "We're done. But if I need to reach you?"

"I'll be at the office."

PETER FLANNERY, ATTORNEY-AT-LAW was stenciled in faded gold into the door's pebbled glass. There was a hole in the glass the size of a fist. Someone had patched it up with gray duct tape. The tape looked old.

I kept the brim of my cap low. My insides ached from my ordeal with the big Asian guy. We had heard my name on the radio station that promises the world in exchange for twenty-two minutes. I was officially a wanted man.

Hard to wrap ye olde brain around that one. I was in huge trouble and yet that all seemed strangely remote, as though that were happening to someone with whom I was vaguely acquainted. I, me, the guy right here, didn't care much. I had a single focus: finding Elizabeth. The rest felt like scenery.

Tyrese was with me. Half a dozen people were scattered about the waiting room. Two wore elaborate neck braces. One had a bird in a cage. I had no idea why. No one bothered to glance up at us, as though they'd weighed the effort of sliding their eyes in our direction against the possible benefits and decided, hey, it isn't worth it.

The receptionist wore a hideous wig and looked at us as though we'd just plopped out of a dog's behind.

I asked to see Peter Flannery.

"He's with a client." She wasn't clacking gum, but it was close.

Tyrese took over then. Like a magician with a great sleight of hand, he flourished a roll of cash thicker than my wrist. "Tell him we be offering a retainer." Then, grinning, he added, "One for you too, we get in to see him right away."

Two minutes later, we were ushered into Mr. Flannery's inner sanctum. The office smelled of cigar smoke and Lemon Pledge. Snap-together furniture, the kind you might find at Kmart or Bradlees, had been stained dark, feigning rich oak and mahogany and working about as well as a Las Vegas toupee. There were no school diplomas on the wall, just that phony nonsense people put up to impress the easily impressed. One commemorated Flannery's membership in the "International Wine-tasting Association." Another ornately noted that he attended a "Long Island Legal Conference" in 1996. Big wow. There were sun-faded photos of a younger Flannery with what I guessed were either celebrities or local politicians, but nobody I recognized. The office staple of a golf foursome photo mounted wood-plaque-like adorned a prize spot behind the desk.

"Please," Flannery said with a big wave of his hand. "Have a seat, gentlemen."

I sat. Tyrese stayed standing, crossed his arms, and leaned against the back wall.

"So," Flannery said, stretching the word out like a wad of chaw, "what can I do for you?"

Peter Flannery had that athlete-gone-to-seed look. His once-golden locks had thinned and fled. His features were malleable. He wore a rayon three-piece suit—I hadn't seen one in a while—and the vest even had the pocket watch attached to a faux gold chain.

"I need to ask you about an old case," I said.

His eyes still had the ice blue of youth, and he aimed them my way. On the desk, I spotted a photograph of Flannery with a plump woman and a girl of maybe fourteen who was definitely in the throes of awkward adolescence. They were all smiling, but I saw a wince there too, as though they were bracing for a blow.

"An old case?" he repeated.

"My wife visited you eight years ago. I need to know what it was about."

Flannery's eyes flicked toward Tyrese. Tyrese still had the folded arms and showed him nothing more than the sunglasses. "I don't understand. Was this a divorce case?"

"No," I said.

"Then...?" He put his hands up and gave me the I'd-like-to-help shrug. "Attorney-client confidentiality. I don't see how I can help you."

"I don't think she was a client."

"You're confusing me, Mr.—" He waited for me to fill in the blank.

"Beck," I said. "And it's doctor, not mister."

His double chin went slack at my name. I

wondered if maybe he had heard the news reports. But I didn't think that was it.

"My wife's name is Elizabeth."

Flannery said nothing.

"You remember her, don't you?"

Again he flipped a glance at Tyrese.

"Was she a client, Mr. Flannery?"

He cleared his throat. "No," he said. "No, she wasn't a client."

"But you remember meeting her?"

Flannery shifted in his chair. "Yes."

"What did you discuss?"

"It's been a long time, Dr. Beck."

"Are you saying you don't remember?"

He didn't answer that one directly. "Your wife," he said. "She was murdered, wasn't she? I remember seeing something about it on the news."

I tried to keep us on track. "Why did she come here, Mr. Flannery?"

"I'm an attorney," he said, and he almost puffed out his chest.

"But not hers."

"Still," he said, trying to gain some sort of leverage, "I need to be compensated for my time." He coughed into his fist. "You mentioned something about a retainer."

I looked over my shoulder, but Tyrese was already on the move. The cash roll was out and he was peeling bills. He tossed three Ben Franklins on the desk, gave Flannery a hard sunglass glare, and then stepped back to his spot.

Flannery looked at the money but didn't

touch it. He bounced his fingertips together and then flattened his palms against each other. "Suppose I refuse to tell you."

"I can't see why you would," I said. "Your communications with her don't fall under privilege, do they?"

"I'm not talking about that," Flannery said. His eyes pierced mine and he hesitated. "Did you love your wife, Dr. Beck?"

"Very much."

"Have you remarried?"

"No," I said. Then: "What does that have to do with anything?"

He settled back. "Go," he said. "Take your money and just go."

"This is important, Mr. Flannery."

"I can't imagine how. She's been dead for eight years. Her killer is on death row."

"What are you afraid to tell me?"

Flannery didn't answer right away. Tyrese again peeled himself off the wall. He moved closer to the desk. Flannery watched him and surprised me with a tired sigh. "Do me a favor," he said to Tyrese. "Stop with the posturing, okay? I've repped psychos who make you look like Mary Poppins."

Tyrese looked as though he might react, but that wouldn't help. I said his name. He looked at me. I shook my head. Tyrese backed off. Flannery was plucking at his lower lip. I let him. I could wait.

"You don't want to know," he said to me after a while.

"Yeah, I do."

"It can't bring your wife back."

"Maybe it can," I said.

That got his attention. He frowned at me, but something there softened.

"Please," I said.

He swiveled his seat to the side and tilted way back, staring up at window blinds that had turned yellow and crusty sometime during the Watergate hearings. He folded his hands and rested them on his paunch. I watched the hands rise and fall as he breathed.

"I was a public defender back then," he began. "You know what that is?"

"You defended the indigent," I said.

"Something like that. The Miranda rights—they talk about having the right to counsel if you can afford one. I'm the guy you get when you can't."

I nodded, but he was still looking at the blinds.

"Anyway, I was assigned one of the most prominent murder trials in the state."

Something cold wormed into my stomach. "Whose?" I asked.

"Brandon Scope's. The billionaire's son. Do you remember the case?"

I froze, terrified. I could barely breathe. Little wonder Flannery's name had seemed familiar. Brandon Scope. I almost shook my head, not because I didn't remember the case, but because I wanted him to say anything but that name.

For the sake of clarity, let me give you the newspaper account: Brandon Scope, age thirty-three, was robbed and murdered eight years ago. Yes, eight years ago. Maybe two months before Elizabeth's murder. He was shot twice and dumped near a housing project in Harlem. His money was gone. The media played all the violins on this one. They made much of Brandon Scope's charitable work. They talked about how he helped street kids, how he preferred working with the poor to running Daddy's multinational conglomerate, that kind of spin. It was one of those murders that "shock a nation" and lead to plenty of finger-pointing and hand-wringing. A charitable foundation had been set up in young Scope's name. My sister, Linda, runs it. You wouldn't believe the good she does there.

"I remember it," I said softly.

"Do you remember that an arrest was made?"

"A street kid," I said. "One of the kids he helped, right?"

"Yes. They arrested Helio Gonzalez, then age twenty-two. A resident of Barker House in Harlem. Had a felony sheet that read like a Hall of Famer's career stats. Armed robbery, arson, assault, a real sunshine, our Mr. Gonzalez."

My mouth was dry. "Weren't the charges eventually dropped?" I asked.

"Yes. They didn't have much really. His fingerprints were found at the scene, but so were plenty of others. There were strands of Scope's hair and even a speck of matching blood found where Gonzalez lived. But Scope had been to the building before. We could have easily claimed that was how that material got there. Nonetheless, they had enough for an arrest, and the cops were sure something more would break."

"So what happened?" I asked.

Flannery still wouldn't look at me. I didn't like that. Flannery was the kind of guy who lived for the Willy Loman world of shined shoes and eye contact. I knew the type. I didn't want anything to do with them, but I knew them.

"The police had a solid time of death," he continued. "The M.E. got a good liver temperature reading. Scope was killed at eleven. You might be able to stretch it a half hour in either direction, but that was about it."

"I don't understand," I said. "What does this have to do with my wife?"

He bounced the fingertips again. "I understand that your wife worked with the poor as well," he said. "In the same office with the victim, as a matter of fact."

I didn't know where this was going, but I knew I wasn't going to like it. For the most fleeting of seconds, I wondered if Flannery was right, if I really didn't want to hear what he had to say, if I should just pick myself out of the chair and forget all about this. But I said, "So?"

"That's noble," he said with a small nod. "Working with the downtrodden."

"Glad you think so."

"It's why I originally went into law. To help the poor."

I swallowed down the bile and sat a little straighter. "Do you mind telling me what my wife has to do with any of this?"

"She freed him."

"Who?"

"My client. Helio Gonzalez. Your wife freed him."

I frowned. "How?"

"She gave him an alibi."

My heart stopped. So did my lungs. I almost pounded on my chest to get the inner workings started up again.

"How?" I asked.

"How did she give him an alibi?"

I nodded numbly, but he still wasn't looking. I croaked out a yes.

"Simple," he said. "She and Helio had been together during the time in question."

My mind started to flail, adrift in the ocean, no life preserver in reach. "I never saw anything about this in the papers," I said.

"It was kept quiet."

"Why?"

"Your wife's request, for one. And the D.A.'s office didn't want their wrongful arrest made more public. So it was all done as quietly as possible. Plus there were, uh, problems with your wife's testimony."

"What problems?"

"She sort of lied at first."

More flailing. Sinking under. Coming to the surface. Flailing. "What are you talking about?"

"Your wife claimed that she was doing

some career counseling with Gonzalez at the charity office at the time of the murder. Nobody really bought that."

"Why not?"

He cocked a skeptical eyebrow. "Career counseling at eleven at night?"

I nodded numbly.

"So as Mr. Gonzalez's attorney, I reminded your wife that the police would investigate her alibi. That, for example, the counseling offices had security cameras and there would be tapes of the comings and goings. That was when she came clean."

He stopped.

"Go on," I said.

"It's obvious, isn't it?"

"Tell me anyway."

Flannery shrugged. "She wanted to spare herself—and you, I guess—the embarrassment. That was why she insisted on secrecy. She was at Gonzalez's place, Dr. Beck. They'd been sleeping together for two months."

I didn't react. No one spoke. In the distance, I heard a bird squawk. Probably the one in the waiting room. I got to my feet. Tyrese took a step back.

"Thank you for your time," I said in the calmest voice you ever heard.

Flannery nodded at the window blinds.

"It's not true," I said to him.

He didn't respond. But then again, I hadn't expected him to.

33

Carlson sat in the car. His tie was still knotted meticulously. His suit jacket was off, hung on a wooden hanger on the backseat hook. The air-conditioning blew loud and hard. Carlson read the autopsy envelope: Elizabeth Beck, Case File 94-87002. His fingers started unwinding the string. The envelope opened. Carlson extracted the contents and spread them out on the passenger seat.

What had Dr. Beck wanted to see?

Stone had already given him the obvious answer: Beck wanted to know if there was anything that might incriminate him. That fit into their early theories, and it had, after all, been Carlson who'd first started questioning the accepted scenario on Elizabeth Beck's murder. He had been the first to believe that the killing was not what it appeared to be—that indeed it was Dr. David Beck, the husband, who had planned the murder of his wife.

So why had he stopped buying it?

He had carefully reviewed the holes now poking through that theory, but Stone had been equally convincing in patching them back up. Every case has holes. Carlson knew that. Every case has inconsistencies. If it doesn't, ten to one you've missed something.

So why did he now have doubts about Beck's guilt?

Perhaps it had something to do with the case becoming too neat, all the evidence suddenly lining up and cooperating with their theory. Or maybe his doubts were based on something as unreliable as "intuition," though Carlson had never been a big fan of that particular aspect of investigative work. Intuition was often a way of cutting corners, a nifty technique of replacing hard evidence and facts with something far more elusive and capricious. The worst investigators Carlson knew relied on so-called intuition.

He picked up the top sheet. General information. Elizabeth Parker Beck. Her address, her birth date (she'd been twenty-five when she died), Caucasian female, height five seven, weight 98 pounds. Thin. The external examination revealed that rigor mortis had resolved. There were blisters on the skin and fluid leaks from the orifices. That placed the time of death at more than three days. The cause of death was a knife wound to the chest. The mechanism of death was loss of blood and dramatic hemorrhaging of the right aorta. There were also cut wounds on her hands and fingers, theoretically because she tried to defend herself against a knife attack.

Carlson took out his notebook and Mont Blanc pen. He wrote *Defensive knife wounds?!?!* and then he underlined it several times. Defensive wounds. That wasn't KillRoy's style. KillRoy tortured his victims. He bound them with rope, did whatever, and once they were too far gone to care, he killed them.

Why would there be defensive knife wounds on her hands?

Carlson kept reading. He scanned through hair and eye color, and then, halfway down the second page, he found another shocker.

Elizabeth Beck had been branded post-mortem.

Carlson reread that. He took out his note-book and scratched down the word *post-mortem*. That didn't add up. KillRoy had always branded his victims while they were alive. Much was made at trial about how he liked the smell of sizzling flesh, how he enjoyed the screams of his victims while he seared them.

First, the defensive wounds. Now this. Something wasn't meshing.

Carlson took off his glasses and closed his eyes. Mess, he thought to himself. Mess upset him. Logic holes were expected, yes, but these were turning into gaping wounds. On the one hand, the autopsy supported his orig-inal hypothesis that Elizabeth Beck's murder had been staged to look like the work of KillRoy. But now, if that were true, the theory was coming unglued from the other side.

He tried to take it step by step. First, why would Beck be so eager to see this file? On the surface, the answer was now obvious. Anybody who scrutinized these results would realize that there was an excellent chance that KillRoy had not murdered Elizabeth Beck. It was not a given, however. Serial killers, despite what you might read, are not creatures of habit. KillRoy could have changed his M.O. or sought some diversity. Still, with what Carlson was reading here, there was enough to make one ponder.

But all of this just begged what had become the big question: Why hadn't anybody noticed these evidentiary inconsistencies back then?

Carlson sorted through possibilities. KillRoy had never been prosecuted for Elizabeth Beck's murder. The reasons were now pretty clear. Perhaps the investigators suspected the truth. Perhaps they realized that Elizabeth Beck didn't fit, but publicizing that fact would only aid KillRoy's defense. The problem with prosecuting a serial killer is that you cast a net so wide, something is bound to slither out. All the defense has to do is pick apart one case, find discrepancies with one murder, and bang, the other cases are tainted by association. So without a confession, you rarely try him for all the murders at once. You do it step by step. The investigators, realizing this, probably just wanted the murder of Elizabeth Beck to go away.

But there were big problems with that scenario too.

Elizabeth Beck's father and uncle—two men in law enforcement—had seen the body. They had in all likelihood seen this autopsy report. Wouldn't they have wondered about the inconsistencies? Would they have let her murderer go free just to secure a conviction on KillRoy? Carlson doubted it.

So where did that leave him?

He continued through the file and stumbled across yet another stunner. The car's air-conditioning was seriously chilling him now, reaching bone. Carlson slid down a window and pulled the key out of the ignition. The top of the sheet read: Toxicology Report. According to the tests, cocaine and heroin had been found in Elizabeth Beck's bloodstream; moreover, traces were found in the hair and tissues, indicating that her use was more than casual.

Did that fit?

He was thinking about it, when his cell phone rang. He picked it up. "Carlson."

"We got something," Stone said.

Carlson put down the file. "What?"

"Beck. He's booked on a flight to London out of JFK. It leaves in two hours."

"I'm on my way."

Tyrese put a hand on my shoulder as we walked. "Bitches," he said for the umpteenth time. "You can't trust them."

I didn't bother replying.

It surprised me at first that Tyrese would be able to track down Helio Gonzalez so quickly, but the street network was as developed as any other. Ask a trader at Morgan Stanley to locate a counterpart at Goldman Sachs and it would be done in minutes. Ask me to refer a patient to pretty much any other doctor in the state, and it takes one phone call. Why should street felons be different?

Helio was fresh off a four-year stint upstate for armed robbery. He looked it too. Sunglasses, a doo-rag on his head, white T-shirt under a flannel shirt that had only the top button buttoned so that it looked like a cape or bat wings. The sleeves were rolled up, revealing crude prison tattoos etched onto his forearm and the prison muscles coiling thereunder. There is an unmistakable look to prison muscles, a smooth, marblelike quality as opposed to their puffier health club counterparts.

We sat on a stoop somewhere in Queens. I couldn't tell you where exactly. A Latin rhythm tah-tah-tahhed, the beat driving into my chest. Dark-haired women sauntered by in too-clingy spaghetti-strap tops. Tyrese nodded at me. I turned to Helio. He had a smirk on his face. I took in the whole package and one word kept popping into my brain: scum. Unreachable, unfeeling scum. You looked at him, and you knew that he would continue to leave serious destruction in his wake. The question was how much. I realized that this view was not charitable. I realized, too, that based on surfaces, the very same could be said for Tyrese. That didn't matter. Elizabeth may have believed in the redemption for the street-hardened or morally anesthetized. I was still working on it.

"Several years ago, you were arrested for the murder of Brandon Scope," I began. "I know you were released, and I don't want to cause you any trouble. But I need to know the truth."

Helio took off his sunglasses. He flicked a glance at Tyrese. "You bring me a cop?"

"I'm not a cop," I said. "I'm Elizabeth Beck's husband."

I wanted a reaction. I didn't get one.

"She's the woman who gave you the alibi."

"I know who she is."

"Was she with you that night?"

Helio took his time. "Yeah," he said slowly, smiling at me with yellow teeth. "She was with me all night."

"You're lying," I said.

Helio looked back over at Tyrese. "What is this, man?"

"I need to know the truth," I said.

"You think I killed that Scope guy?"

"I know you didn't."

That surprised him.

"What the hell is going on here?" he said.

"I need you to confirm something for me."

Helio waited.

"Were you with my wife that night, yes or no?"

"What you want me to say, man?"

"The truth."

"And if the truth is she was with me all night?"

"It's not the truth," I said.

"What makes you so sure?"

Tyrese joined in. "Tell the man what he wants to know."

Helio took his time again. "It's like she said. I did her, all right? Sorry, man, but that's what happened. We were doing it all night."

I looked at Tyrese. "Leave us alone a second, okay?"

Tyrese nodded. He got up and walked to his car. He leaned against the side door, arms folded, Brutus by his side. I turned my gaze back to Helio.

"Where did you first meet my wife?"

"At the center."

"She tried to help you?"

He shrugged, but he wouldn't look at me.

"Did you know Brandon Scope?"

A flicker of what might have been fear crossed his face. "I'm going, man."

"It's just you and me, Helio. You can frisk me for a wire."

"You want me to give up my alibi?"

"Yeah."

"Why would I do that?"

"Because someone is killing everyone connected with what happened to Brandon Scope. Last night, my wife's friend was murdered in her studio. They grabbed me today, but Tyrese intervened. They also want to kill my wife."

"I thought she was dead already."

"It's a long story, Helio. But it's all coming back. If I don't find out what really happened, we're all going to end up dead."

I didn't know if this was true or hyperbole. I didn't much care either.

"Where were you that night?" I pressed.

"With her."

"I can prove you weren't," I said.

"What?"

"My wife was in Atlantic City. I have her old charge records. I can prove it. I can blow your alibi right out of the water, Helio. And I'll do it. I know you didn't kill Brandon Scope. But so help me, I'll let them execute you for it if you don't tell me the truth."

A bluff. A great big bluff. But I could see that I'd drawn blood.

"Tell me the truth, and you stay free," I said.

"I didn't kill that dude, I swear it, man."

"I know that," I said again.

He thought about it. "I don't know why she did it, all right?"

I nodded, trying to keep him talking.

"I robbed a house out in Fort Lee that night. So I had no alibi. I thought I was going down for it. She saved my ass."

"Did you ask her why?"

He shook his head. "I just went along. My lawyer told me what she said. I backed her up. Next thing I knew, I was out."

"Did you ever see my wife again?"

"No." He looked up at me. "How come you so sure your wife wasn't doing me?"

"I know my wife."

He smiled. "You think she'd never cheat?"

I didn't reply.

Helio stood up. "Tell Tyrese he owes me one."

He chuckled, turned, walked away.

34

No luggage. An e-ticket so she could check in by machine rather than with a person. She waited in a neighboring terminal, keeping her eye on the departure screen, waiting for the On Time next to her flight to evolve into Boarding.

She sat in a chair of molded plastic and looked out onto the tarmac. A TV blared CNN. "Next up *Headline Sports*." She made her mind blank. Five years ago, she had spent time in a small village outside Goa, India. Though a true hellhole, the village had something of a buzz about it because of the one-hundred-year-old yogi who lived there. She had spent time with the yogi. He had tried to teach her meditation techniques, pranayama breathing, mind cleansing. But none of it ever really stuck. There were moments when she could sink away into blackness. More often, though, wherever she sank, Beck was there.

She wondered about her next move. There was no choice really. This was about preservation. Preservation meant fleeing. She had made a mess and now she was running away again, leaving others to clean it up. But what other option was there? They were onto her. She had been careful as hell, but they had still been watching. Eight years later.

A toddler scrambled toward the plate-glass window, his palms hitting it with a happy splat. His harried father chased him down and scooped him up with a giggle. She watched and her mind scrambled to the obvious what-could-have-beens. An old couple sat to her right, chatting amiably about nothing. As teenagers, she and Beck would watch Mr. and Mrs. Steinberg stroll up Downing Place arm in arm, every night without fail, long after their children had grown and fled the nest. That would be their lives, Beck had promised. Mrs. Steinberg died when she was eighty-two. Mr. Steinberg, who had been in amazingly robust health, followed four months later. They say that happens a lot with the elderly, that—to paraphrase Springsteen— two hearts become one. When one dies, the other follows. Was that how it was with her and David? They had not been together sixty-one years like the Steinbergs, but when you think about it in relative terms, when you consider that you barely have any memories of your life before age five, when you figure that she and Beck had been inseparable since they were seven, that they could barely unearth any memory that didn't include the other, when you think of the time spent together not just in terms of years but in life percentages, they had more vested in each other than even the Steinbergs.

She turned and checked the screen. Next to British Airways Flight 174, the word Boarding started to flash.

Her flight was being called.

Carlson and Stone, along with their local buddies Dimonte and Krinsky, stood with the British Airways reservation manager.

"He's a no-show," the reservation manager, a blue-and-white-uniformed woman with a kerchief, a beautiful accent, and a name tag reading Emily told them.

Dimonte cursed. Krinsky shrugged. This was not unexpected. Beck had been successfully eluding a manhunt all day. It was a long shot that he would be dumb enough to try to board a flight using his real name.

"Dead end," Dimonte said.

Carlson, who still had the autopsy file clutched against his hip, asked Emily, "Who is your most computer-literate employee?"

"That would be me," she said with a competent smile.

"Please bring up the reservation," Carlson said.

Emily did as he requested.

"Can you tell me when he booked the flight?"

"Three days ago."

Dimonte leapt on that one. "Beck planned to run. Son of a bitch."

Carlson shook his head. "No."

"How do you figure?"

"We've been assuming that he killed Rebecca Schayes to shut her up," Carlson explained. "But if you're going to leave the country,

271

why bother? Why take the risk of waiting three days and trying to get away with another murder?"

Stone shook his head. "You're overthinking this one, Nick."

"We're missing something," Carlson insisted. "Why did he all of a sudden decide to run in the first place?"

"Because we were onto him."

"We weren't onto him three days ago."

"Maybe he knew it was a matter of time."

Carlson frowned some more.

Dimonte turned to Krinsky. "This is a waste of time. Let's get the hell out of here." He looked at Carlson. "We'll leave a couple of uniforms around just in case."

Carlson nodded, only half listening. When they left, he asked Emily, "Was he traveling with anyone?"

Emily hit some keys. "It was a solo booking."

"How did he book it? In person? On the phone? Did he go through a travel agency?"

She clicked the keys again. "It wasn't through a travel agency. That much I can tell you because we'd have a marking to pay a commission. The reservation was made directly with British Airways."

No help there. "How did he pay?"

"Credit card."

"May I have the number, please?"

She gave it to him. He passed it over to Stone. Stone shook his head. "Not one of his cards. At least, not one we know about."

"Check it out," Carlson said.

Stone's cell phone was already in his hand. He nodded and pressed the keypad.

Carlson rubbed his chin. "You said he booked his flight three days ago."

"That's correct."

"Do you know what time he booked it?"

"Actually yes. The computer stamps it in. Six-fourteen in the P.M."

Carlson nodded. "Okay, great. Can you tell me if anyone else booked at around the same time?"

Emily thought about it. "I've never tried that," she said. "Hold on a moment, let me see something." She typed. She waited. She typed some more. She waited. "The computer won't sort by booking date."

"But the information is in there?"

"Yes. Wait, hold up." Her fingers started clacking again. "I can paste the information onto a spreadsheet. We can put fifty bookings per screen. It will make it faster."

The first group of fifty had a married couple who booked the same day but hours earlier. Useless. The second group had none. In the third group, however, they hit bingo.

"Lisa Sherman," Emily pronounced. "Her flight was booked the same day, eight minutes later."

It didn't mean anything on its own, of course, but Carlson felt the hair on the back of his neck stand up.

"Oh, this is interesting," Emily added.

"What?"

"Her seat assignment."

"What about it?"

"She was scheduled to sit next to David Beck. Row sixteen, seats E and F."

He felt the jolt. "Has she checked in?"

More typing. The screen cleared. Another came up. "As a matter of fact, she has. She's probably boarding as we speak."

She adjusted her purse strap and stood. Her step was brisk, her head high. She still had the glasses and the wig and implants. So did the photograph of Lisa Sherman in her passport.

She was four gates away when she heard a snippet of the CNN report. She stopped short. A man wheeling an industrial-size piece of carry-on ran into her. He made a rude hand gesture as though she'd cut him off on a freeway. She ignored him and kept her eyes on the screen.

The anchorwoman was doing the report. In the right-hand corner of the screen was a photograph of her old friend Rebecca Schayes side by side with an image of...of Beck.

She hurried closer to the screen. Under the images in a bloodred font were the words *Death in the Darkroom.*

"...David Beck, suspected in the slaying. But is that the only crime they believe he's committed? CNN's Jack Turner has more."

The anchorwoman disappeared. In her place, two men with NYPD windbreakers rolled out a black body bag on a stretcher. She recognized the building at once and almost gasped. Eight years. Eight years had passed, but Rebecca still had her studio in the same location.

A man's voice, presumably Jack Turner's, began his report: "It's a twisted tale, this murder of one of New York's hottest fashion photographers. Rebecca Schayes was found dead in her darkroom, shot twice in the head at close range." They flashed a photograph of Rebecca smiling brightly. "The suspect is her longtime friend, Dr. David Beck, an uptown pediatrician." Now Beck's image, no smile, lit up the screen. She almost fell over.

"Dr. Beck narrowly escaped arrest earlier today after assaulting a police officer. He is still at large and assumed armed and dangerous. If you have any information on his whereabouts..." A phone number appeared in yellow. Jack Turner read out the number before continuing.

"But what has given this story an added twist are the leaks coming out of Manhattan's Federal Building. Presumably, Dr. Beck has been linked to the murder of two men whose bodies were recently unearthed in Pennsylvania, not far from where Dr. Beck's family has a summer residence. And the biggest shocker of all: Dr. David Beck is also a suspect in the eight-year-old slaying of his wife, Elizabeth."

A photograph of a woman she barely recognized popped up. She suddenly felt naked, cornered. Her image vanished as they went back to the anchorwoman, who said, "Jack, wasn't it believed that Elizabeth Beck was the victim of serial killer Elroy 'KillRoy' Kellerton?"

"That's correct, Terese. Authorities aren't doing much talking right now, and officials deny the reports. But the leaks are coming to us from very reliable sources."

"Do the police have a motive, Jack?"

"We haven't heard one yet. There has been some speculation that there may have been a love triangle here. Ms. Schayes was married to a Gary Lamont, who remains in seclusion. But that's little more than conjecture at this point."

Still staring at the TV screen, she felt the tears start welling up.

"And Dr. Beck is still at large tonight?"

"Yes, Terese. The police are asking for the public's cooperation, but they stress that no one should approach him on their own."

Chatter followed. Meaningless chatter.

She turned away. Rebecca. Oh God, not Rebecca. And she'd gotten married. Had probably picked out dresses and china patterns and done all those things they used to mock. How? How had Rebecca gotten tangled up in all this? Rebecca hadn't known anything.

Why had they killed her?

Then the thought hit her anew: What have I done?

She had come back. They had started looking for her. How would they have gone about that? Simple. Watch the people she was closest to. Stupid. Her coming back had put everyone she cared about in danger. She had messed up. And now her friend was dead.

"British Airways Flight 174, departing for London. All rows may now board."

There was no time to beat herself up. Think. What should she do? Her loved ones were in danger. Beck—she suddenly remembered his silly disguise—was on the run. He was up against powerful people. If they were trying to frame him for murder—and that seemed pretty obvious right now—he'd have no chance.

She couldn't just leave. Not yet. Not until she knew that Beck was safe.

She turned and headed for an exit.

When Peter Flannery finally saw the news reports on the David Beck manhunt, he picked up the phone and dialed a friend at the D.A.'s office.

"Who's running the Beck case?" Flannery asked.

"Fein."

A true ass, Flannery thought. "I saw your boy today."

"David Beck?"

"Yeah," Flannery said. "He paid me a visit."

"Why?"

Flannery kicked back his BarcaLounger. "Maybe you should put me through to Fein."

35

When night fell, Tyrese found me a room at the apartment of Latisha's cousin. We couldn't imagine that the police would unearth my connection with Tyrese, but why take the chance?

Tyrese had a laptop. We hooked it up. I checked my email, hoping for a message from my mysterious mailer. Nothing under my work account. Nothing under my home account. I tried the new one at bigfoot.com. Nothing there either.

Tyrese had been looking at me funny since we'd left Flannery's office. "I ask you something, Doc?"

"Go ahead," I said.

"When that mouthpiece said about that guy being murdered—"

"Brandon Scope," I added.

"Yeah, him. You look like someone hit you with a stun gun."

It had felt it. "You're wondering why?"

Tyrese shrugged.

"I knew Brandon Scope. He and my wife shared an office at a charitable foundation in the city. And my father grew up with and worked for his father. In fact, my father was in charge of teaching Brandon about the family holdings."

"Uh-huh," Tyrese said. "What else?"

"That's not enough?"

Tyrese waited. I turned to face him. He kept his eyes steady and for a moment I thought he could see all the way to the blackest corners of my soul. Thankfully, the moment passed. Tyrese said, "So what do you want to do next?"

"Make a few phone calls," I said. "You sure they can't be traced back here?"

"Can't see how. Tell you what, though. We'll do it with a conference call to another cell phone. Make it that much harder."

I nodded. Tyrese set it up. I had to dial another number and tell somebody I didn't know what numbers to dial. Tyrese headed for the door. "I'm gonna check on TJ. I'll be back in an hour."

"Tyrese?"

He looked back. I wanted to say thanks, but somehow it didn't feel right. Tyrese understood. "Need you to stay alive, Doc. For my kid, see?"

I nodded. He left. I checked my watch before dialing Shauna's cell phone. She answered on the first ring. "Hello?"

"How's Chloe?" I asked.

"Great," she said.

"How many miles did you walk?"

"At least three. More like four or five." Relief coursed through me. "So what's our next—"

I smiled and disconnected the phone. I dialed up my forwarding buddy and gave him another number. He mumbled something about not being a goddamn operator, but he did as I asked.

Hester Crimstein answered as though she were taking a bite out of the receiver. "What?"

"It's Beck," I said quickly. "Can they listen in, or do we have some kind of attorney-client protection here?"

There was a strange hesitation. "It's safe," she said.

"I had a reason for running," I began.

"Like guilt?"

"What?"

Another hesitation. "I'm sorry, Beck. I screwed up. When you ran like that, I freaked out. I said some stupid things to Shauna, and I quit as your attorney."

"Never told me," I said. "I need you, Hester."

"I won't help you run."

"I don't want to run anymore. I want to surrender. But on our terms."

"You're not in any position to dictate terms, Beck. They're going to lock you up tight. You can forget bail."

"Suppose I offer proof I didn't kill Rebecca Schayes."

Another hesitation. "You can do that?"

"Yes."

"What sort of proof?"

"A solid alibi."

"Provided by?"

"Well," I said, "that's where it gets interesting."

Special Agent Carlson picked up his cell phone. "Yeah."

"Got something else," his partner Stone said.
"What?"

"Beck visited a cheap mouthpiece named Flannery a few hours ago. A black street kid was with him."

Carlson frowned. "I thought Hester Crimstein was his attorney."

"He wasn't looking for legal representation. He wanted to know about a past case."

"What case?"

"Some all-purpose perp named Gonzalez was arrested for killing Brandon Scope eight years ago. Elizabeth Beck gave the guy a hell of an alibi. Beck wanted to know all about it."

Carlson felt his head doing a double spin. How the hell...?

"Anything else?"

"That's it," Stone said. "Say, where are you?"

"I'll talk to you later, Tom." Carlson hung up the phone and pressed in another number.

A voice answered, "National Tracing Center."

"Working late, Donna?"

"And I'm trying to get out of here, Nick. What do you want?"

"A really big favor."

"No," she said. Then with a big sigh, "What?"

"You still have that thirty-eight we found in the Sarah Goodhart safety-deposit box?"

"What about it?"

He told her what he wanted. When he finished, she said, "You're kidding, right?"

"You know me, Donna. No sense of humor."

"Ain't that the truth." She sighed. "I'll put in a request, but there's no way it'll get done tonight."

"Thanks, Donna. You're the best."

When Shauna entered the building's foyer, a voice called out to her.

"Excuse me. Miss Shauna?"

She looked at the man with the gelled hair and expensive suit. "And you are?"

"Special Agent Nick Carlson."

"Nighty-night, Mr. Agent."

"We know he called you."

Shauna patted her mouth in a fake yawn. "You must be proud."

"Ever hear the terms aiding and abetting and accessory after the fact?"

"Stop scaring me," she said in an exaggerated monotone, "or I might just make wee-wee right here on the cheap carpeting."

"You think I'm bluffing?"

She put out her hands, wrists together. "Arrest me, handsome." She glanced behind him. "Don't you guys usually travel in pairs?"

"I'm here alone."

"So I gather. Can I go up now?"

Carlson carefully adjusted his glasses. "I don't think Dr. Beck killed anyone."

That stopped her.

"Don't get me wrong. There's plenty of evidence he did it. My colleagues are all convinced he's guilty. There is still a massive manhunt going on."

"Uh-huh," Shauna said with more than a hint of suspicion in her voice. "But somehow you see through all that?"

"I just think something else is going on here."

"Like what?"

"I was hoping you could tell me."

"And if I suspect that this is a trick?"

Carlson shrugged. "Not much I can do about that."

She mulled it over. "It doesn't matter," she said. "I don't know anything."

"You know where he's hiding."

"I don't."

"And if you did?"

"I wouldn't tell you. But you already know that."

"I do," Carlson said. "So I guess you won't tell me what all that talk about walking his dog was about."

She shook her head. "But you'll find out soon enough."

"He'll get hurt out there, you know. Your friend assaulted a cop. That makes it open season on him."

Shauna kept her gaze steady. "Not much I can do about that."

"No, I guess not."

"Can I ask you something?"

"Shoot," Carlson said.

"Why don't you think he's guilty?"

"I'm not sure. Lots of little things, I guess." Carlson tilted his head. "Did you know that Beck was booked on a flight to London?"

Shauna let her eyes take in the lobby, trying to buy a second or two. A man entered and smiled appreciatively at Shauna. She ignored him. "Bull," she said at last.

"I just came from the airport," Carlson continued. "The flight was booked three days ago. He was a no-show, of course. But what was really odd was that the credit card used to purchase the ticket was in the name of Laura Mills. That name mean anything to you?"

"Should it?"

"Probably not. We're still working on it, but apparently it's a pseudonym."

"For whom?"

Carlson shrugged. "Do you know a Lisa Sherman?"

"No. How does she fit in?"

"She was booked on the same flight to London. In fact, she was supposed to sit next to our boy."

"Another no-show?"

"Not exactly. She checked in. But when they called the flight, she never boarded. Weird, don't you think?"

"I don't know what to think," Shauna said.

"Unfortunately, nobody could give us an ID on Lisa Sherman. She didn't check any luggage and she used an e-ticket machine. So we started running a background check. Any guess what we found?"

Shauna shook her head.

"Nothing," Carlson replied. "It looks like another pseudonym. Do you know the name Brandon Scope?"

Shauna stiffened. "What the hell is this?"

"Dr. Beck, accompanied by a black man, visited an attorney named Peter Flannery today. Flannery defended a suspect in the murder of Brandon Scope. Dr. Beck asked him about that and about Elizabeth's role in his release. Any clue why?"

Shauna started fumbling in her purse.

"Looking for something?"

"A cigarette," she said. "You have one?"

"Sorry, no."

"Damn." She stopped, met his eye. "Why are you telling me all this?"

"I have four dead bodies. I want to know what's going on."

"Four?"

"Rebecca Schayes, Melvin Bartola, Robert Wolf—those are the two men we found at the lake. And Elizabeth Beck."

"KillRoy killed Elizabeth."

Carlson shook his head.

"What makes you so sure?"

He held up the manila folder. "This, for one."

"What is it?"

"Her autopsy file."

Shauna swallowed. Fear coursed through her, tingling her fingers. The final proof, one way or the other. She tried very hard to keep her voice steady. "Can I take a look?"

"Why?"

She didn't reply.

"And more important, why was Beck so eager to see it?"

"I don't know what you mean," she said, but

the words rang hollow in her own ears and, she was sure, his.

"Was Elizabeth Beck a drug user?" Carlson asked.

The question was a total surprise. "Elizabeth? Never."

"You're sure?"

"Of course. She worked with drug addicts. That was part of her training."

"I know a lot of vice cops who enjoy a few hours with a prostitute."

"She wasn't like that. Elizabeth was no Goody Two-shoes, but drugs? Not a chance."

He held up the manila envelope again. "The tox report showed both cocaine and heroin in her system."

"Then Kellerton forced them into her."

"No," Carlson said.

"What makes you so sure?"

"There are other tests, Shauna. Tissue and hair tests. They show a pattern of use going back several months at the least."

Shauna felt her legs weaken. She slumped against a wall. "Look, Carlson, stop playing games with me. Let me see the report, okay?"

Carlson seemed to consider it. "How about this?" he said. "I'll let you see any one sheet in here. Any one piece of information. How about that?"

"What the hell is this, Carlson?"

"Good night, Shauna."

"Whoa, whoa, hold up a sec." She licked her lips. She thought about the strange emails. She thought about Beck's running from the cops.

She thought about the murder of Rebecca Schayes and the toxicology report that couldn't be. All of a sudden, her convincing demonstration on digital imaging manipulation didn't seem so convincing.

"A photograph," she said. "Let me see a photograph of the victim."

Carlson smiled. "Now, that's very interesting."

"Why's that?"

"There are none in here."

"But I thought—"

"I don't understand it either," Carlson interrupted. "I've called Dr. Harper. He was the M.E. on this one. I'm seeing if he can find out who else has signed out for this file. He's checking as we speak."

"Are you saying someone stole the photographs?"

Carlson shrugged. "Come on, Shauna. Tell me what's going on."

She almost did. She almost told him about the emails and the street cam link. But Beck had been firm. This man, for all his fancy talk, could still be the enemy. "Can I see the rest of the file?"

He moved it toward her slowly. The hell with blasé, she thought. She stepped forward and grabbed it from his hand. She tore it open and found the first sheet. As her eyes traveled down the page, a block of ice hardened in her stomach. She saw the body's height and the weight and stifled a scream.

"What?" Carlson asked.

She didn't reply.

A cell phone rang. Carlson scooped it out of his pants pocket. "Carlson."

"It's Tim Harper."

"Did you find the old logs?"

"Yes."

"Did someone else sign out Elizabeth Beck's autopsy?"

"Three years ago," Harper said. "Right after it was placed into cold storage. One person signed it out."

"Who?"

"The deceased's father. He's also a police officer. His name is Hoyt Parker."

36

Larry Gandle sat across from Griffin Scope. They were outside in the garden portico behind Scope's mansion. Night had taken serious hold, blanketing the manicured grounds. The crickets hummed an almost pretty melody, as though the super-rich could even manipulate that. Tinkling piano music spilled from the sliding glass doors. Lights from inside the house provided a modicum of illumination, casting shadows of burnt red and yellow.

Both men wore khakis. Larry wore a blue Polo shirt. Griffin had on a silk button-down from his tailor in Hong Kong. Larry waited, a beer cooling his hand. He watched the older man sitting in perfect copper-penny silhouette, facing his vast backyard, his nose tilted up slightly, his legs crossed. His right hand dangled over the arm of the chair, amber liquor swirling in his snifter.

"You have no idea where he is?" Griffin asked.

"None."

"And these two black men who rescued him?"

"I have no idea how they're involved. But Wu is working on it."

Griffin took a sip of his drink. Time trudged by, hot and sticky. "Do you really believe she's still alive?"

Larry was about to launch into a long narrative, offering evidence for and against, showing all the options and possibilities. But when he opened his mouth, he simply said, "I do."

Griffin closed his eyes. "Do you remember the day your first child was born?"

"Yes."

"Did you attend the birth?"

"I did."

"We didn't do that in our day," Griffin said. "We fathers paced in a waiting room with old magazines. I remember the nurse coming out to get me. She brought me down the hall and I still remember turning the corner and seeing Allison holding Brandon. It was the strangest feeling, Larry. Something welled up inside me so that I thought I might burst. The feeling was almost too intense, too over-whelming. You couldn't sort through or comprehend it. I assume that all fathers experience something similar."

He stopped. Larry looked over. Tears ran down the old man's cheeks, sparkling off the low light. Larry remained still.

"Perhaps the most obvious feelings on that day are joy and apprehension—apprehension in the sense that you are now responsible for this little person. But there was something else there too. I couldn't put my finger on it exactly. Not then anyway. Not until Brandon's first day of school."

Something caught in the old man's throat. He coughed a bit and now Larry could see more tears. The piano music seemed softer now. The crickets hushed as though they were listening too.

"We waited together for the school bus. I held his hand. Brandon was five years old. He looked up at me in that way children do at that age. He wore brown pants that already had a grass stain on the knee. I remember the yellow bus pulling up and the sound the door made when it opened. Then Brandon let go of my hand and started climbing up the steps. I wanted to reach out and snatch him back and take him home, but I stood there, frozen. He moved inside the bus and I heard that noise again and the door slid closed. Brandon sat by a window. I could see his face. He waved to me. I waved back and as the bus pulled away,

I said to myself, 'There goes my whole world.' That yellow bus with its flimsy metal sides and its driver I didn't know from Adam chariotted away what was in effect everything to me. And at that moment, I realized what I had felt the day of his birth. Terror. Not just apprehension. Cold, stark terror. You can fear illness or old age or death. But there's nothing like that small stone of terror that sat in my belly as I watched that bus pull away. Do you understand what I'm saying?"

Larry nodded. "I think I do."

"I knew then, at that moment, that despite my best efforts, something bad could happen to him. I wouldn't always be there to take the blow. I thought about it constantly. We all do, I guess. But when it happened, when—" He stopped and finally faced Larry Gandle. "I still try to bring him back," he said. "I try to bargain with God, offering him anything and everything if he'll somehow make Brandon alive. That won't happen, of course. I understand that. But now you come here and tell me that while my son, my whole world, rots in the ground...she lives." He started shaking his head. "I can't have that, Larry. Do you understand?"

"I do," he said.

"I failed to protect him once. I won't fail again."

Griffin Scope turned back to his garden. He took another sip of his drink. Larry Gandle understood. He rose and walked back into the night.

At ten o'clock, Carlson approached the front door of 28 Goodhart Road. He didn't worry much about the late hour. He had seen downstairs lights on and the flicker of a television, but even without that, Carlson had more important worries than someone's beauty sleep.

He was about to reach for the bell when the door opened. Hoyt Parker was there. For a moment they both stood, two boxers meeting at center ring, staring each other down as the referee reiterated meaningless instructions about low blows and not punching on the break.

Carlson didn't wait for the bell. "Did your daughter take drugs?"

Hoyt Parker took it with little more than a twitch. "Why do you want to know?"

"May I come in?"

"My wife is sleeping," Hoyt said, slipping outside and closing the door behind him. "You mind if we talk out here?"

"Suit yourself."

Hoyt crossed his arms and bounced on his toes a bit. He was a burly guy in blue jeans and a T-shirt that fit less snugly ten pounds ago. Carlson knew that Hoyt Parker was a veteran cop. Cute traps and subtlety would not work here.

"Are you going to answer my question?" Carlson asked.

"Are you going to tell me why you want to know?" Hoyt replied.

Carlson decided to change tactics. "Why did you take the autopsy pictures from your daughter's file?"

"What makes you think I took them?" There was no outrage, no loud, phony denials.

"I looked at the autopsy report today," Carlson said.

"Why?"

"Pardon me?"

"My daughter has been dead for eight years. Her killer is in jail. Yet you decide to look at her autopsy report today. I'd like to know why."

This was going nowhere and going there fast. Carlson decided to give a little, put down his guard, let him wade in, see what happened. "Your son-in-law visited the county M.E. yesterday. He demanded to see his wife's file. I was hoping to find out why."

"Did he see the autopsy report?"

"No," Carlson said. "Do you know why he'd be so eager to see it?"

"No idea."

"But you seemed concerned."

"Like you, I find the behavior suspicious."

"More than that," Carlson said. "You wanted to know if he'd actually gotten his hands on it. Why?"

Hoyt shrugged.

"Are you going to tell me what you did with the autopsy pictures?"

"I don't know what you're talking about," he replied in a flat voice.

"You were the only person to sign out this report."

"And that proves what?"

"Were the photographs there when you viewed the file?"

Hoyt's eyes flickered, but there was little delay. "Yes," he said. "Yes, they were."

Carlson couldn't help but smile. "Good answer." It had been a trap, and Hoyt had avoided it. "Because if you answered no, I'd have to wonder why you didn't report it then and there, wouldn't I?"

"You have a suspicious mind, Agent Carlson."

"Uh-huh. Any thoughts on where those photos might be?"

"Probably misfiled."

"Right, sure. You don't seem very upset over it."

"My daughter's dead. Her case is closed. What's to get upset about?"

This was a waste of time. Or maybe it wasn't. Carlson wasn't getting much information, but Hoyt's demeanor spoke volumes.

"So you still think KillRoy murdered your daughter?"

"Without question."

Carlson held up the autopsy report. "Even after reading this?"

"Yes."

"The fact that so many of the wounds were postmortem doesn't trouble you?"

"It gives me comfort," he said. "It means my daughter suffered less."

"That's not what I mean. I'm talking in terms of the evidence against Kellerton."

"I don't see anything in that file that contradicts that conclusion."

"It's not consistent with the other murders."

"I disagree," Hoyt said. "What was not consistent was the strength of my daughter."

"I'm not sure I follow."

"I know that Kellerton enjoyed torturing his victims," Hoyt said. "And I know that he usually branded them while they were still alive. But we theorized that Elizabeth had tried to escape or, at the very least, fought back. The way we saw it, she forced his hand. He had to subdue her and in doing so, he ended up killing her. That explains the knife wounds on her hands. That explains why the branding was postmortem."

"I see." A surprise left hook. Carlson tried to keep on his feet. It was a good answer—a hell of a good answer. It made sense. Even the smallest victims can make plenty of trouble. His explanation made all the apparent inconsistencies wonderfully consistent. But there were still problems. "So how do you explain the tox report?"

"Irrelevant," Hoyt said. "It's like asking a rape victim about her sexual history. It doesn't matter if my daughter was a teetotaler or a crack fiend."

"Which was she?"

"Irrelevant," he repeated.

"Nothing's irrelevant in a murder investigation. You know that."

Hoyt took a step closer. "Be careful," he said.

"You threatening me?"

"Not at all. I'm just warning you that you shouldn't be so quick to victimize my daughter a second time."

They stood there. The final bell had sounded. They were now waiting for a decision that would be unsatisfactory no matter how the judges leaned.

"If that's all," Hoyt said.

Carlson nodded and took a step back. Parker reached for the doorknob.

"Hoyt?"

Hoyt turned back around.

"So there's no misunderstanding," Carlson said. "I don't believe a word you just said. We clear?"

"Crystal," Hoyt said.

37

When Shauna arrived at the apartment, she collapsed onto her favorite spot on the couch. Linda sat next to her and patted her lap. Shauna laid her head down. She closed her eyes as Linda caressed her hair.

"Is Mark okay?" Shauna asked.

"Yes," Linda said. "Do you mind telling me where you were?"

"Long story."

"I'm only sitting here waiting to hear about my brother."

"He called me," Shauna said.

"What?"

"He's safe."

"Thank God."

"And he didn't kill Rebecca."

"I know that."

Shauna turned her head to look up. Linda was blinking her eyes. "He's going to be okay," Shauna said.

Linda nodded, turned away.

"What is it?"

"I took those pictures," Linda said.

Shauna sat up.

"Elizabeth came to my office. She was hurt pretty badly. I wanted her to go to a hospital. She said no. She just wanted to make a record of it."

"It wasn't a car accident?"

Linda shook her head.

"Who hurt her?"

"She made me promise not to tell."

"Eight years ago," Shauna said. "Tell me."

"It's not that simple."

"Like hell it's not." Shauna hesitated. "Why would she go to you anyway? And how can you think of protecting..." Her voice faded away. She looked at Linda hard. Linda didn't flinch, but Shauna thought about what Carlson had told her downstairs.

"Brandon Scope," Shauna said softly.

Linda didn't reply.

"He's the one who beat her up. Oh Christ,

no wonder she came to you. She wanted to keep it a secret. Me or Rebecca, we would have made her go to the police. But not you."

"She made me promise," Linda said.

"And you just accepted that?"

"What was I supposed to do?"

"Drag her ass down to the police station."

"Well, we can't all be as brave and strong as you, Shauna."

"Don't give me that crap."

"She didn't want to go," Linda insisted. "She said that she needed more time. That she didn't have enough proof yet."

"Proof of what?"

"That he assaulted her, I guess. I don't know. She wouldn't listen to me. I couldn't just force her."

"Oh right—and that was likely."

"What the hell does that mean?"

"You were involved in a charity financed by his family with his face at the helm," Shauna said. "What would happen if it got out that he beat up a woman?"

"Elizabeth made me promise."

"And you were only too happy to keep your mouth shut, right? You wanted to protect your damn charity."

"That's not fair—"

"You put it over her well-being."

"Do you know how much good we do?" Linda shouted. "Do you know how many people we help?"

"On the blood of Elizabeth Beck," Shauna said.

Linda slapped her across the face. The slap stung. They stared at each other, breathing hard. "I wanted to tell," Linda said. "She wouldn't let me. Maybe I was weak, I don't know. But don't you dare say something like that."

"And when Elizabeth was kidnapped at the lake—what did you think, for crying out loud?"

"I thought it might be connected. I went to Elizabeth's father. I told him what I knew."

"What did he say?"

"He thanked me and said he knew about it. He also told me not to say anything because the situation was delicate. And then when it became clear that KillRoy was the murderer—"

"You decided to keep silent."

"Brandon Scope was dead. What good would dragging his name through the mud do?"

The phone rang. Linda reached for it. She said hello, paused, and then she handed the phone to Shauna. "For you."

Shauna didn't look at her as she took the receiver. "Hello?"

"Meet me down at my office," Hester Crimstein told her.

"Why the hell should I?"

"I'm not big on apologies, Shauna. So let's just agree that I'm a big fat idiot and move on. Grab a taxi and come down here. We've got an innocent man to rescue."

Assistant District Attorney Lance Fein stormed into Crimstein's conference room looking like a sleep-deprived weasel on too many amphetamines. The two homicide detectives Dimonte and Krinsky followed in his wake. All three had faces taut as piano wire.

Hester and Shauna stood on the other side of the table. "Gentlemen," Hester said with a sweep of her hand, "please have a seat."

Fein eyed her, then shot a look of pure disgust at Shauna. "I'm not here for you to jerk me around."

"No, I'm sure you do enough of that in the privacy of your own home," Hester said. "Sit."

"If you know where he is—"

"Sit, Lance. You're giving me a headache."

Everyone sat. Dimonte put his snakeskin boots up on the table. Hester took both hands and knocked them off, never letting her smile falter. "We are here, gentlemen, with one aim: saving your careers. So let's get to it, shall we?"

"I want to know—"

"Shh, Lance. I'm talking here. Your job is to listen and maybe nod and say things like 'Yes, ma'am' and 'Thank you, ma'am.' Otherwise, well, you're toast."

Lance Fein gave her the eye. "You're the one helping a fugitive escape justice, Hester."

"You're sexy when you talk tough, Lance.

Actually, you're not. Listen up, okay, because I don't want to have to repeat myself. I'm going to do you a favor, Lance. I'm not going to let you look like a total idiot on this. An idiot, okay, nothing to be done about that, but maybe, if you listen carefully, not a total idiot. You with me? Good. First off, I understand you have a definitive time of death on Rebecca Schayes now. Midnight, give or take a half hour. We pretty clear on that?"

"So?"

Hester looked at Shauna. "You want to tell him?"

"No, that's okay."

"But you're the one who did all the hard work."

Fein said, "Cut the crap, Crimstein."

The door behind them opened. Hester's secretary brought the sheets of paper over to her boss along with a small cassette tape. "Thank you, Cheryl."

"No problem."

"You can go home now. Come in late tomorrow."

"Thanks."

Cheryl left. Hester took out her half-moon reading glasses. She slipped them on and started reading the pages.

"I'm getting tired of this, Hester."

"You like dogs, Lance?"

"What?"

"Dogs. I'm not a big fan of them myself. But this one... Shauna, you have that photograph?"

"Right here." Shauna held up a large photograph of Chloe for all to see. "She's a bearded collie."

"Isn't she cute, Lance?"

Lance Fein stood. Krinsky stood too. Dimonte didn't budge. "I've had enough."

"You leave now," Hester said, "and this dog will piss all over your career like it's a fire hydrant."

"What the hell are you talking?"

She handed two of the sheets to Fein. "That dog proves Beck didn't do it. He was at Kinko's last night. He entered with the dog. Caused quite a ruckus, I understand. Here are four statements from independent witnesses positively IDing Beck. He rented some computer time while there—more precisely, from four past midnight to twelve twenty-three A.M., according to their billing records." She grinned. "Here, fellas. Copies for all of you."

"You expect me to take these at face value?"

"Not all. Please, by all means, follow up."

Hester tossed a copy at Krinsky and another at Dimonte. Krinsky gathered it up and asked if he could use a phone.

"Sure," Crimstein said. "But if you're going to make any toll calls, kindly charge it to the department." She gave him a sickly sweet smile. "Thanks so much."

Fein read the sheet, his complexion turning to something in the ash-gray family.

"Thinking about expanding the time of death a bit?" Hester asked. "Feel free, but guess what? There was bridge construction that night. He's covered."

Fein was actually quaking. He muttered something under his breath that might have rhymed with "witch."

"Now, now, Lance." Hester Crimstein made a tsk-tsk noise. "You should be thanking me."

"What?"

"Just think of how I could have sandbagged you. There you are, all those cameras, all that delightful media coverage, ready to announce the big arrest of this vicious murderer. You put on your best power tie, make that big speech about keeping the streets safe, about what a team effort the capture of this animal was, though really you should be getting all the credit. The flashbulbs start going off. You smile and call the reporters by their first names, all the while imagining your big oak desk in the governor's mansion—and then bam, I lower the boom. I give the media this airtight alibi. Imagine, Lance. Man, oh, man, do you owe me, or what?"

Fein shot daggers with his eyes. "He still assaulted a police officer."

"No, Lance, he didn't. Think spin, my friend. Fact: You, Assistant District Attorney Lance Fein, jumped to the wrong conclusion. You hunted down an innocent man with your storm troopers—and not just an innocent man, but a doctor who chooses to work for lower pay with the poor instead of in the lucrative private sector." She sat back, smiling. "Oh, this is good, let me see. So while using dozens of city cops at Lord-knows-what

303

expense, all with guns drawn and chasing down this innocent man, one officer, young and beefy and gung-ho, traps him in an alleyway and starts pounding on him. Nobody else is in sight, so this young cop takes it upon himself to make this scared man pay. Poor, persecuted Dr. David Beck, a widower I might add, did nothing but lash out in self-defense."

"That'll never sell."

"Sure it will, Lance. I don't want to sound immodest, but who's better at spin than yours truly? And wait, you haven't heard me wax philosophical on the comparisons between this case and Richard Jewell, or on the overzealousness of the D.A.'s office, or how they were so eager to pin this on Dr. David Beck, hero to the downtrodden, that they obviously planted evidence at his residence."

"Planted?" Fein was apoplectic. "Are you out of your mind?"

"Come on, Lance, we know Dr. David Beck couldn't have done it. We have a proof-positive alibi in the testimony of four—ah, hell, we'll dig up more than four before this is through—independent, unbiased witnesses that he didn't do it. So how did all that evidence get there? You, Mr. Fein, and your storm troopers. Mark Fuhrman will look like Mahatma Gandhi by the time I'm through with you."

Fein's hands tightened into fists. He gulped down a few breaths and made himself lean back. "Okay," he began slowly. "Assuming this alibi checks out—"

"Oh it will."

"*Assuming* it does, what do you want?"

"Well now, that's an awfully good question. You're in a bind, Lance. You arrest him, you look like an idiot. You call off the arrest, you look like an idiot. I'm not sure I see any way around it." Hester Crimstein stood, started pacing as though working a closing. "I've looked into this and I've thought about it and I think I've found a way to minimize the damage. Care to hear it?"

Fein glared some more. "I'm listening."

"You've done one thing smart in all this. Just one, but maybe it's enough. You've kept your mug away from the media. That's because, I imagine, it would be a tad embarrassing trying to explain how this doctor escaped your dragnet. But that's good. Everything that has been reported can be blamed on anonymous leaks. So here's what you do, Lance. You call a press conference. You tell them that the leaks are false, that Dr. Beck is being sought as a material witness, nothing more than that. You do not suspect him in this crime—in fact, you're certain he didn't commit it—but you learned that he was one of the last people to see the victim alive and wanted to speak with him."

"That'll never fly."

"Oh it'll fly. Maybe not straight and true, but it'll stay aloft. The key will be me, Lance. I owe you one because my boy ran. So I, the enemy of the D.A.'s office, will back you up. I'll tell the media how you cooperated with us, how you made sure that my client's rights were not abused, that Dr. Beck and I wholeheartedly support your investigation and look forward to working with you."

Fein kept still.

"It's like I said before, Lance. I can spin for you or I can spin against you."

"And in return?"

"You drop all these silly assault and resisting charges."

"No way."

Hester motioned him toward the door. "See you in the funny pages."

Fein's shoulders slumped ever so slightly. His voice, when he spoke, was soft. "If we agree," he said, "your boy will cooperate? He'll answer all my questions?"

"Please, Lance, don't try to pretend you're in any condition to negotiate. I've laid out the deal. Take it—or take your chances with the press. Your choice. The clock is ticking." She bounced her index finger back and forth and made a tick-tock sound.

Fein looked at Dimonte. Dimonte chewed his toothpick some more. Krinsky got off the phone and nodded at Fein. Fein in turn nodded at Hester. "So how do we handle this?"

38

woke up and lifted my head and almost screamed. My muscles were two steps beyond stiff and sore; I ached in parts of my body I didn't know I had. I tried to swing my legs out of bed. Swing was a bad idea. A very bad idea. Slow. That was the ticket this morning.

My legs hurt most, reminding me that despite my quasi-marathon of yesterday, I was pathetically out of shape. I tried to roll over. The tender spots where the Asian guy had attacked felt as though I'd ripped sutures. My body longed for a couple of Percodans, but I knew that they would put me on Queer Street, and that's not where I wanted to be right now.

I checked my watch. Six A.M. It was time for me to call Hester back. She picked up on the first ring.

"It worked," she said. "You're free."

I felt only mild relief.

"What are you going to do?" she asked.

A hell of a question. "I'm not sure."

"Hold on a sec." I heard another voice in the background. "Shauna wants to talk to you."

There was a fumbling sound as the phone changed hands, and then Shauna said, "We need to talk."

Shauna, never one for idle pleasantries or subtleties, still sounded uncharacteristically strained and maybe even—hard to imagine— scared. My heart started doing a little giddyap.

"What is it?"

"This isn't for the phone," she said.

"I can be at your place in an hour."

"I haven't told Linda about, uh, you know."

"Maybe it's time to," I said.

"Yeah, okay." Then she added with surprising tenderness, "Love you, Beck."

"Love you too."

I half crouched, half crawled toward the shower. Furniture helped support my stiff-legged stumble and keep me upright. I stayed under the spray until the hot water ran out. It helped ease the soreness, but not a lot.

Tyrese found me a purple velour sweat suit from the Eighties Al Sharpton collection. I almost asked for a big gold medallion.

"Where you gonna go?" he asked me.

"To my sister's for now."

"And then?"

"To work, I guess."

Tyrese shook his head.

"What?" I asked.

"You up against some bad dudes, Doc."

"Yeah, I kinda put that together."

"Bruce Lee ain't gonna let this slide."

I thought about that. He was right. Even if I wanted to, I couldn't just go home and wait for Elizabeth to make contact again. In the first place, I'd had enough with the passive; gentle repose simply was not on the Beck agenda anymore. But equally important, the men in that van were not about to forget the matter and let me go merrily on my way.

"I watch your back, Doc. Brutus too. Till this is over."

I was about to say something brave like "I can't ask you to do that" or "You have your own life to lead," but when you thought about it, they could either do this or deal drugs. Tyrese wanted to help—perhaps even needed to help— and let's face it, I needed him. I could warn him off, remind him of the danger, but he understood these particular perils far better than I did. So in the end, I just accepted with a nod.

Carlson got the call from the National Tracing Center earlier than he expected.

"We were able to run it already," Donna said.

"How?"

"Heard of IBIS?"

"Yeah, a little." He knew that IBIS stood for Integrated Ballistic Identification System, a new computer program that the Bureau of Alcohol, Tobacco and Firearms used to store bullet and shell casings. Part of the ATF's new Ceasefire program.

"We don't even need the original bullet anymore," she went on. "They just had to send us the scanned images. We can digitize and match them right on the screen."

"And?"

"You were right, Nick," she said. "It's a match."

Carlson disconnected and placed another call. When the man on the other end picked up, he asked, "Where's Dr. Beck?"

39

Brutus hooked up with us on the sidewalk. I said, "Good morning." He said nothing. I still hadn't heard the man speak. I slid into the backseat. Tyrese sat next to me and grinned. Last night he had killed a man. True, he had done so in defense of my life, but from his casual demeanor, I wasn't even sure he remembered pulling the trigger. I more than anyone should understand what he was going through, but I didn't. I'm not big on moral absolutes. I see the grays. I make the calls. Elizabeth had a clearer view of her moral compass. She would be horrified that a life had been lost. It wouldn't have mattered to her that the man was trying to kidnap, torture, and probably kill me. Or maybe it would. I don't really know anymore. The hard truth is, I didn't know everything about her. And she certainly didn't know everything about me.

My medical training insists that I never make that sort of moral call. It's a simple rule of triage: The most seriously injured gets treated first. It doesn't matter who they are or what they've done. You treat the most grievously wounded. That's a nice theory, and I understand the need for such thinking. But if, say, my nephew Mark were rushed in with a stab wound and some serial pedophile who stabbed him came in at the same time with a life-threatening bullet in the brain, well, come on. You make the call, and in your heart of hearts, you know that the call is an easy one.

You might argue that I'm nesting myself on an awfully slippery slope. I would agree with you, though I might counter that most of life is lived out there. The problem was, there were repercussions when you lived in the grays—not just theoretical ones that taint your soul, but the brick-and-mortar ones, the unforeseeable destruction that such choices leave behind. I wondered what would have happened if I had told the truth right from the get-go. And it scared the hell out of me.

"Kinda quiet, Doc."

"Yeah," I said.

Brutus dropped me off in front of Linda and Shauna's apartment on Riverside Drive.

"We'll be around the corner," Tyrese said. "You need anything, you know my number."

"Right."

"You got the Glock?"

"Yes."

Tyrese put a hand on my shoulder. "Them or you, Doc," he said. "Just keep pulling the trigger."

No grays there.

I stepped out of the car. Mothers and nannies ambled by, pushing complicated baby strollers that fold and shift and rock and play songs and lean back and lean forward and hold more than one kid, plus an assortment of diapers, wipes, Gerber snacks, juice boxes (for the older sibling), change of clothing, bottles, even car first-aid kits. I knew all this from my own practice (being on Medicaid did not preclude one from affording the high-end Peg Perego strollers), and I found this spectacle of bland normalcy cohabiting in the same realm as my recent ordeal to be something of an elixir.

I turned back toward the building. Linda and Shauna were already running toward me. Linda got there first. She wrapped her arms around me. I hugged her back. It felt nice.

"You're okay?" Linda said.

"I'm fine," I said.

My assurances did not stop Linda from repeating the question several more times in several different ways. Shauna stopped a few feet away. I caught her eye over my sister's shoulder. Shauna wiped tears from her eyes. I smiled at her.

We continued the hugs and kisses through the elevator ride. Shauna was less effusive than usual, staying a bit out of the mix. An outsider might claim that this made sense, that Shauna was giving the sister and brother some space during this tender reunion. That outsider wouldn't know Shauna from Cher. Shauna was wonderfully consistent. She was prickly, demanding, funny, bighearted, and loyal beyond all reason. She never put on masks or pretenses. If your thesaurus had an antonym section and you looked up the phrase "shrinking violet," her lush image would stare back at you. Shauna lived life in your face. She wouldn't take a step back if smacked across the mouth with a lead pipe.

Something inside me started to tingle.

When we reached the apartment, Linda and Shauna exchanged a glance. Linda's arm slipped off me. "Shauna wants to talk to you alone first," she said. "I'll be in the kitchen. You want a sandwich?"

"Thanks," I said.

Linda kissed me and gave me one more squeeze, as though making sure I was still there and of substance. She hurried out of the room. I looked over at Shauna. She kept her distance. I put out my hands in a "Well?" gesture.

"Why did you run?" Shauna asked.

"I got another email," I said.

"At that Bigfoot account?"

"Yes."

"Why did it come in so late?"

"She was using code," I said. "It just took me time to figure it out."

"What kind of code?"

I explained about the Bat Lady and the Teenage Sex Poodles.

When I finished, she said, "That's why you were using the computer at Kinko's? You figured it out during your walk with Chloe?"

"Yes."

"What did the email say exactly?"

I couldn't figure out why Shauna was asking all these questions. On top of what I've already said, Shauna was strictly a big-picture person. Details were not her forte; they just muddied and confused. "She wanted me to meet her at Washington Square Park at five yesterday," I said. "She warned me that I'd be followed. And then she told me that no matter what, she loved me."

"And that's why you ran?" she asked. "So you wouldn't miss the meeting?"

I nodded. "Hester said I wouldn't get bail until midnight at the earliest."

"Did you get to the park in time?"

"Yes."

Shauna took a step closer to me. "And?"

"She never showed."

"And yet you're still convinced that Elizabeth sent you that email?"

"There's no other explanation," I said.

She smiled when I said that.

"What?" I asked.

"You remember my friend Wendy Petino?"

"Fellow model," I said. "Flaky as a Greek pastry."

Shauna smiled at the description. "She took me to dinner once with her"—she made quote marks with her fingers—"spiritual guru. She claimed that he could read minds and tell the future and all that. He was helping her communicate with her dead mother. Wendy's mother had committed suicide when she was six."

I let her go on, not interrupting with the

314

obvious "what's the point?" Shauna was taking her time here, but I knew that she'd get to it eventually.

"So we finish dinner. The waiter serves us coffee. Wendy's guru—he had some name like Omay—he's staring at me with these bright, inquisitive eyes, you know the type, and he hands me the bit about how he senses—that's how he says it, senses—that maybe I'm a skeptic and that I should speak my mind. You know me. I tell him he's full of shit and I'm tired of him stealing my friend's money. Omay doesn't get angry, of course, which really pisses me off. Anyway, he hands me a little card and tells me to write anything I want on it—something significant about my life, a date, a lover's initials, whatever I wanted. I check the card. It looks like a normal white card, but I still ask if I can use one of my own. He tells me to suit myself. I take out a business card and flip it over. He hands me a pen, but again I decide to use my own—in case it's a trick pen or something, what do I know, right? He has no problem with that either. So I write down your name. Just Beck. He takes the card. I'm watching his hand for a switch or whatever, but he just passes the card to Wendy. He tells her to hold it. He grabs my hand. He closes his eyes and starts shaking like he's having a seizure and I swear I feel something course through me. Then Omay opens his eyes and says, 'Who's Beck?' "

She sat down on the couch. I did likewise.

"Now, I know people have good sleight of

hand and all that, but I was there. I watched him up close. And I almost bought it. Omay had special abilities. Like you said, there was no other explanation. Wendy sat there with this satisfied smile plastered on her face. I couldn't figure it out."

"He did research on you," I said. "He knew about our friendship."

"No offense, but wouldn't he guess I'd put my own son's name or maybe Linda's? How would he know I'd pick you?"

She had a point. "So you're a believer now?"

"Almost, Beck. I said I almost bought it. Ol' Omay was right. I'm a skeptic. Maybe it all pointed to him being psychic, except I knew he wasn't. Because there are no such things as psychics—just like there are no such things as ghosts." She stopped. Not exactly subtle, my dear Shauna.

"So I did some research," she went on. "The good thing about being a famous model is that you can call anyone and they'll talk to you. So I called this illusionist I'd seen on Broadway a couple of years ago. He heard the story and then he laughed. I said what's so funny. He asked me a question: Did this guru do this after dinner? I was surprised. What the hell could that have to do with it? But I said yes, how did you know? He asked if we had coffee. Again I said yes. Did he take his black? One more time I said yes." Shauna was smiling now. "Do you know how he did it, Beck?"

I shook my head. "No clue."

316

"When he passed the card to Wendy, it went over his coffee cup. Black coffee, Beck. It reflects like a mirror. That's how he saw what I'd written. It was just a dumb parlor trick. Simple, right? Pass the card over your cup of black coffee and it's like passing it over a mirror. And I almost believed him. You understand what I'm saying here?"

"Sure," I said. "You think I'm as gullible as Flaky Wendy."

"Yes and no. See, part of Omay's con is the want, Beck. Wendy falls for it because she wants to believe in all that mumbo-jumbo."

"And I want to believe Elizabeth is alive?"

"More than any dying man in a desert wants to find an oasis," she said. "But that's not really my point either."

"Then what is?"

"I learned that just because you can't see any other explanation doesn't mean that one doesn't exist. It just means you can't see it."

I leaned back and crossed my legs. I watched her. She turned away from my gaze, something she never does. "What's going on here, Shauna?"

She wouldn't face me.

"You're not making any sense," I said.

"I think I was pretty damn clear—"

"You know what I mean. This isn't like you. On the phone you said you needed to talk to me. Alone. And for what? To tell me that my dead wife is, after all, still dead?" I shook my head. "I don't buy it."

Shauna didn't react.

317

"Tell me," I said.

She turned back. "I'm scared," she said in a tone that made the hair on the back of my neck stand up.

"Of what?"

The answer didn't come right away. I could hear Linda rustling around in the kitchen, the tinkling of plates and glasses, the sucking pop when she opened the refrigerator. "That long warning I just gave you," Shauna finally continued. "That was as much for me as for you."

"I don't understand."

"I've seen something." Her voice died out. She took a deep breath and tried again. "I've seen something that my rational mind can't explain away. Just like in my story about Omay. I know there has to be another explanation, but I can't find it." Her hands started moving, her fingers fidgeting with buttons, pulling imaginary threads off her suit. Then she said it: "I'm starting to believe you, Beck. I think maybe Elizabeth is still alive."

My heart leapt into my throat.

She rose quickly. "I'm going to mix a mimosa. Join me?"

I shook my head.

She looked surprised. "You sure you don't want—"

"Tell me what you saw, Shauna."

"Her autopsy file."

I almost fell over. It took me a little time to find my voice. "How?"

"Do you know Nick Carlson from the FBI?"

"He questioned me," I said.

"He thinks you're innocent."

"Didn't sound that way to me."

"He does now. When all that evidence started pointing at you, he thought it was all too neat."

"He told you that?"

"Yes."

"And you believed him?"

"I know it sounds naïve, but yeah, I believed him."

I trusted Shauna's judgment. If she said that Carlson was on the level, he was either a wonderful liar or he'd seen through the frame-up. "I still don't understand," I said. "What does that have to do with the autopsy?"

"Carlson came to me. He wanted to know what you were up to. I wouldn't tell him. But he was tracking your movements. He knew that you asked to see Elizabeth's autopsy file. He wondered why. So he called the coroner's office and got the file. He brought it with him. To see if I could help him out on that."

"He showed it to you?"

She nodded.

My throat was dry. "Did you see the autopsy photos?"

"There weren't any, Beck."

"What?"

"Carlson thinks someone stole them."

"Who?"

She shrugged. "The only other person to sign out the file was Elizabeth's father."

Hoyt. It all circled back to him. I looked at her. "Did you see any of the report?"

Her nod was more tentative this time.

"And?"

"It said Elizabeth had a drug problem, Beck. Not just that there were drugs in her system. He said that the reports showed the abuse was long-term."

"Impossible," I said.

"Maybe, maybe not. That alone wouldn't be enough to convince me. People can hide drug abuse. It's not likely, but neither is her being alive. Maybe the tests were wrong or inconclusive. Something. There are explanations, right? It can somehow be explained away."

I licked my lips. "So what couldn't be?" I asked.

"Her height and weight," Shauna said. "Elizabeth was listed as five seven and under a hundred pounds."

Another sock in the gut. My wife was five four and closer to a hundred fifteen pounds. "Not even close," I said.

"Not even."

"She's alive, Shauna."

"Maybe," she allowed, and her gaze flicked toward the kitchen. "But there's something more."

Shauna turned and called out Linda's name. Linda stepped into the doorway and stayed there. She looked suddenly small in her apron. She wrung her hands and wiped them on the apron front. I watched my sister, puzzled.

"What's going on?" I said.

Linda started speaking. She told me about the photographs, how Elizabeth had come to her to take them, how she'd been only too happy to keep her secret about Brandon Scope. She didn't sugarcoat or offer explanations, but then again, maybe she didn't have to. She stood there and poured it all out and waited for the inevitable blow. I listened with my head down. I couldn't face her, but I easily forgave. We all have our blind spots. All of us.

I wanted to hug her and tell her that I understood, but I couldn't quite pull it off. When she'd finished, I merely nodded and said, "Thanks for telling me."

My words were meant to be a dismissal. Linda understood. Shauna and I sat there in silence for almost a full minute.

"Beck?"

"Elizabeth's father has been lying to me," I said.

She nodded.

"I've got to talk to him."

"He didn't tell you anything before."

True enough, I thought.

"Do you think it'll be different this time?"

I absentmindedly patted the Glock in my waistband. "Maybe," I said.

Carlson greeted me in the corridor. "Dr. Beck?" he said.

Across town at the same time, the district

attorney's office held a press conference. The reporters were naturally skeptical of Fein's convoluted explanation (vis-à-vis me), and there was a lot of backpedaling and finger-pointing and that sort of thing. But all that seemed to do was confuse the issue. Confusion helps. Confusion leads to lengthy reconstruction and clarification and exposition and several other "tions." The press and their public prefer a simpler narrative.

It probably would have been a rougher ride for Mr. Fein, but by coincidence, the D.A.'s office used this very same press conference to release indictments against several high-ranking members of the mayor's administration along with a hint that the "tentacles of corruption"—their phrase—may even reach the big man's office. The media, an entity with the collective attention span of a Twinkie-filled two-year-old, immediately focused on this shiny new toy, kicking the old one under the bed.

Carlson stepped toward me. "I'd like to ask you a few questions."

"Not now," I said.

"Your father owned a gun," he said.

His words rooted me to the floor. "What?"

"Stephen Beck, your father, purchased a Smith and Wesson thirty-eight. The registration showed that he bought it several months before he died."

"What does that have to do with anything?"

"I assume you inherited the weapon. Am I correct?"

"I'm not talking to you." I pressed the elevator button.

"We have it," he said. I turned, stunned. "It was in Sarah Goodhart's safety-deposit box. With the pictures."

I couldn't believe what I was hearing. "Why didn't you tell me this before?"

Carlson gave me a crooked smile.

"Oh right, I was the bad guy back then," I said. Then, making a point of turning away, I added, "I don't see the relevance."

"Sure you do."

I pressed the elevator button again.

"You went to see Peter Flannery," Carlson continued. "You asked him about the murder of Brandon Scope. I'd like to know why."

I pressed the call button and held it down. "Did you do something to the elevators?"

"Yes. Why did you see Peter Flannery?"

My mind made a few quick deductions. An idea—a dangerous thing under the best of circumstances—came to me. Shauna trusted this man. Maybe I could too. A little anyway. Enough. "Because you and I have the same suspicions," I said.

"What's that?"

"We're both wondering if KillRoy murdered my wife."

Carlson folded his arms. "And what does Peter Flannery have to do with that?"

"You were tracking down my movements, right?"

"Yes."

"I decided to do the same with Elizabeth's.

From eight years ago. Flannery's initials and phone number were in her day planner."

"I see," Carlson said. "And what did you learn from Mr. Flannery?"

"Nothing," I lied. "It was a dead end."

"Oh, I don't think so," Carlson said.

"What makes you say that?"

"Are you familiar with how ballistic tests work?"

"I've seen them on TV."

"Put simply, every gun makes a unique imprint on the bullet it fires. Scratches, grooves—unique to that weapon. Like finger-prints."

"That much I know."

"After your visit to Flannery's office, I had our people run a specific ballistic match on the thirty-eight we found in Sarah Goodhart's safety-deposit box. Know what I found?"

I shook my head, but I knew.

Carlson took his time before he said, "Your father's gun, the one you inherited, killed Brandon Scope."

A door opened and a mother and her teen son stepped into the hall. The teen was in mid-whine, his shoulder slumped in adolescent defi-ance. His mother's lips were pursed, her head held high in the don't-wanna-hear-it posi-tion. They came toward the elevator. Carlson said something into a walkie-talkie. We both stepped away from the elevator bank, our eyes locked in a silent challenge.

"Agent Carlson, do you think I'm a killer?"

"Truth?" he said. "I'm not sure anymore."

I found his response curious. "You're aware, of course, that I'm not obligated to speak to you. In fact, I can call Hester Crimstein right now and nix everything you're trying to do here."

He bristled, but he didn't bother denying it. "What's your point?"

"Give me two hours."

"To what?"

"Two hours," I repeated.

He thought about it. "Under one condition."

"What?"

"Tell me who Lisa Sherman is."

That genuinely puzzled me. "I don't know the name."

"You and she were supposed to fly out of the country last night."

Elizabeth.

"I don't know what you're talking about," I said. The elevator dinged. The door slid open. The pursed-lips mom and her slumped adolescent stepped inside. She looked back at us. I signaled for her to hold the door.

"Two hours," I said.

Carlson nodded grudgingly. I hopped into the elevator.

40

Y ou're late!" the photographer, a tiny man with a fake French accent, shouted at Shauna. "And you look like—*comment dit-on?*—like something flushed through the toilette."

"Up yours, Frédéric," Shauna snapped back, not knowing or caring if that was his name. "Where you from anyway, Brooklyn?"

He threw his hands up. "I cannot work like this!"

Aretha Feldman, Shauna's agent, hurried over. "Don't worry, François. Our makeup man will work magic on her. She always looks like hell when she arrives. We'll be right back." Aretha grabbed Shauna's elbow hard but never let up the smile. To Shauna, sotto voce, she said, "What the hell is wrong with you?"

"I don't need this crap."

"Don't play prima donna with me."

"I had a rough night, okay?"

"Not okay. Get in that makeup chair."

The makeup artist gasped in horror when he saw Shauna. "What are those bags under your eyes?" he cried. "Are we doing a shoot for Samsonite luggage now?"

"Ha-ha." Shauna moved toward the chair.

"Oh," Aretha said. "This came for you." She held an envelope in her hand.

Shauna squinted. "What is it?"

"Beats me. A messenger service dropped it off ten minutes ago. Said it was urgent."

She handed the envelope to Shauna. Shauna took it in one hand and flipped it over. She looked at the familiar scrawl on the front of the envelope—just the word "Shauna"—and felt her stomach clench.

Still staring at the handwriting, Shauna said, "Give me a second."

"Now's not the time—"

"A second."

The makeup artist and agent stepped away. Shauna slit open the seal. A blank white card with the same familiar handwriting fell out. Shauna picked it up. The note was brief: "Go to the ladies' room."

Shauna tried to keep her breath even. She stood.

"What's wrong?" Aretha said.

"I have to pee," she said, the calmness in her voice surprising even her. "Where's the head?"

"Down the hall on the left."

"I'll be right back."

Two minutes later, Shauna pushed the bathroom door. It didn't budge. She knocked. "It's me," she said. And waited.

A few seconds later, she heard the bolt slide back. More silence. Shauna took a deep breath and pushed again. The door swung open. She stepped onto the tile and stopped cold. There, across the room, standing in front of the near stall, was a ghost.

Shauna choked back a cry.

The brunette wig, the weight loss, the wire-framed spectacles—none of it altered the obvious.

"Elizabeth..."

"Lock the door, Shauna."

Shauna obeyed without thought. When she turned around, she took a step toward her old friend. Elizabeth shrunk back.

"Please, we don't have much time."

For perhaps the first time in her life, Shauna was at a loss for words.

"You have to convince Beck I'm dead," Elizabeth said.

"A little late for that."

Her gaze swept the room as though looking for an escape route. "I made a mistake coming back. A stupid, stupid mistake. I can't stay. You have to tell him—"

"We saw the autopsy, Elizabeth," Shauna said. "There's no putting this genie back in the bottle."

Elizabeth's eyes closed.

Shauna said, "What the hell happened?"

"It was a mistake to come here."

"Yeah, you said that already."

Elizabeth started chewing on her lower lip. Then: "I have to go."

"You can't," Shauna said.

"What?"

"You can't run away again."

"If I stay, he'll die."

"He's already dead," Shauna said.

"You don't understand."

"Don't have to. If you leave him again, he

328

won't survive. I've been waiting eight years for him to get over you. That's what's supposed to happen, you know. Wounds heal. Life goes on. But not for Beck." She took a step toward Elizabeth. "I can't let you run away again."

There were tears in all four eyes.

"I don't care why you left," Shauna said, inching closer. "I just care that you're back."

"I can't stay," she said weakly.

"You have to."

"Even if it means his death?"

"Yeah," Shauna said without hesitation. "Even if. And you know what I'm saying is true. That's why you're here. You know you can't leave again. And you know I won't let you."

Shauna took another step.

"I'm so tired of running," Elizabeth said softly.

"I know."

"I don't know what to do anymore."

"Me neither. But running isn't an option this time. Explain it to him, Elizabeth. Make him understand."

Elizabeth lifted her head. "You know how much I love him?"

"Yeah," Shauna said, "I do."

"I can't let him get hurt."

Shauna said, "Too late."

They stood now, a foot apart. Shauna wanted to reach out and hold her, but she stayed still.

"Do you have a number to reach him?" Elizabeth said.

"Yeah, he gave me a cell—"

"Tell him Dolphin. I'll meet him there tonight."

"I don't know what the hell that means."

Elizabeth quickly slid past her, peeked out the bathroom door, slithered through it. "He'll understand," she said. And then she was gone.

41

As usual, Tyrese and I sat in the backseat. The morning sky was a charcoal ash, the color of tombstone. I directed Brutus where to turn off after we crossed the George Washington Bridge. Behind his sunglasses, Tyrese studied my face. Finally he asked, "Where we going?"

"My in-laws'."

Tyrese waited for me to say more.

"He's a city cop," I added.

"What's his name?"

"Hoyt Parker."

Brutus smiled. Tyrese did likewise.

"You know him?"

"Never worked with the man myself, but, yeah, I heard the name."

"What do you mean, worked with the man?"

Tyrese waved me off. We hit the town border. I had gone through several surreal experiences over the past three days—chalk "driving through my old neighborhood with two drug dealers in a car with tinted windows" as another. I gave Brutus a few more directions before we pulled up to the memory-laden split-level on Goodhart.

I stepped out. Brutus and Tyrese sped off. I made it to the door and listened to the long chime. The clouds grew darker. A lightning bolt ripped the sky at the seam. I pressed the chime again. Pain traveled down my arm. I still ached all over hell from yesterday's combination of torture and overexertion. For a moment, I let myself wonder what would have happened if Tyrese and Brutus hadn't shown up. Then I shoved that thought away hard.

Finally I heard Hoyt say, "Who is it?"

"Beck," I said.

"It's open."

I reached for the knob. My hand stopped an inch before touching the brass. Weird. I had visited here countless times in my life, but I never remembered Hoyt asking who it was at the door. He was one of the guys who preferred direct confrontation. No hiding in the bushes for Hoyt Parker. He feared nothing, and dammit, he would prove it every step of the way. You ring his bell, he opens the door and faces you full.

I looked behind me. Tyrese and Brutus were gone—no smarts in loitering in front of a cop's house in a white suburb.

"Beck?"

No choice. I thought about the Glock. As

I put my left hand on the knob, I put my right closer to my hip. Just in case. I turned the knob and pushed the door. My head leaned through the crack.

"I'm in the kitchen," Hoyt called out.

I stepped all the way inside and closed the door behind me. The room smelled of a lemon disinfectant, one of those plug-in-a-socket cover-up brands. I found the odor cloying.

"You want something to eat?" Hoyt asked.

I still couldn't see him. "No, thanks."

I waded across the semi-shag toward the kitchen. I spotted the old photographs on the mantel, but this time I didn't wince. When my feet reached linoleum, I let my eyes take in the room. Empty. I was about to turn back when I felt the cold metal against my temple. A hand suddenly snaked around my neck and jerked back hard.

"You armed, Beck?"

I didn't move or speak.

With the gun still in place, Hoyt dropped the arm from my neck and patted me down. He found the Glock, pulled it out, skidded it across the linoleum.

"Who dropped you off?"

"A couple of friends," I managed to say.

"What sort of friends?"

"What the hell is this, Hoyt?"

He backed off. I turned around. The gun was pointed at my chest. The muzzle looked enormous to me, widening like a giant mouth readying to swallow me whole. It was hard to wrest my gaze from that cold, dark tunnel.

"You come here to kill me?" Hoyt asked.

"What? No." I forced myself to look up. Hoyt was unshaven. His eyes were red-tinged, his body was swaying. Drinking. Drinking a lot.

"Where's Mrs. Parker?" I asked.

"She's safe." An odd reply. "I sent her away."

"Why?"

"I think you know."

Maybe I did. Or was starting to.

"Why would I want to hurt you, Hoyt?"

He kept the gun pointed at my chest. "Do you always carry a concealed weapon, Beck? I could have you thrown in jail for that."

"You've done worse to me," I replied.

His face fell. A low groan escaped his lips.

"Whose body did we cremate, Hoyt?"

"You don't know shit."

"I know that Elizabeth is still alive," I said.

His shoulders slumped, but the weapon stayed right in place. I saw his gun hand tense, and for a moment, I was sure he was going to shoot. I debated jumping away, but it wasn't as though he couldn't nail me with the second round.

"Sit down," he said softly.

"Shauna saw the autopsy report. We know it wasn't Elizabeth in that morgue."

"Sit down," he repeated, raising the gun a bit, and I believe that he might have shot me if I didn't obey. He led me back to the living room. I sat on the hideous couch that had witnessed so many memorable moments, but I had the feeling that they would be pretty much Bic flicks next to the bonfire about to engulf this room.

Hoyt sat across from me. The weapon was still up and centered at my middle. He never let his hand rest. Part of his training, I supposed. Exhaustion bled from him. He looked like a balloon with a slow leak, deflating almost imperceptibly.

"What happened?" I asked.

He didn't answer my question. "What makes you think she's alive?"

I stopped. Could I have been wrong here? Was there any way he didn't know? No, I decided quickly. He had seen the body at the morgue. He had been the one who identified her. He had to be involved. But then I remembered the email.

Tell no one....

Had it been a mistake to come here?

Again no. That message had been sent before all this—in practically another era. I had to make a decision here. I had to push, take some action.

"Have you seen her?" he asked me.

"No."

"Where is she?"

"I don't know," I said.

Hoyt suddenly cocked his head. He signaled me to silence with a finger to his lips. He stood and crept toward the window. The shades were all drawn. He peeked through the side.

I stood.

"Sit down."

"Shoot me, Hoyt."

He looked at me.

"She's in trouble," I said.

"And you think you can help her?" He made a sneering noise. "I saved both your lives that night. What did you do?"

I felt something in my chest contract. "I got knocked unconscious," I said.

"Right."

"You..." I was having trouble articulating. "You saved us?"

"Sit down."

"If you know where she is—"

"We wouldn't be having this conversation," he finished.

I took another step toward him. Then another. He aimed the gun at me. I did not stop. I walked until the muzzle pressed against my sternum. "You're going to tell me," I said. "Or you're going to kill me."

"You're willing to take that gamble?"

I looked him straight in the eye and really held the stare for perhaps the first time in our long relationship. Something passed between us, though I'm not sure what. Resignation on his part maybe, I don't know. But I stayed put. "Do you have any idea how much I miss your daughter?"

"Sit down, David."

"Not until—"

"I'll tell you," he said softly. "Sit down."

I kept my eyes on his as I backed up to the couch. I lowered myself onto the cushion. He put the gun down on the side table. "You want a drink?"

"No."

"You better have one."

"Not now."

He shrugged and walked over to one of those chintzy pull-down bars. It was old and loose. The glasses were in disarray, tinkling against one another, and I was more certain than ever that this had not been his first foray into the liquor cabinet today. He took his time pouring the drink. I wanted to hurry him, but I had done enough pushing for the time being. He needed this, I figured. He was gathering his thoughts, sorting through them, checking the angles. I expected as much.

He cupped the glass in both hands and sank into the chair. "I never much liked you," he said. "It was nothing personal. You come from a good family. Your father was a fine man, and your mother, well, she tried, didn't she." One hand held the drink while the other ran through his hair. "But I thought your relationship with my daughter was"—he looked up, searching the ceiling for the words—"a hindrance to her growth. Now...well, now I realize how incredibly lucky you both were."

The room chilled a few degrees. I tried not to move, to quiet my breath, anything so as not to disturb him.

"I'll start with the night at the lake," he said. "When they grabbed her."

"Who grabbed her?"

He stared down into his glass. "Don't interrupt," he said. "Just listen."

I nodded, but he didn't see. He was still staring down at his drink, literally looking for answers in the bottom of a glass.

"You know who grabbed her," he said, "or you should by now. The two men they found buried up there." His gaze suddenly swept the room. He snatched up his weapon and stood, checking the window again. I wanted to ask what he expected to see out there, but I didn't want to throw off his rhythm.

"My brother and I got to the lake late. Almost too late. We set up to stop them midway down the dirt road. You know where those two boulders are?"

He glanced toward the window, then back at me. I knew the two boulders. They sat about half a mile down the dirt road from Lake Charmaine. Both huge, both round, both almost the exact same size, both perfectly placed on either side of the road. There were all kinds of legends about how they got there.

"We hid behind them, Ken and me. When they came close, I shot out a tire. They stopped to check it. When they got out of the car, I shot them both in the head."

With one more look out the window, Hoyt moved back to his chair. He put down the weapon and stared at his drink some more. I held my tongue and waited.

"Griffin Scope hired those two men," he said. "They were supposed to interrogate Elizabeth and then kill her. Ken and I got wind of the plan and headed up to the lake to stop them." He put up his hand as if to silence a question, though I hadn't dared open my mouth. "The hows and whys aren't important. Griffin Scope wanted Elizabeth dead. That's all you need to know. And he wouldn't stop because a couple of his boys got killed. Plenty more where they came from. He's like one of those mythical beasts where you cut off the head and it grows two more." He looked at me. "You can't fight that kind of power, Beck."

He took a deep sip. I kept still.

"I want you to go back to that night and put yourself in our position," he continued, moving closer, trying to engage me. "Two men are lying dead on that dirt road. One of the most powerful men in the world sent them to kill you. He has no qualms about taking out the innocent to get to you. What can you do? Suppose we decided to go to the police. What would we tell them? A man like Scope doesn't leave any evidence behind—and even if he did, he has more cops and judges in his pocket than I have hairs on my head. We'd be dead. So I ask you, Beck. You're there. You have two men dead on the ground. You know it won't end there. What do you do?"

I took the question as rhetorical.

"So I presented these facts to Elizabeth, just like I'm presenting them to you now. I told her that Scope would wipe us out to get to her. If she ran away—if she went into hiding, for example—he'd just torture us until we gave her up. Or he'd go after my wife. Or your sister. He'd do whatever it took to make sure Elizabeth was found and killed." He leaned closer to me. "Do you see now? Do you see the only answer?"

I nodded because it was all suddenly transparent. "You had to make them think she was dead."

He smiled, and new goose bumps surfaced all over me. "I had some money saved up. My brother Ken had more. We also had the contacts. Elizabeth went underground. We got her out of the country. She cut her hair, learned to wear disguises, but that was probably overkill. No one was really looking for her. For the past eight years she's been bouncing around third world countries, working for the Red Cross or UNICEF or whatever organization she could hook up with."

I waited. There was so much he hadn't yet told me, but I sat still. I let the implications seep in and shake me at the core. Elizabeth. She was alive. She had been alive for the past eight years. She had been breathing and living and working.... It was too much to compute, one of those incomprehensible math problems that make the computer shut down.

"You're probably wondering about the body in the morgue."

I allowed myself a nod.

"It was pretty simple really. We get Jane Does in all the time. They get stored in pathology until somebody gets bored with them. Then we stick them in a potter's field out on Roosevelt Island. I just waited for the next Caucasian Jane Doe who'd be a near enough match to pop up. It took longer than I expected. The girl was probably a runaway stabbed by her pimp, but, of course, we'll never know for sure. We also couldn't leave Elizabeth's murder open. You need a fall guy, Beck. For closure. We chose KillRoy. It was common knowledge that KillRoy branded the faces with the letter K. So we did that to the corpse. That only left the problem of identification. We toyed around with the idea of burning her beyond recognition, but that would have meant dental records and all that. So we took a chance. The hair matched. The skin tone and age were about right. We dumped her body in a town with a small coroner's office. We made the anonymous call to the police ourselves. We made sure we arrived at the medical examiner's office at the same time as the body. Then all I had to do was make a tearful ID. That's how the large majority of murder victims are identified. A family member IDs them. So I did, and Ken backed me up. Who would question that? Why on earth would a father and uncle lie?"

"You took a hell of a risk," I said.

"But what choice did we have?"

"There had to be other ways."

He leaned closer. I smelled his breath. The loose folds of skin by his eyes drooped low. "Again, Beck, you're on that dirt road with those two bodies—hell, you're sitting here right now with the benefit of hindsight. So tell me: What should we have done?"

I didn't have an answer.

"There were other problems too," Hoyt

added, sitting back a bit. "We were never totally sure that Scope's people would buy the whole setup. Luckily for us, the two lowlifes were supposed to leave the country after the murder. We found plane tickets to Buenos Aires on them. They were both drifters, unreliable types. That all helped. Scope's people bought it, but they kept tabs on us—not so much because they thought she was still alive, but they worried that maybe she had given one of us some incriminating material."

"What incriminating material?"

He ignored the question. "Your house, your phone, probably your office. They've been bugged for the past eight years. Mine too."

That explained the careful emails. I let my eyes wander around the room.

"I swept for them yesterday," he said. "The house is clean."

When he was silent for a few moments, I risked a question. "Why did Elizabeth choose to come back now?"

"Because she's foolish," he said, and for the first time, I heard anger in his voice. I gave him some time. He calmed, the red swells in his face ebbing away. "The two bodies we buried," he said quietly.

"What about them?"

"Elizabeth followed the news on the Internet. When she read that they'd been discovered, she figured, same as me, that the Scopes might realize the truth."

"That she was still alive?"

"Yes."

341

"But if she were overseas, it would still take a hell of a lot to find her."

"That's what I told her. But she said that wouldn't stop them. They'd come after me. Or her mother. Or you. But"—again he stopped, dropped his head—"I don't know how important all that was."

"What do you mean?"

"Sometimes I think she wanted it to happen." He fiddled with the drink, jiggled the ice. "She wanted to come back to you, David. I think the bodies were just an excuse."

I waited again. He drank some more. He took another peek out the window.

"It's your turn," he said to me.

"What?"

"I want some answers now," he said. "Like how did she contact you. How did you get away from the police. Where you think she is."

I hesitated, but not very long. What choice did I really have here? "Elizabeth contacted me by anonymous emails. She spoke in code only I'd understand."

"What kind of code?"

"She made references to things in our past."

Hoyt nodded. "She knew they might be watching."

"Yes." I shifted in my seat. "How much do you know about Griffin Scope's personnel?" I asked.

He looked confused. "Personnel?"

"Does he have a muscular Asian guy working for him?"

Whatever color was left on Hoyt's face

flowed out as though through an open wound. He looked at me in awe, almost as though he wanted to cross himself. "Eric Wu," he said in a hushed tone.

"I ran into Mr. Wu yesterday."

"Impossible," he said.

"Why?"

"You wouldn't be alive."

"I got lucky." I told him the story. He looked near tears.

"If Wu found her, if he got to her before he got to you..." He closed his eyes, wishing the image away.

"He didn't," I said.

"How can you be so sure?"

"Wu wanted to know why I was in the park. If he had her already, why bother with that?"

He nodded slowly. He finished his drink and poured himself another. "But they know she's alive now," he said. "That means they're going to come after us."

"Then we'll fight back," I said with far more bravery than I felt.

"You didn't hear me before. The mystical beast keeps growing more heads."

"But in the end, the hero always defeats the beast."

He scoffed at that one. Deservedly, I might add. I kept my eyes on him. The grandfather clock ding-donged. I thought about it some more.

"You have to tell me the rest," I said.

"Unimportant."

"It's connected with Brandon Scope's murder, isn't it?"

He shook his head without conviction.

"I know that Elizabeth gave an alibi to Helio Gonzalez," I said.

"It's not important, Beck. Trust me."

"Been there, done that, got screwed," I said.

He took another swig.

"Elizabeth kept a safety-deposit box under the name Sarah Goodhart," I said. "That's where they found those pictures."

"I know," Hoyt said. "We were in a rush that night. I didn't know she'd already given the key to them. We emptied their pockets, but I never checked their shoes. Shouldn't have mattered, though. I had no intention of them ever being found."

"She left more in that box than just the photographs," I continued.

Hoyt carefully set down his drink.

"My father's old gun was in there too. A thirty-eight. You remember it?"

Hoyt looked away and his voice was suddenly soft. "Smith and Wesson. I helped him pick it out."

I felt myself start shaking again. "Did you know that Brandon Scope was killed with that gun?"

His eyes shut tight, like a child wishing away a bad dream.

"Tell me what happened, Hoyt."

"You know what happened."

I couldn't stop quaking. "Tell me anyway."

344

Each word came out like body blows. "Elizabeth shot Brandon Scope."

I shook my head. I knew it wasn't true.

"She was working side by side with him, doing that charity work. It was just a question of time before she stumbled across the truth. That Brandon was running all this penny-ante crap, playing at being a tough street guy. Drugs, prostitution, I don't even know what."

"She never told me."

"She didn't tell anyone, Beck. But Brandon found out. He beat the hell out of her to warn her off. I didn't know it then, of course. She gave me the same story about a bad fender-bender."

"She didn't kill him," I insisted.

"It was self-defense. When she didn't stop investigating, Brandon broke into your home, and this time he had a knife. He came at her...and she shot him. Total self-defense."

I couldn't stop shaking my head.

"She called me, crying. I drove over to your place. When I got there"—he paused, his breath caught—"he was already dead. Elizabeth had that gun. She wanted me to call the police. I talked her out of it. Self-defense or not, Griffin Scope would kill her and worse. I told her to give me a few hours. She was shaky, but she finally agreed."

"You moved the body," I said.

He nodded. "I knew about Gonzalez. The punk was on his way to a fulfilling life of crime. I've seen the type enough to know.

345

He'd already gotten off on a technicality for one murder. Who better to frame?"

It was becoming so clear. "But Elizabeth wouldn't let that happen."

"I didn't count on that," he said. "She heard on the news about the arrest, and that was when she decided to make up that alibi. To save Gonzalez from"—sarcastic finger-quote marks—"a grave injustice." He shook his head. "Worthless. If she'd just let that scumbag take the fall, it would have been all over."

I said, "Scope's people found out about her making up that alibi."

"Someone inside leaked it to them, yeah. Then they started sending their own people around, and they found out about her investigation. The rest became obvious."

"So that night at the lake," I said. "It was about revenge."

He mulled that over. "In part, yes. And in part it was about covering up the truth about Brandon Scope. He was a dead hero. Maintaining that legacy meant a lot to his father."

And, I thought, to my sister.

"I still don't get why she kept that stuff in a safety-deposit box," I said.

"Evidence," he said.

"Of what?"

"That she killed Brandon Scope. And that she did it in self-defense. No matter what else happened, Elizabeth didn't want someone else to take the blame for what she did. Naïve, wouldn't you say?"

No, I wouldn't. I sat there and let the truth try to settle in. Not happening. Not yet anyway. Because this wasn't the full truth. I knew that better than anyone. I looked at my father-in-law, the sagging skin, the thinning hair, the softening gut, the still-impressive but eroding frame. Hoyt thought that he knew what had really happened with his daughter. But he had no idea how wrong he was.

I heard a thunderclap. Rain pounded the windows like tiny fists.

"You could have told me," I said.

He shook his head, this time putting more into it. "And what would you have done, Beck? Follow her? Run away together? They would have learned the truth and killed us all. They were watching you. They still are. We told no one. Not even Elizabeth's mother. And if you need proof we did the right thing, look around you. It's eight years later. All she did was send you a few anonymous emails. And look what happened."

A car door slammed. Hoyt pounced toward the window like a big cat. He peered out again. "Same car you arrived in. Two black men inside."

"They're here for me."

"You sure they don't work for Scope?"

"Positive." On cue, my new cell phone rang. I picked it up.

"Everything okay?" Tyrese asked.

"Yes."

"Step outside."

"Why?"

"You trust that cop?"

"I'm not sure."

"Step outside."

I told Hoyt that I had to go. He seemed too drained to care. I retrieved the Glock and hurried for the door. Tyrese and Brutus were waiting for me. The rain had let up a bit, but none of us seemed to care.

"Got a call for you. Stand over there."

"Why?"

"Personal," Tyrese said. "I don't want to hear it."

"I trust you."

"Just do what I say, man."

I moved out of hearing distance. Behind me I saw the shade open up. Hoyt peered out. I looked back at Tyrese. He gestured for me to put the phone to my ear. I did. There was silence and then Tyrese said, "Line clear, go ahead."

The next voice I heard was Shauna's. "I saw her."

I remained perfectly still.

"She said for you to meet her tonight at the Dolphin."

I understood. The line went dead. I walked back to Tyrese and Brutus. "I need to go somewhere on my own," I said. "Where I can't be followed."

Tyrese glanced at Brutus. "Get in," Tyrese said.

42

Brutus drove like a madman. He took one-way streets in the wrong direction. He made sudden U-turns. From the right lane, he'd cut across traffic and make a left through a red light. We were making excellent time.

The MetroPark in Iselin had a train heading toward Port Jervis that left in twenty minutes. I could rent a car from there. When they dropped me off, Brutus stayed in the car. Tyrese walked me to the ticket counter.

"You told me to run away and not come back," Tyrese said.

"That's right."

"Maybe," he said, "you should do the same."

I put my hand out for him to shake. Tyrese ignored it and hugged me fiercely. "Thank you," I said softly.

He released his grip, adjusted his shoulders so that his jacket relaxed down, fixed his sunglasses. "Yeah, whatever." He didn't wait for me to say anything more before heading back to the car.

The train arrived and departed on schedule. I found a seat and collapsed into it. I tried to make my mind go blank. It wouldn't happen. I glanced around. The car was fairly empty. Two college girls with bulky backpacks jabbered in the language of "like" and "you know." My eyes drifted off. I spotted a newspaper—more specifically, a city tabloid—that someone had left on a seat.

I moved over and picked it up. The coveted cover featured a young starlet who'd been arrested for shoplifting. I flipped pages, hoping to read the comics or catch up on sports—anything mindless would do. But my eyes got snagged on a picture of, well, me. The wanted man. Amazing how sinister I looked in the darkened photo, like a Mideast terrorist.

That was when I saw it. And my world, already off kilter, lurched again.

I wasn't actually reading the article. My eyes were just wandering down the page. But I saw the names. For the first time. The names of the men who'd been found dead at the lake. One was familiar.

Melvin Bartola.

It couldn't be.

I dropped the paper and ran, opening those sliding doors until I found a conductor two cars away. "Where's the next stop?" I asked him.

"Ridgemont, New Jersey."

"Is there a library near the station?"

"I wouldn't know."

I got off there anyway.

Eric Wu flexed his fingers. With a small, tight push, he forced the door.

It hadn't taken him long to track down the

350

two black men who'd helped Dr. Beck escape. Larry Gandle had friends in the police department. Wu had described the men to them, and then he went through the proper mug books. Several hours later, Wu spotted the image of a thug named Brutus Cornwall. They made a few calls and learned that Brutus worked for a drug dealer named Tyrese Barton.

Simple.

The chain lock snapped. The door flew open, the knob banging against the wall. Latisha looked up, startled. She was about to scream, but Wu moved fast. He clamped his hand over her mouth and lowered his lips to her ear. Another man, someone Gandle had hired, came in behind him.

"Shh," Wu said almost gently.

On the floor, TJ played with his Hot Wheels. He tilted his head at the noise and said, "Mama?"

Eric Wu smiled down at him. He let Latisha go and knelt to the floor. Latisha tried to stop him, but the other man held her back. Wu rested his enormous hand on the boy's head. He stroked TJ's hair as he turned to Latisha.

"Do you know how I can find Tyrese?" he asked her.

Once off the train, I took a taxi to the rent-a-car place. The green-jacketed agent behind the counter gave me directions to the library. It took maybe three minutes to get there. The Ridgemont library was a modern facility, nouveau colonial brick, picture windows, beech-wood shelves, balconies, turrets, coffee bar. At the reference desk on the second floor, I found a librarian and asked if I could use the Internet.

"Do you have ID?" she asked.

I did. She looked at it. "You have to be a county resident."

"Please," I said. "It's very important."

I expected to see a no-yield, but she softened. "How long do you think you'll be?"

"No more than a few minutes."

"That computer over there"—she pointed to a terminal behind me—"it's our express terminal. Anyone can use it for ten minutes."

I thanked her and hurried over. Yahoo! found me the site for the *New Jersey Journal,* the major newspaper of Bergen and Passaic counties. I knew the exact date I needed. Twelve years ago on January twelfth. I found the search archive and typed in the information.

The Web site went back only six years.

Damn.

I hurried back over to the librarian. "I need to find a twelve-year-old article from the *New Jersey Journal,*" I said.

"It wasn't in their Web archive?"

I shook my head.

"Microfiche," she said, slapping the sides of her chair to rise. "What month?"

"January."

She was a large woman and her walk was labored. She found the roll in a file drawer and then helped me thread the tape through the machine. I sat down. "Good luck," she said.

I fiddled with the knob, as if it were a throttle on a new motorcycle. The microfiche shrieked through the mechanism. I stopped every few seconds to see where I was. It took me less than two minutes to find the right date. The article was on page three.

As soon as I saw the headline, I felt the lump in my throat.

Sometimes I swear that I actually heard the screech of tires, though I was asleep in my bed many miles away from where it happened. It still hurt—maybe not as much as the night I lost Elizabeth, but this was my first experience with mortality and tragedy and you never really get over that. Twelve years later, I still remember every detail of that night, though it comes back to me in a tornado blur—the predawn doorbell, the solemn-faced police officers at the door, Hoyt standing with them, their soft, careful words, our denials, the slow realization, Linda's drawn face, my own steady tears, my mother still not accepting, hushing me, telling me to stop crying, her already frayed sanity giving way, her telling me to stop acting like a baby, insisting that everything was fine, then suddenly, coming close to me, marveling at how big my tears were, too big, she said, tears that big belonged on the face of a child, not a grown-up, touching one, rubbing it between her forefinger and her thumb, stop crying David! growing angrier because I couldn't

353

stop, her screams then, screaming at me to stop crying, until Linda and Hoyt stepped in and shushed her and someone gave her a sedative, not for the first or last time. It all came back to me in an awful gush. And then I read the article and felt the impact jar me in a whole new direction:

CAR DRIVES OVER RAVINE

One Dead, Cause Unknown

Last night at approximately 3:00 AM, a Ford Taurus driven by Stephen Beck of Green River, New Jersey, ran off a bridge in Mahwah, not far from the New York state border. Road conditions were slick due to the snowstorm, but officials have not yet made a ruling on what caused the accident. The sole witness to the accident, Melvin Bartola, a truck driver from Cheyenne, Wyoming —

I stopped reading. Suicide or accident. People had wondered which. Now I knew it was neither.

Brutus said, "What's wrong?"

"I don't know, man." Then, thinking about it, Tyrese added, "I don't want to go back."

Brutus didn't reply. Tyrese sneaked a glance at his old friend. They had started hanging out together in third grade. Brutus hadn't been much of a talker back then either. Probably too busy getting his ass whipped twice a day—home and school—until Brutus figured out the only way he was going to survive was to become the meanest son of a bitch on the block. He started taking a gun to school when he was eleven. He killed for the first time when he was fourteen.

"Ain't you tired of it, Brutus?"

Brutus shrugged. "All we know."

The truth sat there, heavy, unmoving, unblinking.

Tyrese's cell phone trilled. He picked it up and said, "Yo."

"Hello, Tyrese."

Tyrese didn't recognize the strange voice. "Who is this?"

"We met yesterday. In a white van."

His blood turned to ice. Bruce Lee, Tyrese thought. Oh, damn... "What do you want?"

"I have somebody here who wants to say hi."

There was a brief silence and then TJ said, "Daddy?"

Tyrese whipped off his sunglasses. His body went rigid. "TJ? You okay?"

But Eric Wu was back on the line. "I'm looking for Dr. Beck, Tyrese. TJ and I were hoping you could help me find him."

"I don't know where he is."

"Oh, that's a shame."

"Swear to God, I don't know."

"I see," Wu said. Then: "Hold on a moment, Tyrese, would you? I'd like you to hear something."

43

The wind blew, the trees danced, the purple-orange of sunset was starting to give way to a polished pewter. It frightened me how much the night air felt exactly the same as it had eight years ago, the last time I'd ventured near these hallowed grounds.

I wondered if Griffin Scope's people would think to keep an eye on Lake Charmaine. It didn't matter really. Elizabeth was too clever for that. I mentioned earlier that there used to be a summer camp here before Grandpa purchased the property. Elizabeth's clue—Dolphin—was the name of a cabin, the one where the oldest kids had slept, the one deepest in the woods, the one we rarely dared to visit.

The rental car climbed what had once been the camp's service entrance, though it barely existed anymore. From the main road you couldn't make it out, the high grass hiding it like the entrance to the Batcave. We still kept a chain across it, just in case, with a sign that read No Trespassing. The chain and sign were both still there, but the years of neglect showed. I stopped the car, unhooked the chain, wrapped it around the tree.

I slid back into the driver's seat and headed up to the old camp mess hall. Little of it remained. You could still see the rusted, overturned remnants of what had once been ovens and stoves. Some pots and pans littered the ground, but most had been buried over the years. I got out and smelled the sweet of the green. I tried not to think about my father, but in the clearing, when I was able to look down at the lake, at the way the moon's silver sparkled on the crisp surface, I heard the old ghost again and wondered, this time, if it wasn't crying out for revenge.

I hiked up the path, though that, too, was pretty much nonexistent. Odd that Elizabeth would pick here to meet. I mentioned before that she never liked to play in the ruins of the old summer camp. Linda and I, on the other hand, would marvel when we stumbled over sleeping bags or freshly emptied tin cans, wondering what sort of drifter had left them behind and if, maybe, the drifter was still nearby. Elizabeth, far smarter than either of us, didn't care for that game. Strange places and uncertainty scared her.

It took ten minutes to get there. The cabin was in remarkably good shape. The ceiling and walls were all still standing, though the wooden steps leading to the door were little more than splinters. The Dolphin sign was still there, hanging vertically on one nail. Vines and moss and a mélange of vegetation I couldn't name had not been dissuaded by the structure; they burrowed in, surrounded it, slithered through holes and windows, consumed the cabin so that it now looked like a natural part of the landscape.

"You're back," a voice said, startling me.

357

A male voice.

I reacted without thought. I jumped to the side, fell on the ground, rolled, pulled out the Glock, and took aim. The man merely put his hands up in the air. I looked at him, keeping the Glock on him. He was not what I expected. His thick beard looked like a robin's nest after a crow attack. His hair was long and matted. His clothes were tattered camouflage. For a moment, I thought I was back in the city, faced with another homeless panhandler. But the bearings weren't right. The man stood straight and steady. He looked me dead in the eye.

"Who the hell are you?" I said.

"It's been a long time, David."

"I don't know you."

"Not really, no. But I know you." He gestured with his head toward the bunk behind me. "You and your sister. I used to watch you play up here."

"I don't understand."

He smiled. His teeth, all there, were blindingly white against the beard. "I'm the Boogeyman."

In the distance, I heard a family of geese squawk as they glided to a landing on the lake's surface. "What do you want?" I asked.

"Not a damn thing," he said, still smiling. "Can I put my hands down?"

I nodded. He dropped his hands. I lowered my weapon but kept it at the ready. I thought about what he'd said and asked, "How long have you been hiding up here?"

"On and off for"—he seemed to be doing some kind of calculation with his fingers—"thirty years." He grinned at the dumbstruck expression on my face. "Yeah, I've watched you since you were this high." He put his hand at knee level. "Saw you grow up and—" He paused. "Been a long time since you been up here, David."

"Who are you?"

"My name is Jeremiah Renway," he said.

I couldn't place the name.

"I've been hiding from the law."

"So why are you showing yourself now?"

He shrugged. "Guess I'm glad to see you."

"How do you know I won't tell the authorities on you?"

"I figure you owe me one."

"How's that?"

"I saved your life."

I felt the ground beneath me shift. "What?"

"Who do you think pulled you out of the water?" he asked.

I was dumbstruck.

"Who do you think dragged you into the house? Who do you think called the ambulance?"

My mouth opened, but no words came out.

"And"—his smile spread—"who do you think dug up those bodies so someone would find them?"

It took me a while to find my voice. "Why?" I managed to ask.

"Can't say for sure," he said. "See, I did something bad a long time ago. Guess I thought this was a chance at redemption or something."

"You mean you saw...?"

"Everything," Renway finished for me. "I saw them grab your missus. I saw them hit you with the bat. I saw them promise to pull you out if she told them where something was. I saw your missus hand them a key. I saw them laugh and force her into the car while you stayed underwater."

I swallowed. "Did you see them get shot?"

Renway smiled again. "We've chatted long enough, son. She's waiting for you now."

"I don't understand."

"She's waiting for you," he repeated, turning away from me. "By the tree." Without warning, he sprinted into the woods, darting through the brush like a deer. I stood there and watched him vanish in the thicket.

The tree.

I ran then. Branches whipped my face. I didn't care. My legs begged me to let up. I paid them no heed. My lungs protested. I told them to toughen up. When I finally made the right at the semi-phallic rock and rounded the path's corner, the tree was still there. I moved closer and felt my eyes start to well up.

Our carved initials—E.P. + D.B.—had darkened with age. So, too, had the thirteen lines we had carved out. I stared for a moment, and then I reached out and tentatively touched the grooves. Not of the initials. Not of the thirteen lines. My fingers traced down the eight fresh lines, still white and still sticky from sap.

Then I heard her say, "I know you think it's goofy."

My heart exploded. I turned behind me. And there she was.

I couldn't move. I couldn't speak. I just stared at her face. That beautiful face. And those eyes. I felt as though I were falling, plummeting down a dark shaft. Her face was thinner, her Yankee cheekbones more pronounced, and I don't think I had ever seen anything so perfect in all my life.

I reminded myself of the teasing dreams then—the nocturnal moments of escape when I would hold her in my arms and stroke her face and all the while feel myself being pulled away, knowing even as I had been bathing in the bliss that it was not real, that soon I'd be flung back into the waking world. The fear that this might be more of the same engulfed me, crushing the wind out of my lungs.

Elizabeth seemed to read what I was thinking and nodded as if to say "Yeah, this is real." She took a tentative step toward me. I could barely breathe, but I managed to shake my head and point at the carved lines and say, "I think it's romantic."

She muffled a sob with her hand and sprinted toward me. I opened my arms and she jumped in. I held her. I held her as tight as I could. My eyes squeezed shut. I smelled the lilac and cinnamon in her hair. She buried her face into my chest and sobbed. We gripped and regripped. She still...fit. The contours, the grooves of our bodies needed no adjusting. I cupped the back of her head. Her hair was shorter, but the texture hadn't changed. I could feel her shaking and I'm sure she could feel the same emanating from me.

Our first kiss was exquisite and familiar and frighteningly desperate, two people who'd finally reached the surface after misjudging the depth of the water. The years began to melt away, winter giving way to spring. So many emotions ricocheted through me. I didn't sort through them or try to figure them out. I just let it all happen.

She lifted her head and looked into my eyes and I couldn't move. "I'm sorry," she said, and I thought my heart would shatter all over again.

I held her. I held her, and I wondered if I would ever risk letting her go. "Just don't leave me again," I said.

"Never."

"Promise?"

"Promise," she said.

We kept the embrace. I pressed against the wonder of her skin. I touched the muscles in her back. I kissed the swan neck. I even looked up to the heavens as I just held on. How? I wondered. How could this not be another cruel joke? How could she still be alive and back with me?

I didn't care. I just wanted it to be real. I wanted it to last.

But even as I held her against me, the sound of the cell phone, like something from my teasing dreams, started pulling me away. For a moment, I debated not answering it, but with all that had happened, that wasn't really an option. Loved ones had been left lying in our wake. We couldn't just abandon them. We both knew that. Still keeping one arm around Elizabeth—I'd be damned if I was ever going to let her go—I put the phone to my ear and said hello.

It was Tyrese. And as he spoke, I could feel it all start to slip away.

44

We parked in the abandoned lot at Riker Hill Elementary School and cut across the grounds, holding hands. Even in the dark, I could see that very little had changed from the days when Elizabeth and I had frolicked here. The pediatrician in me couldn't help but notice the new safety features. The swing set had stronger chains and harnessed seats now. Soft mulch was spread thickly under the jungle gyms in case a kid fell. But the kickball field, the soccer field, the blacktop with its painted-on hopscotch and four-square courts—they were all the same as when we were kids.

We walked past the window of Miss Sobel's second-grade class, but it was so long ago now that I think neither of us felt more than a ripple of nostalgia. We ducked into the woods, still hand in hand. Neither one of us had taken the path in twenty years, but we still knew the way. Ten minutes later, we were in Elizabeth's backyard on Goodhart Road. I turned to her. She stared at her childhood house with moist eyes.

"Your mother never knew?" I asked her.

She shook her head. She turned to me. I nodded and slowly let go of her hand.

"Are you sure about this?" she asked.

"No choice," I said.

I didn't give her a chance to argue. I stepped away and headed for the house. When I reached the sliding glass door, I cupped my hands around my eyes and peered in. No sign of Hoyt. I tried the back door. It was unlocked. I turned the knob and went inside. No one was there. I was about to head out when I saw a light snap on in the garage. I went through the kitchen and into the laundry room. I opened the door to the garage slowly.

Hoyt Parker sat in the front seat of his Buick Skylark. The engine was off. He had a drink in his hand. When I opened the door, he lifted his gun. Then, seeing me, he lowered it back to his side. I took the two steps down to the cement and reached for the passenger door handle. The car was unlocked. I opened the door and slid in next to him.

"What do you want, Beck?" There was the slur of drink in his speech.

I made a production of settling back in the seat. "Tell Griffin Scope to release the boy," I said.

"I don't know what you're talking about," he replied without an iota of conviction.

"Graft, payola, on the take. Choose your own term, Hoyt. I know the truth now."

"You don't know shit."

"That night at the lake," I said. "When you helped convince Elizabeth not to go to the police."

"We talked about that already."

"But now I'm curious, Hoyt. What were you really afraid of—that they'd kill her or that you'd be arrested too?"

His eyes lazily drifted toward me. "She'd be dead if I hadn't convinced her to run."

"I don't doubt that," I said. "But still it was lucky for you, Hoyt—shooting down two birds with one stone like that. You were able to save her life—and you were able to stay out of jail."

"And why exactly would I go to jail?"

"Are you denying you were on Scope's payroll?"

He shrugged. "You think I'm the only one who took their money?"

"No," I said.

"So why would I be more worried than the next cop?"

"Because of what you'd done."

He finished his drink, looked around for the bottle, poured himself some more. "I don't know what the hell you're talking about."

"Do you know what Elizabeth was investigating?"

"Brandon Scope's illegal activities," he

said. "Prostitution. Underage girls. Drugs. The guy was playing at being Mr. Bad."

"What else?" I said, trying to stop quivering. "What are you talking about?"

"If she kept digging, she might have stumbled across a bigger crime." I took a deep breath. "Am I right, Hoyt?"

His face sagged when I said that. He turned and stared straight out the front windshield.

"A murder," I said.

I tried to follow his gaze, but all I saw were Sears Craftsman tools hanging neatly on a pegboard. The screwdrivers with their yellow-and-black handles were lined up in perfect size order, flat-tops on the left, Phillips head on the right. Three wrenches and a hammer separated them.

I said, "Elizabeth wasn't the first one who wanted to bring Brandon Scope down." Then I stopped and waited, waited until he looked at me. It took some time, but eventually he did. And I saw it in his eyes. He didn't blink or try to hide it. I saw it. And he knew that I saw it.

"Did you kill my father, Hoyt?"

He took a deep swig from the glass, swished it around his mouth, and swallowed hard. Some of the whiskey spilled onto his face. He didn't bother to wipe it away. "Worse," he said, closing his eyes. "I betrayed him."

The rage boiled up in my chest, but my voice stayed surprisingly even. "Why?"

"Come on, David. You must have figured that out by now."

Another flash of fury shot across me. "My father worked with Brandon Scope," I began.

366

"More than that," he interjected. "Griffin Scope had your dad mentor him. They worked very closely together."

"Like with Elizabeth."

"Yes."

"And while working with him, my father discovered what a monster Brandon really was. Am I right?"

Hoyt just drank.

"He didn't know what to do," I continued. "He was afraid to tell, but he couldn't just let it go. The guilt ate at him. That was why he was so quiet the months before his death." I stopped and thought about my father, scared, alone, nowhere to turn. Why hadn't I seen it? Why hadn't I looked past my own world and seen his pain? Why hadn't I reached out to him? Why hadn't I done something to help him?

I looked at Hoyt. I had a gun in my pocket. How simple it would be. Just take out the gun and pull the trigger. Bam. Gone. Except I knew from personal experience that it wouldn't solve a damn thing. Just the opposite, in fact.

"Go on," Hoyt said.

"Somewhere along the line, Dad decided to tell a friend. But not just any friend. A cop, a cop who worked in the city where the crimes were being committed." My blood started boiling, threatening again to erupt. "You, Hoyt."

Something in his face shifted.

"I got it right so far?"

"Pretty much," he replied.

"You told the Scopes, didn't you?"

He nodded. "I thought they'd transfer him or something. Keep him away from Brandon. I never thought..." He made a face, clearly hating the self-justification in his own voice. "How did you know?"

"The name Melvin Bartola, for starters. He was the witness to the supposed accident that killed my father, but, of course, he worked for Scope too." My father's smile flashed in front of me. I tightened my hands into fists. "And then there was the lie you told about saving my life," I continued. "You did go back to the lake after you shot Bartola and Wolf. But not to save me. You looked, you saw no movement, and you figured I was dead."

"Figured you were dead," he repeated. "Not wanted you dead."

"Semantics," I said.

"I never wanted you to get hurt."

"But you weren't very broken up about it either," I said. "You went back to the car and told Elizabeth that I had drowned."

"I was just trying to convince her to disappear," he said. "It helped too."

"You must have been surprised when you heard I was still alive."

"More like shocked. How did you survive anyway?"

"It's not important."

Hoyt settled back as though from exhaustion. "Guess not," he said. His expression veered again and I was surprised when he said, "So what else do you want to know?"

"You're not denying any of this?"

"Nope."

"And you knew Melvin Bartola, right?"

"That's right."

"Bartola tipped you off about the hit on Elizabeth," I said. "I can't figure out what happened exactly. Maybe he had a conscience. Maybe he didn't want her to die."

"Bartola a conscience?" He chuckled. "Please. He was a low-life murdering scum. He came to me because he thought he could double-dip. Collect from the Scopes and from me. I told him I'd double his money and help him out of the country if he helped me fake her death."

I nodded, seeing it now. "So Bartola and Wolf told Scope's people that they were going to lie low after the killing. I wondered why their disappearance didn't raise more eyebrows, but thanks to you, Bartola and Wolf were supposed to go away."

"Yes."

"So what happened? Did you double-cross them?"

"Men like Bartola and Wolf—their word means nothing. No matter how much I paid them, I knew that they'd come back for more. They'd get bored living out of the country or maybe they'd get drunk and boast about it in a bar. I've dealt with this type of garbage my whole life. I couldn't risk that."

"So you killed them."

"Yep," he said without an ounce of regret. I knew it all now. I just didn't know how it

369

was all going to play out. "They're holding a little boy," I said to him. "I promised I'd turn myself in if they let him go. You call them. You help make the trade."

"They don't trust me anymore."

"You've worked for Scope for a long time," I said. "Come up with something."

Hoyt sat there and thought about it. He looked at his tool wall again, and I wondered what he was seeing. Then slowly, he lifted the gun and pointed it at my face. "I think I got an idea," he said.

I didn't blink. "Open the garage door, Hoyt."

He didn't move.

I reached across him to the visor and pressed the garage's remote. The door came to life with a whir. Hoyt watched it rise. Elizabeth stood there, not moving. When it was open all the way, her gaze settled hard on her father's.

He flinched.

"Hoyt?" I said.

His head snapped toward me. With one hand he grabbed my hair. He pressed the gun against my eye. "Tell her to move out of the way."

I stayed still.

"Do it or you die."

"You wouldn't. Not in front of her."

He leaned closer to me. "Just do it, dammit." His voice was more like an urgent plea than a hostile command. I looked at him and felt something strange course through me. Hoyt turned on the ignition. I faced the front and gestured for her to move out of the way. She hesitated, but eventually she stepped to the side. Hoyt waited until she was clear of his path. Then he hit the gas. We flew past her with a jerk. As we hurtled away, I turned and watched out the back window as Elizabeth grew dimmer, fainter, until finally she was gone.

Again.

I sat back and wondered if I would ever see her again. I had feigned confidence before, but I knew the odds. She fought me on it. I explained that I had to do this. I needed to be the one doing the protecting this time. Elizabeth hadn't liked it, but she understood.

In the past few days I'd learned that she was alive. Would I trade my life for that? Gladly. I understood that going in. A strange, peaceful feeling came over me as I drove with the man who betrayed my father. The guilt that had weighed me down for so long finally lifted its hold. I knew now what I had to do—what I had to sacrifice—and I wondered if there was ever any choice, if it had been preordained to end like this.

I turned to Hoyt and said, "Elizabeth didn't kill Brandon Scope."

"I know," he interrupted, and then he said something that shook me to the core: "I did."

I froze.

"Brandon beat up Elizabeth," he went on quickly. "He was going to kill her. So I shot him when he got to the house. Then I framed Gonzalez, just like I said before. Elizabeth knew what I had done. She wouldn't let an innocent man take the fall. So she made up that alibi. Scope's people heard about it and it made them wonder. When they then began to suspect that maybe Elizabeth was the killer"—he stopped, kept his eyes on the road, summoned something from deep inside—"God help me, I let them."

I handed him the cell phone. "Call," I said.

He did. He called a man named Larry Gandle. I had met Gandle several times over the years. His father had gone to high school with mine. "I have Beck," Hoyt told him. "We'll meet you at the stables, but you have to release the kid."

Larry Gandle said something I couldn't make out.

"As soon as we know the kid is safe, we'll be there," I heard Hoyt say. "And tell Griffin I have what he wants. We can end this without hurting me or my family."

Gandle spoke again and then I heard him click off the line. Hoyt handed me back the phone.

"Am I part of your family, Hoyt?"

He aimed the gun at my head again. "Slowly take out your Glock, Beck. Two fingers."

I did as he asked. He hit the electric window slide.

"Toss it out the window."

I hesitated. He pushed the muzzle into my eye. I flipped the gun out of the car. I never heard it land.

We drove in silence now, waiting for the phone to ring again. When it did, I was the one who answered it. Tyrese said in a soft voice, "He's okay."

I hung up, relieved.

"Where are you taking me, Hoyt?"

"You know where."

"Griffin Scope will kill us both."

"No," he said, still pointing the gun at me. "Not both."

45

We turned off the highway and headed into the rural. The number of streetlights dwindled until the only illumination came from the car's headlights. Hoyt reached into the backseat and pulled out a manila envelope.

"I have it here, Beck. All of it."

"All of what?"

"What your father had on Brandon. What Elizabeth had on Brandon."

I was puzzled for a second. He'd had it with him the whole time. And then I wondered. The car. Why had Hoyt gone to the car?

"Where are the copies?" I asked.

He grinned as though happy I had asked. "There aren't any. It's all here."

"I still don't understand."

"You will, David. I'm sorry, but you're my fall guy now. It's the only way."

"Scope won't buy it," I said.

"Yeah, he will. Like you said, I've worked for him a long time. I know what he wants to hear. Tonight it ends."

"With my death?" I asked.

He didn't reply.

"How are you going to explain it to Elizabeth?"

"She might end up hating me," he said. "But at least she'll be alive."

Up ahead, I could see the estate's gated back entrance. Endgame, I thought. The uniformed security guard waved us through. Hoyt kept the gun on me. We started up the drive and then, without warning, Hoyt slammed on the brake.

He spun toward me. "You wearing a wire, Beck?"

"What? No."

"Bullshit, let me see." He reached for my chest. I leaned away. He lifted the gun higher, closed the gap between us, and then started patting me down. Satisfied, he sat back.

"You're lucky," he said with a sneer.

He shifted back into drive. Even in the dark, you could get a feel for the lushness of the grounds. Trees stood silhouetted against the moon, swaying even though there seemed to be no wind. In the distance, I saw a burst of lights. Hoyt followed the road toward them. A faded gray sign told us we'd arrived at the Freedom Trails Stables. We parked in the first spot on the left. I looked out the window. I don't know much about the housing of horses, but this sprawl was impressive. There was one hangar-shaped building large enough to house a dozen tennis courts. The stables themselves were V-shaped and stretched as far as I could see. There was a sprouting fountain in the middle of the grounds. There were tracks and jumps and obstacle courses.

They were also men waiting for us.

With the weapon still on me, Hoyt said, "Get out."

I did. When I closed the door, the slam echoed in the stillness. Hoyt came around to my side of the car and jammed the gun into the small of my back. The smells brought on a quick spell of 4-H-fair déjà vu. But when I saw the four men in front of me, two of whom I recognized, the image fled.

The other two—the two I had never seen before—were both armed with some sort of semiautomatic rifle. They pointed them at us. I barely shuddered. I guess that I was getting used to weapons aimed in my direction. One of the men stood on the far right near the stable entrance. The other was leaning against a car on the left.

The two men I had recognized were huddled together under a light. One was Larry Gandle. The other was Griffin Scope. Hoyt nudged me forward with the gun. As we moved toward them, I saw the door to the big building open.

Eric Wu stepped out.

My heart thumped against my rib cage. I could hear my breath in my ears. My legs tingled. I might be immune to weapon intimidation, but my body remembered Wu's fingers. I involuntarily slowed a step. Wu hardly glanced at me. He walked straight to Griffin Scope and handed him something.

Hoyt made me stop when we were still a dozen yards away. "Good news," he called out.

All eyes turned to Griffin Scope. I knew the man, of course. I was, after all, the son of an old friend and the brother of a trusted employee. Like most everyone else, I'd been in awe of the burly man with the twinkle in his eye. He was the guy you wanted to notice you—a back-slap buy-you-a-drink compadre who had the rare ability to walk the tightrope between friend and employer. It was a mix that rarely worked. The boss either lost respect when he became a friend, or the friend was resented when he suddenly had to be the boss. That wasn't a problem for a dynamo like Griffin Scope. He'd always known how to lead.

Griffin Scope looked puzzled. "Good news, Hoyt?"

Hoyt tried a smile. "Very good news, I think."

"Wonderful," Scope said. He glanced at Wu. Wu nodded but stayed where he was. Scope said, "So tell me this good news, Hoyt. I'm all atwitter."

Hoyt cleared his throat. "First of all, you have to understand. I never meant to harm you. In fact, I went to great lengths to make sure nothing incriminating ever got out. But I also

needed to save my daughter. You can understand that, can't you?"

A shadow flickered across Scope's face.
"Do I understand the desire to protect a
child?" he asked, his voice a quiet rumble. "Yes,
Hoyt, I think I do."

A horse neighed in the distance. All else was
silence. Hoyt licked his lips and held up the
manila envelope.

"What's that, Hoyt?"

"Everything," he replied. "Photographs,
statements, tapes. Everything that my daughter
and Stephen Beck had on your son."

"Are there copies?"

"Only one," Hoyt said.

"Where?"

"In a safe place. An attorney has it. If I
don't call him in an hour and give him the code,
he releases them. I don't mean this as a threat,
Mr. Scope. I would never reveal what I know.
I have as much to lose as anyone."

"Yes," Scope said. "You do at that."

"But now you can leave us alone. You have
it all. I'll send the rest. There is no need to hurt
me or my family."

Griffin Scope looked at Larry Gandle, then
at Eric Wu. The two perimeter men with the
weapons seemed to tense. "What about my son,
Hoyt? Someone shot him down like a dog. Do
you expect me to just let that go?"

"That's just it," Hoyt said. "Elizabeth
didn't do it."

Scope narrowed his eyes in what was supposed to be profound interest, but I thought

377

I saw something else there, something akin to bemusement. "Pray tell," he said. "Then who did?"

I heard Hoyt swallow hard. He turned and looked at me. "David Beck."

I wasn't surprised. I wasn't angry either.

"He killed your son," he continued quickly. "He found out what was going on and he took vengeance."

Scope made a production of gasping and putting his hand on his chest. Then he finally looked at me. Wu and Gandle turned my way too. Scope met my eyes and said, "What do you have to say in your defense, Dr. Beck?"

I thought about it. "Would it do any good to tell you he's lying?"

Scope didn't reply to me directly. He turned to Wu and said, "Please bring me that envelope."

Wu had the walk of a panther. He headed toward us, smiling at me, and I felt a few of my muscles contract instinctively. He stopped in front of Hoyt and put out his hand. Hoyt handed him the envelope. Wu took the envelope with one hand. With the other—I've never seen anyone move so fast—he snatched away Hoyt's gun as though from a child, and tossed it behind him.

Hoyt said, "What the—?"

Wu punched him deep in the solar plexus. Hoyt fell to his knees. We all stood and watched as he dropped to all fours, retching. Wu circled, took his time, and placed his kick squarely on Hoyt's rib cage. I heard something snap. Hoyt rolled onto his back, blinking, his arms and legs splayed.

Griffin Scope approached, smiling down at my father-in-law. Then he held up something in the air. I squinted. It was small and black.

Hoyt looked up, spitting out blood. "I don't understand," he managed.

I could see what was in Scope's hand now. It was a microcassette player. Scope pressed the play button. I heard first my own voice, then Hoyt's:

"Elizabeth didn't kill Brandon Scope."

"I know. I did."

Scope snapped off the tape recorder. Nobody spoke. Scope glared down at my father-in-law. As he did, I realized a number of things. I realized that if Hoyt Parker knew that his house was bugged, he'd also know that it was more than likely that the same would be true of his car. That was why he left the house when he spotted us in the backyard. That was why he waited for me in the car. That was why he interrupted me when I said that Elizabeth didn't kill Brandon Scope. That was why he confessed to the murder in a place where he knew they'd be listening. I realized that when he patted me down, he did indeed feel the wire that Carlson had put on my chest, that he wanted to make sure that the feds, too, would hear everything and that Scope wouldn't bother frisking me. I realized that Hoyt Parker was taking the fall, that while he had done many terrible things, including betraying my father, this had all been a ruse, a last chance at redemption, that in the end, he, not I, would sacrifice himself to save us all. I also realized that for his plan to work, he had to do one more thing. So I stepped away. And even as I heard the FBI helicopters start to descend, even as I heard Carlson's voice through a megaphone shout for everyone to freeze, I watched Hoyt Parker reach into his ankle holster, pull out a gun, and fire it three times at Griffin Scope. Then I watched him turn the gun around.

I shouted "No!" but the final blast smothered it out.

46

We buried Hoyt four days later. Thousands of uniformed cops showed up to pay their respects. The details of what had happened at the Scope estate weren't out yet, and I wasn't sure they ever would be. Even Elizabeth's mother hadn't pushed for answers, but perhaps that had more to do with the fact that she was delirious with joy over her daughter's return from the dead. It made her not want to ask too many questions or look at the cracks too closely. I could relate.

For now, Hoyt Parker had died a hero. And maybe that was true. I'm not the best judge.

Hoyt had written a long confession, basically restating what he had told me in the car. Carlson showed it to me.

"Does this end it?" I asked.

"We still have to make a case against Gandle and Wu and some of the others," he said. "But with Griffin Scope dead, everyone's cutting deals now."

The mythical beast, I thought. You don't chop off its head. You stab it in the heart.

"You were smart to come to me when they kidnapped that little boy," Carlson said to me.

"What was my alternative?"

"Good point." Carlson shook my hand. "Take care of yourself, Dr. Beck."

"You too," I said.

You may want to know if Tyrese ever goes down to Florida and what happens to TJ and Latisha. You may be wondering if Shauna and Linda stay together and what that means to Mark. But I can't tell any of that because I don't know.

This story ends now, four days after the death of Hoyt Parker and Griffin Scope. It is late. Very late. I am lying in bed with Elizabeth, watching her body rise and fall in sleep. I watch her all the time. I don't close my eyes much. My dreams have perversely reversed themselves. It is in my dreams now that I lose her—where she is dead again and I am alone. So I hold her a lot. I am clingy and needy. So is she. But we'll work that out.

As though she feels my eyes on her, Elizabeth rolls over. I smile at her. She smiles back and I feel my heart soar. I remember the day at the lake. I remember drifting on that raft. And I remember my decision to tell her the truth.

"We need to talk," I say.

"I don't think so."

"We're not good at keeping secrets from each other, Elizabeth. It's what caused this mess in the first place. If we had just told each other everything..." I didn't finish.

She nods. And I realize that she knows. That she's always known.

"Your father," I say. "He always thought you killed Brandon Scope."

"That's what I told him."

382

"But in the end—" I stop, start again. "When I said in the car that you didn't kill him, do you think he realized the truth?"

"I don't know," Elizabeth says. "I like to think that maybe he did."

"So he sacrificed himself for us."

"Or he tried to stop you from doing it," she says. "Or maybe he died still thinking I killed Brandon Scope. We'll never really know. And it doesn't matter."

We look at each other.

"You knew," I say, my chest hitching. "From the beginning. You—"

She hushes me with a finger on my lips. "It's okay."

"You put all that stuff in the safety-deposit box," I say, "for me."

"I wanted to protect you," she says.

"It was in self-defense," I say, again remembering the feel of the gun in my hand, the sickening backfire when I pulled the trigger.

"I know," she says, wrapping her arms around my neck and pulling me close. "I know."

You see, I was the one who was home when Brandon Scope broke into our house eight years ago. I was the one lying alone in the bed when he sneaked up with the knife. We struggled. I fumbled for my father's gun. He lunged again. I shot and killed him. And then, in a panic, I ran. I tried to gather my thoughts, figure out what to do. When I came to my senses, when I returned to the house, the body was gone. So was the gun. I wanted to tell her. I was going to at the lake. But in the end, I never said anything about it. Until now.

Like I told you earlier, if I had just told the truth from the get-go...

She pulls me closer.

"I'm here," Elizabeth whispers.

Here. With me. It would take a while to accept that. But I would. We hold each other and drift off to sleep. Tomorrow morning we would wake up together. And the morning after that too. Her face would be the first I'd see every day. Her voice would be the first I'd hear. And that, I knew, would always be enough.